I0780448

OBLITERATION
A Medieval Romance

By Kathryn Le Veque

Part of the Guard of Six series

© Copyright 2025 by Kathryn Le Veque Novels, Inc.
Trade Paperback Edition

Text by Kathryn Le Veque
Cover by Kim Killion

Reproduction of any kind except where it pertains to short quotes in relation to advertising or promotion is strictly prohibited.

All Rights Reserved.

The characters and events portrayed in this book are fictitious. Any similarity to real persons, living or dead, is purely coincidental and not intended by the author.

No AI or ghostwriting was used in the creation of this story, or any story, authored by Kathryn Le Veque. All text, structure, content, ideas, and concept are 100% Human generated solely by the author. It is prohibited to use this material, or any copyrighted material, for AI engine training.

KATHRYN LE VEQUE
NOVELS

WWW.KATHRYNLEVEQUE.COM

ARE YOU SIGNED UP FOR KATHRYN'S BLOG?

You'll get the latest news and information on exclusive giveaways, exclusive excerpts, coming releases, sales, free books, cover reveals and more.

Kathryn's blog followers get it all first. No spam, no junk.

Get the latest info from the reigning Queen of English Medieval Romance!

Sign Up Here

It's another epic Guard of Six novel when one of the Six finds himself with an explosive inheritance that threatens to ruin his reputation as a noble knight.

An inheritance that involves… wine, women, and song??

Sir Jareth de Leybourne is the moral compass for the Guard of Six. He's the wise man of the group, rooted in reality, relying heavily on logic. But Jareth's family has a secret that is about to shake his very foundation.

Jareth's life is proceeding normally when he receives word that his father's brother, a rich nobleman with extravagant tastes, has passed away. Jareth is named as his heir. Summoned to his uncle's lavish manse in the vibrant city of Bristol, Jareth finds himself in possession of a productive shipping business. This business has funded the building of a local church and a college, among other things. It seems that Jareth's uncle was heavily into philanthropy. But there's also another business, far darker, that has made his uncle richer than God.

A brothel.

"Aphrodite's Feast" is a very elegant house of ill repute, so accepted by the populace of Bristol because of the money it gives back to the community that it's the worst-kept secret in town. The women are the most beautiful in England. It is also a gambling hall, so the entire enterprise makes money hand over fist. And a very appalled Jareth finds himself the new owner.

Enter Lady Desdra le Daire.

Desdra ended up at the brothel for reasons beyond her control. She's not one of the working women, but instead, uses her education to run the entire venture. A spinster by choice—because who is going to want a wife who works at a house of ill repute?—she and Jareth go head to head from the first day they meet. But that friction soon turns into something else warm and romantic. However, beneath it all, an even greater enemy lurks.

As it turns out, Jareth's uncle had a very powerful enemy. Now that enemy wants Jareth dead, but in a twist of fate, Desdra stands in the way.

And Jareth must do everything he can to save her.

Join Jareth and Desdra and the fascinating characters of Aphrodite's Feast on a remarkable and unique journey through the seedier side of Medieval England, where the darkest of souls lurk and love always reigns supreme.

GUARD OF SIX

Fortitudo in unitate
Motto: Strength in Unity

We are protectors.
Defenders.
The shield between the king and those who threaten him.
We are the Guard of Six.
Fortitudo in unitate
Strength in unity.

AUTHOR'S NOTE

I will admit that the Guard of Six has really grown on me.

I mean, "all" of the books I write, and the characters I write, grow on me, but the Guard of Six is so unique. They're not family—not brothers or cousins or anything. They're just a bunch of guys with some emotional—or family—baggage who find themselves serving Henry as bodyguards. Guys like that, back in the day, were always the very best swordsmen. Their background usually didn't come into play—all that mattered was how good they were with a sword. Loyalty was usually bought, not by blood or honor. So that's the world the Guard of Six are in, different from most worlds I write about.

A list of the guys to refresh your memory and the novels where their families can be found:

- Torran de Serreaux *(The Unholy Hour—a contemporary novel)*
- Aidric St. John *(The Warrior Poet)*
- Dirk d'Vant *(Tender Is the Knight)*
- Jareth de Leybourne *(Lady of the Moon)*
- Britt de Garr *(Lord of Light)*
- Kent de Poyer *(Netherworld)*

If you've read this series so far, and you've also read my Sons of de Wolfe and/or the de Reyne Domination series, you'll notice that the Guard of Six series runs concurrently to both of those series. In this tale, we've got a little crossover in the appearance of Thor de Reyne, the hero in my novel *One Wylde Knight*. Thor was Henry III's Lord Protector after Patrick de Wolfe (*Nighthawk*) turned down the job, so Thor makes a brief appearance in this novel.

Let's talk a little bit about the historical accuracy of colleges in Medieval times because one is mentioned in this story. Yes, there were colleges in Medieval times, but they were called "universitas." They were a scholastic guild, in fact, that could offer higher education on things like law and medicine and theology. There is evidence of institutions of higher learning in many cultures dating back to the sixth century, so a college was not a new concept. The oldest state-funded university in the world in continuous use is the University of Naples, founded in 1224 A.D. It's still around.

And what would be one of my novels without a cameo from a character from other books? Keep in mind that the Guard of Six runs concurrently, timeline-wise, with several of my series. Henry III ruled for sixty-six years, so that covers a ton of timelines. De Wolfe, De Winter, Lords of Thunder to name a few. This novel sees an appearance by Hugh de Winter, brother of Davyss de Winter from *Lespada*. There is also a mention of an Axminster Angel—if you've read my novel *Lion of Steel*, then you know what they are.

What else can I say about this novel? It moves fast and it's action-packed. We've got bad guys, good guys, better guys, and badder guys ("badder" isn't a word, but for my purposes, we're going to use it). It's also a very sweet story about a man's discovery of the world around him.

The usual pronunciation guide:

Aidric – AID-rick

Desdra – DEZZ-druh

Anosia – ann-NO-see-uh

Prudhoe – Pruh-duh

Ciaran – KEER-in

And with that, enjoy *Obliteration*!

Hugs,

PROLOGUE

Year of Our Lord 1271
Redcliffe Hill Manor
Bristol, England

"QUICKLY. THERE IS not much time."

The words were rasped, the last efforts of a dying man whose breath had become the faint wisps of a fading world and whose blood was now slowing in his very veins as he spoke. A heart that was struggling to beat and a body that had failed him.

Quickly. There is not much time.

That summarized the situation well.

In the chamber that was more lavish than that of a king, he lay upon his silks, feeling their last bit of comfort before he transitioned to a place where no such creature comforts existed. That was his greatest regret. That he couldn't take his life's work—and wealth—with him. Around him, musicians played softly, gently easing him from one life to the next, which would have been a delightful way to go if he were ready.

He wasn't.

But Death waited for no man.

"What would you have of me, my lord?" A woman's soft voice wafted amidst the notes from the harps. "I have my writing kit. I will write whatever you wish."

The man drew in a deep breath, trying to stave off the inevitable. His lungs didn't want to work any longer, but he forced them to. He had something to do and refused to go until he finished it.

"You must send word to my nephew," he said weakly. "He serves the king. His name is Jareth de Leybourne."

The young woman had her writing implements spread out on a nearby table, pushing aside old food and cups with dried wine in the bottom of them. A cat suddenly leapt onto the table, scattering her vellum, and she pushed the beast off as she scrambled to collect her parchment.

"Well?" the old man demanded. "What is happening over there?"

She put the vellum in front of her, grabbing for her quill as the cat jumped up again. Frustrated, she eyed it before dipping her quill in her inkwell.

"Nothing is amiss, my lord," she said. "I will write this missive to your nephew, Sir Jareth."

"And you will send it to Westminster Palace."

"Aye, my lord."

The old man didn't say anything after that. The young woman sat, ink poised above the vellum, as she awaited his great words of wisdom and sacrifice, but he remained silent. Oddly silent. By the time she looked up to see why, she could see a big smile spreading across his old face. He was shaking.

He's laughing! she thought.

"My lord?" she said timidly.

He let out a ragged gasp. "You do not know Jareth," he said.

"A fine man. A very fine man. An elite knight who serves Henry. He is moral and brave. He is worthy of that which I will bestow upon him. But I can tell you that he will *not* like it."

The young woman gazed steadily at him. "He does not like money, my lord?"

The old man weakly shrugged. "A man must have money," he said. "I have more money than almost anyone in England, but alas, I have no sons. My brother, however, has two sons—his heir and Jareth. Jareth will not inherit when his father passes away, so he will become my heir. You will help him when he comes to Bristol, will you not, Desdra?"

Lady Desdra le Daire nodded slowly. "If you wish it, my lord."

"I do," he said. "You are very bright. Brighter than any woman I have ever known. You must explain how everything works to Jareth when he comes."

"I will, my lord."

"And tell him not to give his brother anything."

"I will, my lord."

"Good lass," the old man said, laying his head back against the pillow. He gazed up at the ceiling, one that had been painted with a scene from the Bible on it. It was quite elaborate, with stars made of real gold plastered to the ceiling. "That is where I am going, you know. Up there. To a place with blue skies and gold stars."

Desdra turned her gaze upward, seeing the ceiling as it was illuminated by the light from dozens of tapers. It was truly a work of art.

"I hope so," she said. "You have been kind to so many, my lord. You have done great good for this town. I pray that God has a special place just for you, where you can enjoy your blue skies and gold stars. You have earned it."

He looked at her, his eyes yellowed from the disease that ravaged his body. "You are kind, lass," he said quietly. "Desdra... surely you know that you paid your father's debt a long time ago."

She averted her gaze, looking at the vellum. "I know, my lord."

"You are free to leave."

Her gaze flicked up to him. "And go where?" she said. "Home? Where my father can sell me again to pay his debts, only the next time, the creditor might not be so kind or forgiving? Aye, I know I can leave. I know the debt has long been paid. But this is my home now and I will remain and help your nephew manage your empire. It is a great empire, my lord. You said that he is worthy of it. I can only pray that you are right."

The old man smiled faintly. "You are the keeper of my legacy, are you not?" he said. "You will ensure he is worthy, I am sure, and if he is not..."

"If he is not, then I will know soon enough," she said. "You have been kind and generous with me, my lord. I will repay the favor by ensuring your legacy is preserved. Now... what did you wish to say to Jareth?"

The old man told her.

But he still couldn't do it without laughing.

CHAPTER ONE

Westminster Palace

"JARETH, WATCH OUT!"

Jareth heard the warning before he hit the ground, face first, and a blade whizzed over his head. Infuriated, and with a mouth full of dirt, he managed to kick his legs out and catch his opponent by the ankles.

Stefan de Lohr went down in a heap.

Jareth sat up, spitting clumps from his mouth, as he pounced on Stefan and shoved the man's face into the dirt as well.

"That's what you get, you overgrown child," he said, rolling off the man when he resisted. "Honestly, Stefan. Grabbing my ear and twisting? As if that would force me to capitulate?"

Stefan spat out some dirt of his own as he pushed himself onto his knees. "What's that you say?" he said. "I did not quite hear."

Given that Stefan was mostly deaf, Jareth had learned to speak very loudly to him. They all had. But sometimes Stefan used the deafness to his advantage and pleaded ignorance. Jareth, and the rest of the Guard of Six, had learned that as well.

Stefan may have been hard of hearing, and they knew it was growing worse, but he was anything but ignorant or helpless.

The man was a beast in the best sense of the word.

"I said you are an overgrown child," Jareth shouted at him, watching Stefan grin. "This was to be a training exercise, not a brawl."

Stefan stood up, reaching out a hand to pull Jareth to his feet. "It was great fun, whatever it was," he said. "You may not have the size of some of the others, but you are faster than lightning. That makes you more dangerous."

Jareth turned his nose up at him. "Do not flatter me," he said. "I do not like you and I do not believe you."

Stefan started laughing.

The men known as the Guard of Six had been training in a smaller yard of Westminster Palace beneath a May sun that was surprisingly warm. Tunics were off, shoulders were starting to bronze up and burn, but they were enjoying every moment of it. Training, and practice, was something that had been part of their lives since they were small children because, as English knights, perfect skill and readiness was expected of them.

No one trained more diligently than Jareth. A de Leybourne son, he had an older brother, a father, and an ancestral home named Tyringham Castle deep in the wilds of Cornwall. He'd been raised in that mysterious land that was built on legends and blood, so there was something wild in his soul. He wasn't the largest man in the Guard of Six, as Stefan had mentioned, but he was by far one of the most cunning. Jareth was as wise as he was ethical, as skilled as he was fast.

But he was not a small man by any definition. He was over six feet in height, with enormous shoulders and big arms. But the Guard of Six, by the king's design, comprised some of the biggest, strongest men in the kingdom, so Jareth's height against the others was all relative. He was a big man in any room he entered and certainly the smartest.

He was also the bravest.

And everyone knew it.

Which was why Stefan's comment about him being danger-ous was true. When an enemy sized up the Guard of Six, they often overlooked the man of shorter stature.

And that was a deadly mistake.

"I love you madly, Jareth," Stefan said as Jareth brushed the dirt off his breeches. "You know that you are the air in my lungs, the very blood that flows in me."

Jareth looked at him, his lips pressed in a doubtful line. "You can take that statement and toss it into the river with the rest of the rubbish," he said, watching Stefan laugh. "Train with Dirk for the rest of the day. If you try to twist his ear, he'll cut your fingers off."

The other Guard of Six members were chuckling at the pair, who were, in reality, the best of friends. Stefan had officially joined the Guard of Six earlier in the year when Kent de Poyer, one of the original Six, married and temporarily resigned his post to spend time on the Welsh marches with his new wife's family. Torran de Serreaux, the unofficial leader of the group, was also the Earl of Ashford, so he spent about half of his time at his seat of Kennington Castle in Kent.

That meant the Guard of Six, which had originally started with six men, needed reinforcements.

Those reinforcements had come in the form of Stefan, who was a de Lohr and therefore from one of the most powerful families in England, and another knight who was from the north of England and came with an astonishingly deep pedigree.

Orion Payton-Forrester.

Annoying was where he started. Where he ended, one could only guess. He was big and blond, with a dark blond mustache and a manner that was infinitely charming, bright, and resourceful, but the man was so perfect that he was, predictably, annoying. Even now, as he tried to engage Stefan into practicing some techniques with him, Jareth turned to watch the man. He was the great persuader because he was so persistent that one gave in simply to shut him up. Jareth took a drink of boiled water from a pitcher they had sitting on the stoop, swishing it around his mouth and spitting out the dirt that was still lodged in his teeth. But his gaze never left Orion as he finally convinced Stefan to work with him.

"He knows how to make grown men cry."

Jareth turned to see Aidric St. John walk up beside him. Tall and fair, the man looked like a Dane. He had a big, square jaw and strong features, far more of a follower than a leader, but he was the Six's secret weapon. He was the most vicious member of the group, someone that Stefan and Orion wouldn't spar with, not yet. They didn't know him well enough, but they were learning. Aidric had been watching them like a hawk since they had joined the group, and when Henry traveled and the Guard of Six stayed close to him, as their primary function was as royal bodyguards, Aidric took point because he looked positively terrifying. Stefan and Orion had simply fallen in behind him.

But that was their lot in life these days.

If they wanted to truly be considered part of the Six, they had to earn it.

"Orion, you mean?" Jareth said. Then he snorted. "He's getting better about it. Remember when Britt slapped him early on?"

That had Aidric grinning. "Britt has no patience," he said, referring to Britt de Garr, the least tolerant of the group. "That slap at least forced Orion to think twice about his behavior. He does not vex as he used to."

"True," Jareth said. "And before I forget yet again to tell you, Henry is planning on traveling to Windsor next month to do some hunting, so we will be traveling with him. With Torran and Kent away, I will take command."

That was usual, so Aidric simply nodded. "Any instructions?"

"None yet," Jareth said. "Henry may want us in the hunting party, so be prepared."

"With pleasure."

Hunting was always great sport. As they pondered what fun the journey to Windsor would entail, Stefan and Orion began engaging in swordplay. They were practicing a particular technique, joined by the final members of the Guard of Six in Britt and Dirk d'Vant, another Cornwall native. Aidric ended up with them as well, working beneath the noon sun, and Jareth was thinking of joining them when he caught movement off to his right.

Thor de Reyne was heading in his direction. An enormously powerful knight with black hair and piercing blue eyes, Thor held the title of Lord Protector, the king's personal bodyguard. He worked autonomously from the Guard of Six because he literally stayed by the king's side in all things, while the Guard of Six formed more of a perimeter. Fortunately, they all worked very well together and Jareth liked the suave and debonair Thor a good deal. He considered the man a good friend.

"Did you come to see us beat de Lohr and Payton-Forrester into the ground?" he called to him. "You are not too late if you wish to help."

Thor started to laugh, watching the five members of the Six as they went through their paces. "Is Payton-Forrester being a nuisance again?" he asked.

"A little."

"A little beating now and again might solve that."

"We've tried. He likes it."

That caused Thor to laugh harder. "Then I cannot help you," he said. "But I have come with a missive. It came for you a little while ago."

Jareth looked at him curiously. "Are you a messenger now?"

Thor shook his head. "Nay," he said. "But I was at the gatehouse when it arrived, so I brought it over."

With that, he extended a vellum envelope, carefully folded and sealed. Curious, Jareth looked at the seal—and there were three of them, all in a row—before realizing whose it was.

"My uncle," he said, sounding pleased. "Christ, I haven't spoken to him in years."

Thor watched as Jareth broke all three seals. "Why not?"

"A few reasons, I suppose," Jareth said. "The man is in Bristol. He hasn't come to London in years."

"You can go visit him, you know. Bristol is not that far."

Jareth shrugged. "No need," he said. "He's always come here, and we sup together when he does. We've never been particularly close, but with him, at least the effort is made."

"Unlike your own father."

Jareth shook his head. "Nay," he said without remorse. "My father only had time for my older brother, who only had time for himself. When my father died a few years ago, Jasper inherited everything and I've not heard from him since."

Thor watched the man open up the envelope and inspect

the careful writing. "Pity," he said.

"Not really," Jareth said. "My brother is an arse. In fact, I… Damn…"

He was reading the missive, and Thor looked at him with concern. "Is something amiss in Bristol?"

Jareth didn't answer for a moment. He just kept reading. "It seems so," he said slowly. "It seems that my uncle has died."

"I am sorry for you," Thor said sincerely. "Even if you were not close to the man, a death in the family is regrettable."

Jareth barely nodded as he continued reading. When he was finished, he read the missive again. And again. Finally, he looked up from the vellum, appearing the least bit stunned. Even Thor could see it.

"What is it?" he asked. "What's happened?"

Jareth looked back at the vellum. "He has left me his entire estate."

Thor's eyebrows lifted. "Truly?" he said. "And you were not even close to the man?"

"I did not think so."

"Evidently, your uncle thought differently."

Jareth shook his head. "You do not understand," he said. Then he read the vellum one more time before letting out a guffaw of disbelief. "My God… everything."

"What is everything? What do you mean?"

Jareth had to collect himself before he answered. "My uncle was my mother's brother," he said. "My mother came from a noble family in Bristol, and when my grandfather died, my uncle took over the family business. Shipping, mostly, but there is also a very large merchant stall in the city where things from all over the known world were sold."

Thor failed to see why that had Jareth so rattled. "Congratulations are in order," he said. "It sounds as if you are to be a very wealthy man."

Jareth shook his head. "You do not understand," he said. "This is not just wealth. My uncle has turned the family business into an empire. He built a church in the town center as well as a universitas. Can you imagine that? An institute of higher education. It is called the Temple Generale and it teaches priests and knights in the Biblical arts, architecture, and mathematics. He owns most of Bristol as it is—property and homes. The people who live in those properties work for him or work his land and pay him a percentage. He has more money than most of the warlords in England—combined. Rich does not completely cover how much he has."

Thor grinned. "Well done, old man," he said, clapping Jareth on the arm. "But why are you not more pleased about this?"

Jareth had to pause and think on that question. "Because… hell, because the subject of the man's heir has never come up," he said. "Not from my mother, not even from my father. My father could not stand the man, in fact."

"Why?"

"Because Uncle Chester de Long was twice as smart as my father and twice as ambitious," he said. "Chester could run circles around my father and my father hated him for it. Chester also hates my brother, Jasper, and the feeling is mutual."

"But he does not hate you?" Thor said. "Why?"

Jareth shrugged. "Because I am my mother's son," he said quietly, thinking on the woman he loved dearly. "My mother was a sweet woman, Thor. We share the same dark hair and eyes. My father once said that I have her smile. Uncle Chester adored my mother. Her marriage to my father was arranged and Chester never forgave my grandfather for it. He did not think my father was good enough for her."

Thor understood. "Ah," he said. "The protective older brother."

"Indeed," Jareth said. "Ironic he did not think my father was good enough, because we descend from King Mark of Cornwall. Our bloodlines are royal. But Chester never liked my father. Truthfully, he probably would not have liked any man who married my mother. When my mother died when I was ten years of age, I do not think Uncle Chester ever spoke to my father again. I seemed to be the only one he maintained a relationship with. Still, this missive comes as a… surprise."

A lift of the eyebrows emphasized his last word, and Thor could see that it was a complex family matter. Anything involving relatives usually was.

"What will you do?" he asked quietly.

Jareth lifted his shoulders. "What can I do?" he said. "I cannot ignore this. My uncle had no children, so I suppose I should, at the very least, go to Bristol and settle his affairs."

Thor nodded. "But what about the empire?" he said. "What will you do with it?"

Jareth shook his head. "For all I know, it may not even exist any longer," he said. "Mayhap Uncle Chester let it all fall to pieces."

"Would he?"

"I have no way of knowing until I go to Bristol."

"Then you must tell Henry."

Jareth cast him a long look. "He's already lost Kent," he said. "Torran is only here half of the time. I do not think Henry will be too thrilled if I leave for months on end, but it cannot be helped."

Thor gestured to the vellum. "If I were you, I would tell him now," he said. "You already know you must go. You may as well ask permission."

Jareth knew that, but the missive in his hand caught his attention again and he lifted it, looking at the words again and suspecting his life was going to change from this point forward. It wasn't that the prospect of wealth didn't interest him, because it did. But he wanted it on his own terms, not his uncle's. Chester had sent him a summons from his deathbed, informing him of the path his future was about to take, and Jareth wasn't entirely certain he wanted to go down that road.

He wasn't entirely sure about anything at the moment.

"I will," he said. "But this is something I must ponder. This was not something I had anticipated today. This will take some thought."

Thor understood. Over in the group of training knights, someone had started an actual fight and neither Thor nor Jareth was surprised to see that it was Orion. He had irritated Stefan, who swung his big sword at him, much to Orion's delight. The training was turning into something else.

"This will not end well for Orion," Jareth said, his focus shifting away from his uncle as he watched Stefan stalk Orion. "Stefan may not be able to hear, but he can still fight better than almost anyone in England. If I were Orion, I would be—"

He didn't even get the words out of his mouth before Stefan launched a lightning-fast attack, thrusting with his sword so that all Orion could do was defend himself. Orion was dodging a move that came up from underneath him, turning his sword to counter it, but he failed to see how close Stefan came to him until Stefan's left fist made contact with Orion's jaw.

Down he went.

Much to Orion's chagrin, the laughter from his colleagues could be heard all throughout the yard. Directed at him, no less. Nay, it was not his finest moment.

Training was over for the day.

CHAPTER TWO

"I DID NOT know that Chester de Long was your uncle."

"He is, Your Grace."

"Then I would say that this is excellent fortune for you, yet you do not seem pleased."

The words came from Henry, King of England, the man who had ruled since he'd been nine years of age. If anyone in the history of the Crown had ever truly lost their identity in their birthright, it was Henry. He was England and England was him. He'd long shirked off any sense of individuality, and now was simply a symbol of the idolatry for those who worshipped kings.

Henry *was* England.

He was also quite elderly and ill, and he had been ill for some time. Anyone who knew that, those closest to him, were surprised that his son and heir, Edward, had left for the Levant the previous year on yet another crusade. However, those that knew Edward were not surprised in the least because Edward did as Edward wanted.

Even if it meant he'd never see his father alive again.

Jareth was very aware of all of that, and his focus was on

Henry as the man sat in a cushioned chair in a small reception chamber that was part of the royal apartments. He would often receive the Guard of Six, or other close ministers, there informally, so when Thor came to him with Jareth's request for an audience, Henry was quite willing to give it to him. He liked Jareth, in particular, because the man would sit with him for hours playing chess, something Henry enjoyed and something Jareth was good enough at to make it look like the king won more than he did. Therefore, he was genuinely pleased to hear of Jareth's good fortune with his inheritance.

Even if Jareth himself didn't seem too thrilled.

"Well?" Henry said when Jareth didn't answer quickly enough. "You do not seem entirely pleased. Chester de Long is a very wealthy man who has done much good for Bristol with the universitas he built. Why are you not happy about this?"

Jareth was very nearly receiving a lecture, trying not to look too ungrateful. "You have heard of the school he built, Your Grace?"

Henry frowned. "Of course I have," he said. "Mostly, I know because when he built it, the church was distressed and demanding that he build a cathedral as well, which he did. The universitas is for mathematics and architecture, or at least it was, originally. But the Bishop of Bristol did not like that something important was built without being part of the church, or not at least teaching clergy, so your uncle had to pay for a cathedral as well as adding theology to the universitas. It was quite an uproar, for years, as I recall. Did you not know this?"

Jareth shrugged weakly. "You must remember I do not have much contact with my family, Your Grace," he said. "I did hear something about it when it happened, but I have only visited with my uncle on a handful of occasions when he came to London. We were not particularly close, but closer than he was to my brother. I suppose that is why he made me his heir. At least he had one nephew with whom he still had contact."

"And you are not pleased that you are his heir."

It wasn't a question, but a statement. Even after that lengthy explanation on family dynamics, Henry only seemed to be focused on whether or not Jareth was happy with the news.

A complicated question with a complicated answer.

"I suppose I am unsettled because I am not certain how his directive will affect my life," he said. "I enjoy my position with you, Your Grace. I do not want to leave it. I am happy with my life in London."

Henry seemed to understand that explanation. "While your loyalty is appreciated, I would be the first man to say that you deserve this good fortune," he said. "Your uncle has entrusted you with, by all accounts, a tremendous fortune, so you must not fail him. More importantly, you must not fail yourself. You are duty bound to see this through."

Jareth was listening with an unhappy expression on his face. "But what if it takes me from London for a great length of time?" he said. "What if I am required to remain in Bristol to oversee everything? That is something I did not choose, Your Grace. What if I do not want it?"

Henry grunted at the man's reluctance. Standing behind him, he could see Thor, who seemed concerned for Jareth's position. The man was clearly happy where he was, so the advent of an unexpected inheritance, and everything that entailed, was troubling.

An uncertain future always was.

"I think only an insane man would not want a wealthy inheritance, Jareth, and I do not consider you insane," Henry said. "My suggestion would be that you go to Bristol and discover for yourself everything the inheritance entails. Then, if you do not wish to remain in Bristol, or you do not wish to manage it, then pay someone trustworthy to do it for you. But not someone from Bristol, who knows of it, and not someone who already serves your uncle. Find someone who has no affiliation. It will be safer that way. You do not want someone who will rob you blind because they know what the inheritance is worth and you do not."

Jareth nodded reluctantly. "Sage advice, Your Grace," he said. Then he sighed. "I suppose I should go right away. Whoever was in the employ of my uncle could be robbing me blind as I speak."

"Indeed."

"Would it be inconvenient to you if I were to leave on the morrow?" Jareth said. "Unless you require me for a task, in which case I will remain."

Henry waved him off. "Nay," he said. "You may go. In fact… in fact, I have some thoughts I would like to share with you, Jareth. Would you spare me the time to hear them?"

"My time is yours, Your Grace."

Henry reached for a cup of honeyed wine on the table next to him and took a big swallow. He ended up coughing, spraying some of it out, as a servant moved quickly to help him clean it up. It was indicative of his terrible health and the clumsy way in which his entire left side moved. It was the common opinion among the royal physics that Henry had suffered an apoplectic episode last year, something that weakened his left side. He was still able to walk and move, but it was difficult for him at times. Jareth personally poured the king more sweet wine as the servant finished cleaning the man up.

"Jareth," Henry said, his voice hoarse from the coughing, "a great knight such as yourself should not be reduced to pouring me wine. That is what I wish to speak to you about."

"Your Grace?"

Henry, a man who clearly had something on his mind, took a deep breath. "I do not believe I shall travel away from London again," he said. "I know I told you that I may wish to hunt next month, but I have changed my mind. I am tired, Jareth. I am content to remain here with Eleanor and watch our grandchildren grow. Make no mistake, however—I shall remain in control. There are still things to do. My rule shall be absolute. But I do not see myself taking on any great campaigns or quests again."

Jareth simply nodded, unsure why the man would tell him something like that. "You are a great king, Your Grace," he said. "Should you ever choose to ride again, I will be by your side."

Henry's dark eyes twinkled with warmth, or as much warmth as the man was able to give. "You have stayed by my side through some difficult times," he said. "When I look back upon our history together, you were there for a good deal of it."

"I was, Your Grace."

"My task here still is not complete."

"What do you mean, Your Grace?"

Henry sighed again. "The country is still not entirely stable," he said. "There are still those who remain allied to Simon de Montfort, though he has been dead these many years. There are still those who are not loyal to me, as their king. You know that the treasury has struggled to rebuild after the battles with de Montfort. That has not changed overly, and Edward's quest to the Levant has taken more money than it should. I do not like instability, Jareth. It smacks of failure."

Jareth shook his head. "It smacks of a king who was challenged by a usurper," he said quietly. "In the end, you emerged the victor, as you should. But it will simply take time to rebuild."

Henry pondered that for a moment. "I have been thinking on disbanding the Guard of Six so that you may find more lucrative positions," he said. "Do not look at me with such shock—I simply mean that Torran is now an earl and we do not see him often, and Kent has decided to remain on the Welsh marches with his new wife and family. We will not see him again. I consider you the leader of the Guard of Six now, and there is Aidric and Britt and Dirk. There is also Stefan de Lohr now, and that fiery knight, Payton-Forrester. You are all elite knights, but if I am to no longer travel or engage in battle, your lives will go to waste for want of action, and that is not a fate any of you deserve."

"No man suffers an ill fate when he serves the king," Jareth said. "But it is true that a man's skills will lapse if he does not use them."

"Do you feel that your skills will lapse if you remain with me in my infirm years?"

Jareth shook his head. "Not at all, Your Grace," he said. "I will simply go around starting fights to stave off boredom."

That brought a grin from Henry. "Let us hope it does not come to that," he said. Then he turned to a man off to his right. "William believes I should keep my Six. He has been your advocate, as has Thor. Mayhap I will not disband you at this time because, truthfully, you are a comfort to me. And I need men who are a comfort."

Jareth looked over at William de Valence, one of Henry's

chief advisors. He was French, as many of Henry's advisors were, but he was likable enough. He genuinely seemed to have the king's, and the country's, best interests at heart. As he exchanged a nod with William, Thor, who had been standing well behind Jareth during the conversation, came to stand alongside him.

"Your Grace, may I offer to accompany Jareth on his journey to Bristol?" he said. "I suspect he may need guidance and assistance, and I am certain you do not wish to send the entire Six with him."

Jareth thought that was a good idea, but Henry shook his head. "Nay," he said. "He may take the Six. As I said, I have no plans to go anywhere or do anything for the next month or so, but I would prefer that my Lord Protector remain by my side. Jareth, take the Six with you. It will give them an adventure to stave off the boredom, as you call it. But I will expect you to return as soon as you can."

Jareth dipped his head in acknowledgment. "Aye, Your Grace."

He eyed Thor as he turned to leave, as if to acknowledge the man's disappointment in not being able to travel with him to Bristol. Thor remained behind, indeed disappointed, as Jareth quit the chamber and shut the door behind him. When he was gone, Henry let out a hiss.

"I did not want to say this in front of him, but I fear he is in for a shock when he arrives in Bristol," he said.

Thor looked at him. "Why, Your Grace?" he asked.

It was de Valence who spoke. "Very true, Your Grace," he said.

Thor was looking between them now. "*What* is he facing when he arrives in Bristol?" he said.

William and Henry looked at each other again until Henry gestured toward the man, inviting him to answer Thor's question. As Henry returned to his sweet wine, William spoke.

"Do you know much of Bristol, de Reyne?" he asked.

Thor shook his head. "I've only been there once," he said. "It seemed a nice enough town. Why?"

"Were you told anything about it?"

"Like what?"

That told William what he needed to know because to those who knew much about Bristol, there was one thing that stood out to them. Surely Thor would have said so had he known.

But he hadn't.

William proceeded.

"My wife has property near Bristol," he said. "Some of her family still lives there. Part of my role, as an advisor to the king, is to keep my ear to the ground for information on the nobles who infest England, especially when it is within lands or areas where my family lives. I must know of the people who pay my taxes."

Thor knew he was speaking as a Frenchman who had been greatly opposed by Henry's warlords. "My father is the Earl of Ashington, so I know about people who pay taxes and the character of English nobles," he said, more or less warning de Valence that he was not on the man's side should he speak ill of the English people. "What have you heard of Chester de Long?"

An amused expression drifted across William's face. "Simply that Chester is a man of many enterprises," he said. "The merchant business is only the beginning. That is not where he makes the bulk of his money."

Thor frowned. "Then where does he make it?"

William couldn't keep the smile off his face. "From a place

called Aphrodite's Feast," he said. "That is the true moneymaking establishment in Bristol. It is an enormous place, an old Roman temple converted into a luxurious home. Truthfully, it could put the finest palaces to shame. I have been there before, taken by my wife's father. He is a regular patron of the place that the locals call, simply, The Feast."

"What is it?" Thor asked. "An inn?"

"A *myltenhus*."

Thor stared at him as he realized what the man was saying. "A *what*?" he said, aghast. "A bordel?"

William nodded. "Where women sell their bodies to men for money."

That had Thor's mouth popping open in surprise. "And Jareth has inherited it?"

William shrugged. "If he has inherited all of Chester de Long's businesses, then he has, indeed, inherited it," he said. "I am not entirely sure I have ever heard of any man inheriting something like that, to be truthful. But it must make money the likes of which no other business in England ever has. Thousands of pounds, mayhap on a daily basis. Jareth will not only be rich—he will possess more wealth than God himself."

"Money I could very much use," Henry said softly.

Both Thor and William looked at him. Money was in desperate need by the king and everyone knew it, so now it made some sense as to why Henry seemed so incensed that Jareth didn't want his inheritance.

Jareth had what Henry needed.

"Surely de Long paid taxes, Your Grace," William said. "I know he contributed a good deal to Edward's crusade."

Henry drew in a long, thoughtful breath. "He did," he said. "But so did others. De Long was not unique in that sense. But his wealth is obscene. No one man should be allowed to hoard such an amount."

Thor could see that he was stewing about it, but Thor was stewing about the fact that Jareth had no idea what he was walking into. "Should you not tell Jareth what you know, Your Grace?" he said. "About the bordel, I mean. That is not exactly an inheritance a man can be proud of. Shouldn't he know?"

Henry wasn't as concerned for Jareth as he should have been. He took another sip of his wine. "Why?" he said. "He is going to find out when he arrives. What is the point of telling him now? It will simply make him more reluctant to accept the inheritance than he is already."

"Aye, Your Grace."

"And you will not tell him what you know," Henry said. "It is none of your affair, anyway."

"Nay, Your Grace."

Lost in thought, Henry considered his wine before continuing. "Thor, I am to have an audience with the Bishop of Ely tomorrow," he said. "You are aware of this?"

It was a change of subject that Thor wasn't ready for, because he didn't consider the conversation about Jareth and the bordel finished, but Henry clearly did. Thor nodded to the question.

"I am, Your Grace."

"I want to meet with him alone," Henry said. "I want you to discover whom he is traveling with and whom he intends to bring with him to Westminster. You know the man is here to plead on behalf of some Norfolk warlords who sided with de Montfort those years ago, men who have continued to refuse to support me. You will discover everyone he is bringing because I would not be surprised if some of those warlords come disguised as the bishop's guards."

"Fear not, Your Grace," Thor said. "No one but the bishop shall make it to the hall."

"Go, then," Henry said. "And remember what I told you."

"Your Grace?"

"Not a word of the strumpet house to Jareth."

Thor nodded, his features expressionless, before quitting the chamber. That left William with Henry, just the two of them.

And that was the way Henry wanted it.

"It is going to eat away at de Reyne, not being able to tell Jareth what you told him," Henry said. "But I am withholding the information for a reason."

"Reason, Your Grace?" William said curiously.

Henry nodded, taking another drink of his wine. Just the dregs were left now, and he swirled them around in his cup, watching them float about.

"If Jareth is shocked enough at his inheritance and refuses to accept it, where do you think it will go after that?" he said.

William shrugged. "To his brother? His father?"

"To me," Henry said, looking at him. "Unclaimed property will revert to the Crown."

William understood completely now. "And so will the money it generates."

Henry nodded slowly. "Exactly," he said. "Therefore, let Jareth go to Bristol. Let him see what his uncle has left him—a den of debauchery that no pious knight would want to take responsibility for. But I have no such qualms, considering the income it could bring me, so let him discover this for himself. And when he returns to London and tells me he'll not accept the inheritance, I will most graciously relieve him of this heinous enterprise. And he'll thank me for it."

It was the general consensus that between Henry and his eldest son, Edward, Edward was the more conniving and ambitious of the two. But William de Valence knew better.

In moments like this, Henry was the master.

In more ways than one.

CHAPTER THREE

Redcliffe Hill Manor
Bristol

"THAT'S QUITE A townhome, Jareth. Congratulations."

Aidric was gesturing to a large manse, with a big curtain wall, that was perched on the riverbank. With the blue, breezy sky as a backdrop and birds riding the drafts overhead, Jareth paused to get a good look at what his uncle had left him. A big, gray-stoned edifice with some sections that were wattle and daub, with whitewashed walls and brown-stained beams in patterns, like quatrefoil, which looked like a four-leaf clover. There were other designs, too, carefully carved and then applied to the wall with plaster.

Truthfully, it was a stunning piece of architecture.

"Given the fact that my uncle was wealthy, I suppose I should not be surprised," he finally said. "But… damnation, I am. I truly am."

Those around him started laughing because he was showing genuine shock. Along with Aidric, Stefan and Orion had accompanied him with the rest of the Guard of Six, as Henry had allowed. It was a full complement of some of the most powerful men in England, and exactly nine days after leaving London, they were standing in front of Redcliffe.

It seemed like a dream.

Britt de Garr came over and slapped Jareth on the shoulder, beaming at him. The man had red hair, blue eyes, and the flaming temper to match those vibrant colors. He was big and menacing when he wanted to be, but no man was more loyal to king or country or his companions.

Jareth liked Britt a great deal.

Rounding out the Six was Dirk d'Vant, from the Cornwall d'Vants, a family that had made its name in war and piracy and shipping. He was an enormous blond god of a man, more fearsome with a sword than any of them. He was congenial, and had an air of command about him, but tended to be rather quiet because he spoke with a slight lisp. A very deep voice with a barely noticeable lazy tongue, but Dirk had been self-conscious about it since he was a child, so he tended to be a man of action more than words. But even Dirk was awed by his friend's good fortune.

"God's Blood," he said. "You could rule quite an empire from that home, Jareth. Well deserved, old man."

Jareth was trying to keep the smile off his face. Now that the shock of seeing such a place was wearing off, he could feel the thrill of pleasure filling him. Pleasure in the fact that his uncle's empire was still here, or at least his primary residence was still here, a fine example of a rich man's legacy. They were outside of the gates, in an open area where three roads converged, and there were other cottages around, all of them well kept. It was evidently the higher rent district of Bristol. Everything appeared rather nice and neat. Orion and Stefan were already up by the gate leading into the manse's yard, trying to peer through the slats, when Jareth walked up and pulled on a piece of rope poking through a hole next to the gate.

Somewhere, a bell rang.

Curious, the men gathered around the gate, waiting to see who would appear. No one answered right away, so Jareth rang again. And a third time. Finally, they could hear someone chattering as they came closer to the gate, a running conversation about the virtue of patience or something like it. Whoever it was sounded irritated. The gate on the right had a small window cut into it, and that little wooden square was yanked open.

An eye appeared.

"What are ye wanting?" came the demand.

Jareth put himself in front of the bloodshot eye. "My name is Jareth de Leybourne," he said. "Chester de Long was my uncle. I have a document from him naming me the heir to his properties and I am here to stake my claim. Open the gate and let me in."

The eye widened as it looked him up and down. "Ye?"

"Me."

"Show me the letter!"

Jareth went back over to his horse, digging in his saddlebag before pulling forth the missive. He went back over to the eye, unfolding the vellum to show him the letter.

"See?" he said. "From my Uncle Chester. Now will you open the gate?"

The eye could see the document, and the familiar seal, but he only looked at it briefly before looking at the other men standing around. All of them big and heavily armed.

"Who are the others?" he demanded.

Jareth was quickly running out of patience. "I have told you my name," he said. "I have shown you the document sent to me by my uncle. You will open the gate or the six of us will kick it down and throw you into the river. Do you understand?"

The eye disappeared. Jareth looked at Aidric and the others, a wry expression on his face as he wondered if he was going to have to make good on his threat. But he was saved from a decision when the bolt to the gate was thrown and the panel on the right lurched open.

An old man with dirty white hair stood in the gap.

"My name is Henbury," he said. "I have been the major-domo at Redhill since I was a young man. Ye must understand that men will do or say anything to come inside and rob us."

Jareth couldn't fault the old man being careful. "I assure you, we are not here to rob you," he said. "My uncle has left me this home and his property. I have come to claim my property."

"As ye should," the old man said. "Welcome to Redcliffe Manor."

Everyone stepped in through the gate, looking around. Especially Jareth—he liked what he saw.

"It is well kept," he observed. "This isn't the only property in town, however. Am I correct in my understanding of that?"

"Ye are."

"Then mayhap you can explain everything to me."

The old man shook his head. "Ye must see Desdra for that," he said. "She has been expecting ye."

"Who is Desdra?"

"Lord Chester's scribe."

"Very well," Jareth said. "Will you announce me to Desdra?"

"She is at The Feast, my lord."

Jareth had no idea what that meant. "What feast?"

"*The* Feast. Aphrodite's Feast."

"I do not know what that is or where it is."

The old man pointed back toward the city center, northward. "It is *The Feast*, my lord," he said as if Jareth should already know. "Only the greatest enterprise the world has ever seen. Ye do not know this?"

"Tell me what The Feast is."

The old man looked at him. Then he looked at the men around him. "It is a place for men," he explained. "A place where men find women to take comfort with. And food to eat. The very best food! Aphrodite's Feast is famous for the finest food and drink in all of England. Lord Chester would have Spanish wine brought over—great barrels of it—because the customers demand it."

Jareth still wasn't clear on what he was talking about. "A tavern?" he said.

"Nay," Orion said quietly. He'd been listening to the explanation and had a suspicion what the establishment was all about. "Henbury, is this a place where a man can pay to lie with a woman?"

Henbury nodded without hesitation. "If he wishes," he said. "But he can also pay to dance with her or eat with her. Whatever he desires. Have ye truly not heard of it?"

Orion looked at Jareth. "It seems that your uncle has left you a brothel."

Jareth hadn't expected to hear that. He wasn't naïve by any stretch of the imagination, but Orion had figured it out before he did. Perhaps because a brothel, in his noble family, had never entered his mind. Shocked, he lifted his eyebrows.

"Is *that* what it is?" he said incredulously, looking at Henbury. "A strumpet house?"

He didn't seem pleased, which puzzled Henbury. He could see that the rest of the men were a little surprised by the news, so he once again pointed toward the city center.

"Desdra is there, waiting for ye," he said. "She will tell ye everything. Ye'll find Aphrodite's Feast on the Avenue of the Jews. Where the metalsmiths are."

Jareth just stood there for a moment, astounded. Then he started to shake his head. "I cannot believe this," he said. "My uncle kept *whores*?"

"We do not call them that, my lord," Henbury said. "They are muses."

Jareth was quickly moving beyond surprise to outrage. "It doesn't matter what you call them," he said. "It is all the same. God's Bones, this cannot be true!"

Henbury was genuinely puzzled at the outrage. "The Feast has been in the de Long family for many years," he said. "It wasn't just yer uncle, my lord. His father before him, and his before him. Ye did not know?"

Realizing this enterprise was generational did nothing for Jareth's shock or anger. He looked at the men around him, feeling a great deal of embarrassment. They'd all come to witness his shameful inheritance. The fact that this was some family secret kept from him only made him feel more foolish. After a moment, he closed his eyes and clapped a hand on his forehead.

"I did not know," he muttered. "How is that even possible? Surely my mother knew. My father must have known. And no one bothered to mention it."

Henbury wasn't sure what to say. "Ye must find Desdra, my lord," he said again. "She will tell you everything."

Jareth shook his head quickly. "I am not going anywhere,"

he said. "Bring this Desdra woman to me immediately. I will *not* go to a brothel. I certainly will not own one."

Henbury was coming to realize that the man who identified himself as Lord Chester's nephew was grossly unhappy with the inheritance he'd been given. Perhaps it wasn't the most prestigious bequest, but it was a moneymaker. It also did good for the town. Henbury had been around it for so long that the fact it featured women meant nothing to him. It was simply one business in Lord Chester's empire.

But, clearly, the knight didn't feel that way.

Perhaps Henbury needed to explain a little more than he had.

"It is not as bad as that, my lord," he said. "Aphrodite's Feast is well respected, even by the church. They do not mind it."

Jareth was incredulous. "How can they not mind it?"

"Because it is more than what ye think," Henbury said. "Come inside and I'll explain it all to ye. Then ye can proceed into town, as ye'll be fully informed."

Jareth was quite sure he wouldn't be proceeding anywhere that had to do with a brothel, but he took the man up on his invitation to go inside the manse. The ride from London had been tiring and he was ready to sit and rest. But before he could do that, he took the opportunity to inspect the grounds and the manse itself. At close range, he wasn't disappointed with what he saw.

Redcliffe Hill Manor was astonishing.

It was enough to take his mind off the brothel for the moment. He walked the yard of the manse with his friends, with Henbury trailing after him, and he inspected the stables and the few outbuildings there were. Then he went inside the manse only to discover that the entire thing was furnished in absolute riches. Cushions on the chairs, tapestries on the walls, and curtains on the windows. The feasting table had lion's heads carved at each corner, and above the hearth, on a long wooden mantel, sat a dozen plates of pewter and at least one plate of gold with a few semiprecious stones embedded in it.

"Incredible," Stefan said, standing near Jareth. "My family is wealthy, so when I say that this is an astonishing display of wealth, you can believe it."

Jareth glanced at him, though it was difficult for him to tear his eyes away from what he was seeing. "I knew the man was rich, but this is beyond anything I could imagine," he said. "And this was built from the shipping business?"

"Not all of it, my lord," Henbury said, speaking on something he knew about. "What ye mostly see is the wealth from Aphrodite's Feast."

Jareth was reminded of that which he'd been happy to forget. With a sigh, he turned to the old man. "No brothel can bring in this kind of coinage."

"The Feast can."

Jareth didn't want to hear that. "I am not sure how much plainer I can be," he said. "I do not want this Feast place. No moral man would."

Henbury stiffened. "Lord Chester was an exceedingly moral man, my lord," he said. "Ye do not understand about The Feast. Ye do not understand that it provides positions for women who have nowhere to go. Women who are widows or spinsters. It gives them the opportunity to earn a living so they are not destitute."

Jareth wasn't sold. "Earn a living by receiving money for… favors."

Henbury shrugged. "Only if they wish to," he said. "They are not forced to do anything they do not wish to do. Most of them simply sing or dance or have conversations with men who pay them for such things. Women are creatures of beauty and companionship, and for those who do not know the benefits of such things, at Aphrodite's Feast, they can pay for the privilege and the woman can feed herself and her children. Is that not better than starving?"

"I do not know," Jareth said with irritation. "Is it? Are you telling me that my uncle made money off their misfortune?"

By this time, all of the Six were listening to Henbury's explanation and Jareth's stubborn, but understandable, reaction. It was Aidric who finally leaned into Jareth.

"Mayhap you had better see for yourself," he muttered. "You may as well inspect that which you are going to refuse. Only a fool wouldn't discover the truth, because if what that man is telling you is true, your uncle left you the riches of Midas."

Jareth looked at him, his lips pressed in a stubborn line, but he refrained from retorting. Aidric was right and he knew it. He glanced at Britt and Dirk, seeing that they were agreeing with Aidric. Jareth was usually the wise and levelheaded one of the group, but in this case, he realized he hadn't been. He was ready to refuse something outright that he didn't even know anything about. After a moment, he nodded reluctantly.

"Very well," he said, though he was clearly unhappy. "I suppose I should examine it before making a decision. Where did you say it was?"

Henbury pointed toward the city center again, a bend on the River Avon. "That way," he said. "Ye will pass Bristol Castle and continue on into the city. When ye come to the Avenue of the Jews, which is next to the river, ye will find it. Ye cannot miss it. It is the largest building on the street."

Jareth was already looking in that direction. "Bristol Castle," he repeated thoughtfully. "One of Henry's properties. Who is the commander?"

Aidric spoke up. "The last I heard, the House of de Winter had taken it over," he said. "But that was a year or two ago. I do not know if it has changed hands."

Jareth cocked an eyebrow. "I would be willing to wager that the commander of the castle knows about The Feast."

It was a logical suggestion. At least Jareth was willing to be reasonable and not rely on his anger and stubbornness for the moment. That was some progress. As Aidric had said, he may as well inspect what he was going to refuse.

The day was about to make an interesting turn.

CHAPTER FOUR

BRISTOL CASTLE OCCUPIED a prime location at the bend of the River Avon. It had an enormous moat around it that was fed not only from the River Avon, but also from the River Frome, which ran slightly to the north and bisected the town. It was an impressive property of stone and battlements, and extremely defensible. There were several gatehouses because there were several bridges across the moat, all of them disposable in the case of an attack. They could either be burned or pushed into the river.

Jareth had to admit that it was a remarkable castle. It wasn't large, but it was sturdy and well maintained. The six knights went to what looked to be the main gatehouse, with a rather narrow bridge that spanned the moat, about fifteen feet above the murky green water. The horses could only go across single file, so Jareth went first. When he came to the gatehouse, he called up to the sentries and identified himself and the men that were with him. He asked to see the commander of the castle, in the name of the king, and identified himself further as a royal knight. His tunic, and the standards of the others, confirmed it. But he didn't have to go to so much trouble—someone in the gatehouse recognized his name.

They ran off to fetch the commander.

As the Six stood there in single file, waiting for admittance, Jareth found himself looking off toward the city center, which was not far from the castle. It was off to the west and he could see many small fishing vessels moored on the banks of the river. He knew that the River Avon eventually wound its way to the sea, making Bristol a port city. The birds were circling above the vessels, diving down to pilfer from the catches brought ashore or capture loose fish scattered on the rocky bank. His gaze then moved to the city with its sturdy buildings and well-kept avenues.

It was the city his mother had grown up in.

Odd how he'd never spent any time here. His world had only been his father's side of the family, and Cornwall had been their domain. As Jareth continued to wait for the commander to appear, thoughts of his father had his focus returning to his uncle and everything the man had left him.

He wondered if he'd ever get over the shock.

Truthfully, Jareth was still having a difficult time believing that in all of his years, he had never heard of the fact that his uncle and his grandfather had a brothel for a business. He knew about the shipping, and he knew about the merchant business, and if he thought hard enough, he could recall his mother saying something about other ventures in the city, but there had never been any mention of a brothel. He was coming to wonder if his mother had even known.

Part of him hoped that she hadn't.

So, how *did* he feel about the inheritance? The more he thought about it, the more resistant he was. The more shocked and embarrassed he was. Unfortunately, it wasn't as if he could pick and choose what he wanted to inherit versus what he didn't want to inherit. The inheritance laws in England were strict for a reason, but that usually pertained to property of the nobility so dying old men who controlled their world couldn't do what they wanted with it. The law always had the last word. He didn't think there was any law that said a nephew had to accept a brothel as part of an inheritance from an uncle who was lesser nobility. Chester de Long, as far as he knew, had only inherited a very minor title from his father, Lord Easton. It was only a regional title with no real clout in the grand scheme of things, but it occurred to Jareth that now *he* was Lord Easton. That would have been a proud moment if the title hadn't come with a trollop house.

He wondered if this day could get any worse.

As he was mulling over the shameful course his life had taken, the portcullis began to lift. He dismounted his horse to greet the commander only to be faced with a man he hadn't seen in a couple of years.

Hugh de Winter grinned brightly at the sight of Henry's personal bodyguards.

"Jareth!" he said happily, running over to hug the man. "Welcome to Bristol! And you brought the Six with you!"

Jareth smiled weakly at the younger brother of Davyss de Winter, head of what was commonly known as the de Winter war machine, an army so powerful that Henry had depended on it regularly for the vast majority of his reign. During the time of Simon de Montfort's rebellion, the strength from Davyss and the de Winter army had been invaluable.

Jareth had to admit that he was glad to see Hugh.

"Are you the garrison commander now?" he said, surprised. "We'd heard that de Winter had taken over the property, but to see a de Winter himself at the helm? Astonishing."

Hugh was an emotional and exuberant man, never afraid to give his opinion or question something he didn't like. He was the embodiment of honesty even if honesty wasn't the best course of action. No man in his right mind would resist or be aggressive toward Hugh for two very good reasons—he was hell with a sword and his brother was even worse.

No man challenged a de Winter and lived to tell the tale.

But a challenge was clearly the last thing from Hugh's mind as he moved to Aidric and Britt and finally Dirk, greeting them happily.

"Gentle knights, welcome," he said, shaking hands. "In answer to your question, Jareth, I'm not the garrison commander. I am here to relieve Andrew Catesby. You remember Andrew?"

Jareth did indeed remember the tall blond knight who had served the House of de Winter for years. "I know him," he said. "Andrew is the commander?"

Hugh nodded. "He is," he said. "But his father passed away recently, so Andrew and his brother, Edmund, have gone home to bury their father. I am here until such time as they return."

"Then I am glad to find you here," Jareth said. "How's the outpost? Quiet?"

Hugh nodded. "For the most part," he said. "There are some politically opposed families in the area that must be watched so they do not get into a tangle, and there are also pirates who roam the waters this time of year, so I'm told."

"You haven't seen them?"

"Nay," Hugh said. "None of them. Too bad, too. I was hoping to have a little party with one or more of them."

Jareth smirked. "I can only imagine the hospitality you

would show them."

Hugh laughed. "Only the best," he insisted. "But let us speak of other things. I must know why all of you are here. And where are Torran and Kent?"

"Torran is the Earl of Keddington now," Jareth said. "Surely you knew that."

Hugh nodded. "I remember hearing he had married well," he said. "And Kent?"

"He married a woman from the Welsh marches and has chosen to stay there for the time being," Jareth said. "In their absence, we are joined by Orion Payton-Forrester and Stefan de Lohr. Of course, you know them."

Hugh hadn't caught sight of either one of those men because he'd been focused on those from the original Guard of Six. But the mention of Stefan and Orion saw the smile vanishing from his face.

"I know de Lohr," he said as if the name left a bad taste in his mouth. "They are kin to the Earl of East Anglia, a man who tries to rule over my brother's lands any chance he gets. Stefan, I'll not speak with you at all, do you hear me?"

Stefan hadn't, so Britt had to tell him what had been said. That had Stefan rolling his eyes. "No great loss," he said. "I like Davyss better than his idiot brother, anyway."

Hugh heard him. His dark eyebrows flew up in outrage. "Is that so?" he said. "Just for that, everyone can have wine but you. Oh, and Payton-Forrester. That bastard still owes me money from a game of chance at The Pox over three years ago."

The Pox was the infamous tavern on the banks of the River Thames. It was a gambling hall, but also a drinking hall. Every fighting man in England had been there at one time or another because not only could they find a game of chance there, any time of the day or night, but The Pox also had the finest food around. Odd for such a seedy place. Orion, much like Stefan, didn't care much for Hugh.

"I paid you and you know it," he said loudly. "And I wouldn't drink your wine if it was the last drink in England. If you've had your grimy fingers on it, then it's probably rank."

That only succeeded in making Hugh angrier. "You *never* paid me."

"I paid for your meals and your room for four days and nights," Orion said. "You agreed it was payment enough."

"I never did!"

Orion started to charge forward, jabbing a finger at Hugh. "Then let us settle this here and now, you cheat," he said. "Davyss de Winter's pissy little brother will not call me a liar and emerge unscathed."

Britt and Stefan held him back as Jareth and Aidric pushed Hugh back into the gatehouse. "Come," Jareth said, trying to distract him. "I've come here with a question I need answered. Do not let Orion distract you."

Hugh didn't appreciate being pushed around, but Jareth was doing a good job of it because he was quite strong. He wasn't the tallest man around, but he had a strength that rivaled that of Samson's.

"What question?" he said as they entered the bailey of Bristol Castle. Digging his heels in, he came to a halt. "Stop shoving, Jareth. What question do you have?"

"What do you know about Aphrodite's Feast?"

That wasn't a question Hugh had been expecting. A bit bewildered by the rapid shift in focus, he furrowed his brow and looked at Jareth strangely.

"The Feast?" he repeated. "Why do you ask?"

"Just tell me what you know."

The subject seemed to have Hugh properly distracted from Orion, because his entire demeanor changed. "It's a fantasy world," he said. "It's a place of beautiful women, wine, and song. It's a place where a man can have anything he wants for a price."

"Then you've been there?"

"Of course I've been there," Hugh said. "Why? Are you heading there now? I will go with you if you are. But Payton-Forrester is *not* invited."

Hugh didn't seem at all distressed talking about it. In fact, he seemed eager to go. His words, his explanation of Aphrodite's Feast, mirrored Henbury's. Jareth scratched his forehead, trying to figure out how to phrase the situation he found himself in.

"But it's a brothel," he said. "Isn't it?"

Hugh snorted. "You've never seen a brothel like this in your life," he said. "It's more than a brothel, Jareth. It's a place that makes you think you've died and gone to heaven."

"But you *have* paid a woman to have her in your bed… haven't you?"

Hugh shook his head. "Nay, because I promised my brother I would not, since he is trying to solicit a marriage for me with Roger Mortimer's daughter," he said. "I promised him I would keep myself clean of scandal, at least for the time being. But that has not stopped me from going to The Feast and spending time with an utterly divine creature named Melaina. She sings like an angel and lets me eat my meals off her belly. Literally, she lies on the table and lets me eat whatever I want off her belly. It's the most seductive thing you've ever seen."

"So… you like the place?"

"Love it. Why the questions?"

"Because I have inherited it."

Hugh's eyes widened. He stared at Jareth until his mouth finally popped open. "You inherited Chester de Long's property?" he gasped. "*You?*"

"Me."

"My God, how?"

"He is my mother's brother. He had no heirs, so he chose me."

That had Hugh throwing his arms around Jareth's neck jubilantly. "Such great fortune for you, my friend!" he said. "We must go to The Feast and celebrate this instant!"

But Jareth wasn't quite so jubilant. "Wait," he said, pushing Hugh away. "It is utterly shameful that I have inherited a brothel. I do not want to 'celebrate' it."

Hugh was puzzled by the reaction. "Have you even been there?" he said. "Do you know what you are saying?"

Jareth sighed sharply. "Nay, I've not been there, but I know that inheriting a brothel is scandalous at best," he said. "Why would you be so happy for me to be shamed like that?"

"It is not a shame, I assure you."

"What would your mother say if you inherited such a place?"

Hugh shrugged. "Lady Katherine de Winter would never visit a place like that herself, but she also would not discourage me from having a source of income," he said. "A very *big* source. Do you understand that, Jareth? If you do not, then I cannot explain it to you. We must go to The Feast immediately so you can see it for yourself."

That was what everyone had been telling him. Jareth knew he had little choice in the matter. Evidently, Aphrodite's Feast was something that had to be seen to be believed, so he resigned himself to the fact that everyone wanted to see the place except him.

The whole situation was positively ridiculous.

"Very well," he said, openly perturbed. "Let us go see this thing that I do not want. Lead the way, Hugh."

Gleefully, Hugh did.

CHAPTER FIVE

Aphrodite's Feast

IT WAS A business.

From the top of its stone towers to the bottom of its storage vault, the legendary establishment known as Aphrodite's Feast had always been treated like a business because it was. It was a place where women who needed to earn a living could earn it with some dignity. Given the fact that it was technically a brothel, perhaps that seemed like the paradox, but it wasn't. Aphrodite's Feast was a well-run and well-supplied establishment, and in this case, it supplied what many men were looking for.

The company of a beautiful woman.

In truth, there had been a brothel on this location for centuries. Aphrodite's Feast had been given its name because it was built on an ancient Roman temple dedicated to the wine god, Bacchus. Although that seemed strange, given the region, which was not a wine-producing region, it was nonetheless true that the temple had been dedicated to the god of drunks. It was equally possible that was why the temple had been so widely used when the Romans occupied western England. Those who appreciated drink kept the temple in good repair, and that included a massive mosaic on the floor depicting a great feast with many beautiful women. Hence the name of the establishment—Aphrodite's Feast.

Sometime after the Romans, during the Dark Ages, it had fallen into some disrepair, but an enterprising person saw the value in it and used the building as both an inn and a brothel. They had reinforced the walls and built more rooms, and more stories, and as the centuries passed, the building continued to be reinforced and built upon until the ancestors of Chester de Long won the property in a game of chance.

It was the House of de Long that had turned it into a refuge for the seagoing men who would travel down the mouth of the River Avon and throw their anchors in the bend of the river near Bristol Castle. Back then, Aphrodite's Feast had been a place of rest and respite and food, and eventually, they added women to give comfort to those who'd been at sea for a very long time. The establishment became so popular, in fact, that they leaned in heavily to the "companion women" aspect of it, and that was how it became a brothel.

But it wasn't just any brothel.

There were rules.

It seemed that the wife of a de Long ancestor had a conscience. She was a benevolent woman known for giving alms to the poor, but she also saw that there were many widowed or destitute women who needed a way to support their families. Relying on the charity of others never supplied enough for a family to survive, and that was the truth. Committing oneself to the church as a beguine guaranteed a life of discomfort and loneliness. Therefore, Lady Matilda de Long offered them the opportunity to earn money at Aphrodite's Feast by becoming a companionable woman for men who were in need of such things.

But the guidelines were strict.

Lady de Long was specific with the women seeking a way to earn money. Their presence was purely for entertainment—men paid them well to eat with them, talk to them, perhaps sing with them or even dance. She never, under any circumstances, forced them into providing sexual favors, which was why the church didn't outright condemn the business. Even they saw that it was a way for destitute women to earn, something incredibly difficult in the society of the day.

However, that didn't mean that sexual favors weren't given. It had always been the longstanding policy that anything sexual was purely at the discretion of the woman. If she wanted to, she could. Any sexual relations between the women and the clients were always consensual, unheard of for a brothel. But if the women were abused in any way, perhaps if a man forced himself upon her, then justice was very swift. There was a team of eight men and an overseer at Aphrodite's Feast known as The Guardians, whose sole responsibility was the safety of the women and punishing anyone who got out of hand. Depending on the level of abuse, men could find themselves with a cut throat and tossed into the river.

At Aphrodite's Feast, there were no second chances when the women were abused.

And everybody knew it.

Therefore, it was quite a different place, in more ways than one. In addition to the unique manner in which it did business, Aphrodite's Feast was more elegantly appointed than the finest palaces on the planet. There were beautiful pieces of art, the finest food to be had, and the women who worked there were finely clothed and healthy. In a smaller port city like Bristol, perhaps a usual brothel wouldn't have so much business, but Aphrodite's Feast was unique in that men specifically traveled to Bristol to visit it. It wasn't usual in the least. It was like nothing in the known world.

It was, in fact, a world of its own.

And it was a world where Desdra le Daire lived. It was *her* world. On days like today, it was a world she was grateful for as she tended to the accounts from the previous day. That was her role in Aphrodite's Feast—not as a companion woman, or a cook, or any number of tasks women undertook at the establishment—a role that saw her handle the business end of things. That was what she was suited for because she was well educated, so that was what she accomplished.

Truthfully, in the weeks following Lord Chester's passing, she had been determined more than ever to protect the man's legacy. His entire *family's* legacy. He wasn't even a relative, but he had been the one person in her life who had shown her kindness, and she would return the favor. She knew nothing about this nephew to whom he'd left everything, but with God as her witness, she was going to protect Chester's legacy even from him.

"Desi!"

A young woman burst into the chamber, seemingly frantic. Startled from her daydreams, Desdra nearly dropped her quill.

"God's Bones," she said, putting her hand over her chest to still her rapid heart. "Why did you do that? What is so important, Melaina?"

Melaina wasn't her real name. The woman had bottomless brown eyes, curly brown hair, and she was clad in a garment that looked like the ones worn by the women on the mosaic—

flowing and white, in this case muslin. She was also young, and excitable, and she found herself at Aphrodite's Feast because she had elderly grandparents to support. Thanks to their granddaughter, they weren't going to starve in their old age.

"He's here!" Melaina gasped, rushing over to grasp Desdra by the hand. "Quickly! Come and look!"

"Who?" Desdra demanded.

"Lord Chester's nephew!"

That had Desdra up from her chair, allowing herself to be dragged across the chamber to the arched windows that faced the street below. That muddy, well-traveled street that paralleled the River Avon as it wound its way through town. There were people down there going about their business because Aphrodite's Feast was located in a busier section of town. Having once been a temple centuries ago, it was natural that, over the years, other buildings were built up around it.

This section of town happened to be, ironically, gold- and silversmiths. There were even a few jewelers. When Aphrodite's Feast first came into existence, men without the coin to spend on the ladies inside would go around town and try to sell their valuables. They were almost inevitably sold to the Jews, gold- and silversmiths, and upon realizing why these men were seeking to sell their possessions, the smithies moved their business locations to the block containing the brothel. That way, a man could sell what he needed to sell immediately and go straight into the establishment.

It was a very lucrative arrangement.

There were some people either passing along the street or attending the businesses down the avenue, but there was also a big group of men riding expensive horses right at the entrance to Aphrodite's Feast. Desdra could see them looking up at the building in awe. When they saw her, on the second floor directly above the entry, she ducked back, looking at Melaina with chagrin.

"How do you know it is the nephew?" she said. "Did he announce himself?"

Melaina nodded eagerly. "Aye," she said. "To The Guardians at the door. He said his name was Sir Jareth de Leybourne."

Hearing that name was a blow. Desdra knew that was, indeed, the nephew, because she had been the one to send him Chester's missive. She hadn't expected to see the man nearly so soon.

He was here!

"Botheration," she spat. "He did not even have the courtesy to send word of his arrival."

Melaina watched her as she rushed toward the chamber door. Skittish, she quickly followed. "What do you intend to do?" she said.

Desdra was already on the stairwell, heading down the stone steps that were scrubbed with sand so they wouldn't be slippery.

"Berate him for not notifying us that he was coming," she said as she took the stairs too fast. "Then I shall invite him in and introduce him to Lord Chester's grand holding."

At the base of the stairs was a door, one that could be locked from the inside, and she opened it, spilling out into the grand entry of the building. The entry, in fact, was three stories tall, with the first and second floors having some of the remnants of the Roman pillars from so long ago. The floor was not mosaic in the entry, but rather rough-cut stone that had been smoothed until it created a level floor. There were marble statues that had been brought all the way from Rome, not in the best repair, but a de Long ancestor had paid a craftsman to smooth them down and make them positively glow. Heads were missing, hands were missing, but it didn't matter.

The statues were magnificent.

As Desdra headed for the entry door, she passed by tapestries with silk tassels and chairs made from wood with gold leaf and expensive velvet cushions. Velvets were nearly unheard of except to royalty, but through their shipping business, Chester had managed to get his hands on a stretch of the fabric, which he'd promptly had fashioned into cushions for the impressive entry and a tunic he was buried in.

But Desdra didn't pay attention to the riches. She was used to seeing them. When she came to the entry, she was greeted by the commander of The Guardians, a man who called himself Zeus.

"I'm told Lord Chester's nephew has arrived," she said.

Zeus, with his long, graying hair and broad shoulders, resembled the historical descriptions of his namesake. "Aye," he said, his gaze moving to the street beyond the door. "I was shown the missive with Lord Chester's seal on it, and the garrison commander from Bristol Castle also confirmed his identity. It is he."

Desdra realized that she was disappointed to hear that. "I see," she said. "I suppose I should get this over with, then."

With that, she stepped through the doorway, onto the white marble walkway that led from the front door to the street. It was Italian marble, something that Chester had shipped all the way from Rome. As she drew close to the group of men standing on the avenue, looking up at the creation that was Aphrodite's Feast, she took a moment to look them over. Surprisingly, it was a collection of exceptionally handsome men, all of them, and that included Hugh de Winter, whom she recognized. At least four of the men were quite tall, with blond hair in varying shades, and then there was a big man with auburn hair. Standing over near the corner of the building was Hugh, pointing up at the structure and speaking to the man next to him. When Hugh moved out of the way to comment on the stone in front of the building, Desdra got a good look at the man he'd been speaking to.

He wasn't as tall as some of the others in the group, but he was still head and shoulders taller than her average height, and powerfully built. His shoulders were quite broad, his arms enormous, and his hands large. He had brown hair that he kept closely cropped except around the crown, which was neatly combed back, and a dark beard that embraced his square jaw. When he turned to look at her, she swore that she saw Chester in the shape of his brown eyes.

The nephew.

Something about the man made her suck in her breath. He was quite perfect looking, in her opinion, and she was surrounded by men on a daily basis. He seemed so clean and neat. Virtue seemed to radiate from him, and she had no idea why she should think that simply by looking at him. When Hugh caught sight of her, he grabbed the man by the arm and began to pull him in her direction.

The introduction between them was something she would remember for the rest of her life.

CG

THIS IS DESDRA?

Jareth wasn't exactly sure what he had been expecting, but it wasn't this. He'd never expected this. The legendary woman who seemed to hold all of the information he was eager for turned out to be a goddess of sorts.

For a moment, he was actually stunned silent.

For starters, she was young and beautiful. *Quite* beautiful, if he were to admit it. She had light brown hair that had a tight wave to it, indicative of hair that was probably quite curly on occasion. It was very long, past her buttocks, and the ends of it had been bleached blonde by the sun and elements and age. She'd probably never cut it in her life, so all that fine blonde hair at the end was here from her youth, more than likely. She had it pulled back and secured at the nape of her neck, but she made no move to secure it other than that. Even as he walked toward her, he could see that long hair behind her blowing gently in the breeze.

But the hair wasn't the only thing that had his attention. She had an oval face with a delicately square jaw, beautifully shaped lips, and an upturned nose. Her eyes were the same color as the dress she wore, a dark blue gown that displayed her lovely neck.

Truly, he was astonished.

"Jareth? Did you hear me?"

It was Hugh. Jareth had been staring at Desdra so intently that he hadn't really heard what the man had said, but he didn't want to admit it. He had to think quickly, suspecting that Hugh had said nothing more than her name.

Desdra le Daire.

"I did," he said stiffly, tearing his gaze away from Desdra. "Thank you for the introduction. Lady Desdra, I am Jareth de Leybourne. Chester was my uncle."

Desdra curtsied, a practiced gesture. "Welcome to Bristol, my lord," she said. "And welcome to Aphrodite's Feast. Please accept my condolences on the passing of your uncle. He was well loved here. We miss him greatly."

Jareth nodded faintly, unable to tear his gaze away from her this time. She had a sweet voice, soft yet firm, and the tone and timbre perfectly reflected her physical appearance.

"Thank you," he said. "I have come to speak to you about his estate. I understand that you can tell me everything I need to know."

Desdra nodded quickly. "Of course, my lord," she said. "If you and your men will come with me, I will show you everything."

Jareth didn't even bother to motion to the others to follow him. He simply followed Desdra as she turned back for the structure. That beautiful hair and the curve of her torso had his attention as she walked in front of him. He wasn't about to take his eyes off her and look at the men around him because he might miss something. The way she moved was fluid. As they walked on the marble, he heard footsteps behind him but didn't turn to see who it was.

He just kept following.

"The building that is now Aphrodite's Feast used to be a temple in the days of old," Desdra said, entering the building with the herd of men behind her. "To the left, in this big chamber, is the reason for the name. You will see an ancient mosaic that comprises the floor, a feast for Bacchus, but he is surrounded with goddesses, all of them happily drinking, and that is where the name comes from—Aphrodite's Feast."

Six heads popped into the doorway of the room she was indicating. Just as she'd explained, there was an elaborate mosaic on the floor of a feast with many beautiful women and a male in the center of it all with a cup of wine in his hand. The chamber itself wasn't huge, but it was still a feasting room.

There were tables and food in it. A doorway on the north side of the chamber led to a larger room beyond.

"And this," Desdra said, continuing to the chamber directly across from the feasting room, "is a reception chamber. This is where men who have come to Aphrodite's Feast gather and await their companion."

All six of them moved across the entry to the chamber opposite the mosaic chamber. Inside the reception hall, heights of luxury existed. Satin lounges, satin-cushioned chairs, tables with food and wine, and carpets upon the floor. Orion entered the hall and crouched down to touch a rug that had come all the way from Baghdad. It was a spectacular piece. Everywhere in the chamber was an example of not only the de Long wealth, but the reach their shipping business had.

It was a Hall of Wonders.

Tables with works of art were everywhere. The group wandered into the chamber, looking at everything, but no one was looking with more interest than Jareth. He made his way over to a beautifully carved table that held the statue of a big, bulky creature with a long nose and elaborate dressing over its back and head. Jareth peered closely at it.

"What is that?" he asked.

Desdra, who had been walking behind him, came to stand next to him. "It is called an olifant," she said. "It hails from a land far to the east, so far that it would take years to reach it. There are great herds of these olifants, I am told, and some men tame them and ride them like horses."

Jareth's eyebrows lifted, in both approval and understanding. "Remarkable," he said. "Have you ever seen one?"

Desdra smiled faintly, shaking her head. "Nay," she said. "I would like to, mayhap someday. I'm told that when they are born, they are tiny and adorable. I would like to see a little one."

Jareth's gaze lingered on her moment before he turned away, moving to the next table, which stood on its own against a wall. The table itself was made from dark wood, elaborately carved, and atop it sat a statue carved from ivory. It was a horse, but a very distinctive one. Every muscle could be seen as the animal reared up, its mouth open, its expression fierce. The hooves were painted gold.

"And this?" Jareth said, pointing at it. "Where is this from?"

"A place even further away than the land of the olifant," Desdra said. "This is an ivory statue from a land called Cathay. Lord Chester was particularly fond of the land and its culture, so much so that he did a good deal of trading with men from that land in Damascus. Their treasures are miraculous and great. Would you like to see more?"

Jareth nodded, and she motioned to him to follow. He caught Aidric's attention, who caught the others', and the six of them followed Desdra through a corridor and toward the rear of the establishment. There, she paused at a closed door long enough to find a key on her chatelaine ring to open it.

"Why is this chamber locked?" Jareth asked.

Desdra turned the tumblers in the old lock and opened the door. "Because Lord Chester's greatest treasures are in here," she said. "He only displayed it to his friends or finest patrons."

With that, she opened the door. Beyond was a magical chamber that contained more marble statues. It also contained tables with gold bowls or other precious treasures upon them. Desdra led them to the rear of the chamber, near the arched windows that overlooked the east, where something tall was covered up with a big piece of linen fabric. Reaching up, Desdra pulled the fabric off and set it aside.

Two six-foot-tall statues of men in strange armor, with strange faces, loomed over them, as they were standing on a platform. A pole at their backs secured them from falling. Jareth studied them, moving forward to scrutinize both without touching them.

All the while, Desdra was watching him.

"These are two ancient warriors that Lord Chester purchased from a man who had come from the ancient land of Cathay," she said softly. "From a city called Xi'an. He said that these were the bodies of ancient warriors buried with their king. Men who fought in ancient times, in ancient ways. Lord Chester felt they were the most valuable thing he had."

Now, all of the Guard of Six was crowding around the two figures. Even Hugh was crowding up because he'd never seen these before. Aidric reached out to touch one, feeling it under his fingers, before thumping on it gently.

"It feels like plaster," he said to Jareth, to the rest of them. "My lady, did you say this was a body? That it had once been alive?"

Desdra shrugged. "It was a body in the sense that it was made to look like someone who had once lived," she said. "It is made of baked earth, so it can break, I assure you. That is why Lord Chester has them both tied to a post."

Jareth was looking at the face of the figure in front of him. "Earthenware, you say?"

"Aye, my lord."

Jareth reached out to timidly touch the chin of the statue he was looking at. "My God," he muttered. "I can see hair on his face. Utterly remarkable."

He caught her looking at him, but she was quick to look away, focusing on the sculpture. "As the story goes, these two statues were part of a great army for an ancient king," she said. "They were found buried in a burial mound and brought to the Levant to help educate the people on other lands and other countries. But the merchant who brought them told Lord Chester that the Muslims viewed these men as idols, as sacrilege, so he could not sell them. Lord Chester bought them and brought them here. As you can see, he treats them carefully."

Jareth immediately looked to the windows, which were close by. "Then they should be kept away from the windows," he said. "Moisture and weather can affect them."

Desdra turned to the windows also. "I know," she said. "But he preferred to keep them where there was the best light. He always made a great show out of displaying them to a select few."

It made sense, sort of. Uncle Chester had wanted the two statues illuminated well when he showed them off. With a nod acknowledging the reason, Jareth continued inspecting the statues because they were unlike anything he had ever seen. The entire Guard of Six was crowding up around them, so Desdra went to stand by the door, waiting for them to tire of their inspection.

But, as she quickly learned, they were never tired of inspecting something exceptional.

It wasn't only Jareth, but the rest of them. They were all curious about Aphrodite's Feast, and that included every nook and every cranny and every chamber they came across. The building itself was three stories tall, and there were a total of twenty-seven rooms over those three stories, so there was a good deal to see. Desdra took them through the chambers, the corridors, the staircases, and finally down to the kitchens, which were in the lower level. Given that they were so close to the river, it could make for damp conditions, but the kitchens were otherwise quite fine because they were lined with stone, which tended to keep the moisture out.

The cook was a man who had also served Lord Chester's father. He had two assistants, and between the three of them, they fed up to fifty people every single day. Even now, they were busy making cheese tarts, something that Jareth and the others were quite drawn toward. They had been riding most of the day, as it was, and they had not yet stopped to break their fast. When Jareth mentioned that to Desdra, she asked the cook to feed the men. Being the snob that he was, however, the cook didn't seem too apt to do it until Desdra informed him that Jareth was the new Lord of Aphrodite's Feast. Of course, that had the man presenting everything he could for Jareth and his men to eat.

And all of it was delicious.

Along with the cheese tarts there were different types of bread, some sweet and some savory. There were copious amounts of butter, stewed fruit, and even honey. Evidently, the night before, they had roasted half of a pig, and this morning, the cook had made a stew with the leftover pork, beans, carrots, onions, and garlic. He doled out hot bowls of it as Jareth and the others ate the cheese tarts and the bread, and by the time the stew was presented, the rich smell of pork filled the entire kitchen.

As the eating was going on, Desdra simply sat back and tried to become accustomed to the men who would now be part of her life. She wasn't entirely sure if all of these men were sworn to Jareth or if they were simply his companions or friends. She knew that Hugh was from Bristol Castle, so he wasn't part of Jareth's group, but the men he had with him were incredibly intelligent and well spoken, every one of them. They didn't seem like men who would be sworn to a simple knight.

Gradually, she began to figure it out.

When the cook brought out some of Uncle Chester's fine Spanish wine, the men began to drink freely. And talk. The wine was quite delicious, and very expensive, and they enjoyed it immensely. It also had the ability to get a man drunk quickly, so the conversation went from something relatively quiet and neutral to something boisterous and, truthfully, hilarious at times. Desdra began to realize that the men were sworn to none other than King Henry himself, who was also Jareth's liege, because she knew that the missive she had sent him from Chester had gone to Westminster Palace. Therefore, she deduced they were all men who served the king directly.

Very powerful men.

And in the middle of it was Jareth.

By the time the wine was nearly finished, she had been watching him for the better part of three hours. He was quiet for the most part, although he seemed to have a lot to say. The only time he got loud was when someone else got loud with him or he experienced some kind of jest or insult. There was a big blond knight at the end of the table in the kitchen that no one seemed to like and it was that man most of all who seemed to bring out Jareth's loud side. His name was Orion, like the huntsman from Greek mythology. At one point, Hugh tried to throw a punch at the same man, but he was stopped by the others, who accused him of being drunk and tried to take his wine away. That caused him to grab the pitcher and try to run off with it. When they wouldn't let him, he climbed under the table with it and wouldn't give it to anyone, which effectively ended their meal at the table. He ended up drinking what was left in the pitcher underneath the table and only coming out when it was gone.

That had Jareth slapping him on the side of the head.

Everyone burst into laughter.

At that point, Jareth seemed to realize that they had completely ignored Desdra for quite some time. He was clearly drunk and the alcohol had seemed to loosen his manner quite a bit.

He stood up from the table unsteadily and headed in Desdra's direction.

"Forgive us, my lady," he said, his brown eyes glimmering with mirth. "We've not eaten since last night and I fear my uncle's strong wine has gone straight to our heads. I did not mean to ignore you."

Desdra smiled timidly, standing up from the stool she'd been sitting on. "I am glad you are enjoying yourselves," she said. "Aphrodite's Feast is made for enjoyment, so you are welcome to partake."

The smile faded from Jareth's lips. "That is something I must speak with you about," he said. "Will you indulge me?"

"Of course, my lord."

"I want to see the ledgers."

She nodded and motioned for him to follow. But everyone wanted to come, and he had to practically fight them off.

"Nay!" he roared. "This belongs to me and I will investigate it privately! This is not a group activity!"

They were giving him trouble, especially Hugh, so Desdra discreetly called for more wine, and that seemed to distract the group. When they were sharing a new bottle all around, Desdra took Jareth out of the kitchen, up the servants' staircase to the level where Chester's solar was located.

Up here, it was quiet but for the usual sounds on the street outside or an occasional gull overhead. He followed Desdra into the solar, coming to an abrupt halt once he entered the chamber. For a moment, he simply stood there and looked at the room—great tapestries, expensive furniture, and the finest art that money could buy. The table that Desdra went to sit behind had lions carved into the legs.

He'd never seen anything like it.

"Now," she said, pulling a few leather-bound books in front of her, "I have ledgers from all of Lord Chester's holdings. Some of these are quite old, from his grandfather's father, but they are all in order. You can see how much revenue the businesses generate and how much they spend."

Jareth wandered over to the table, sitting heavily on a chair because he was perhaps a little drunker than he thought he was. He was actually a *lot* drunker than he thought he was. It was a struggle to clear his head and focus, but he had to try. He was finally here, preparing to hear the details of the situation, and he needed his wits about him.

But all he could seem to do was stare at that exquisite creature at the table.

"Will you tell me something?" he said.

Desdra looked up from the ledgers. "If I can, my lord."

"What do you do here?" he said. Before she could answer, he waved a hand at her. "I do not mean it the way it sounds, but this *is* a brothel, isn't it? It's where women are paid to spread their legs for a man. Please tell me that you are not one of those. Oh, God… Were you my uncle's concubine? Is that why you are in a position of importance?"

Desdra was looking at him in horror. "I am no one's concubine!"

He wasn't quite sure he believed her. "It would be a tragedy if you were," he said. "You are quite a beautiful woman. Did you know that? Surely you must. I can only imagine my uncle saw that you are more beautiful than the rest of the women here and elevated your status."

Desdra's horror turned to shock and then to rage. She could see that the Spanish wine had taken its toll on him, but that didn't excuse him from asking rude and insulting questions.

"It is clear that you are ignorant of your uncle's empire, so I will try to forgive you your words," she said, jaw clenched. "But do not assume, nor ask, such things again. You would be wrong in doing so."

"Wrong?" he said, brow furrowed. "Lady, this *is* a brothel, is it not?"

"It is a place of worship."

"Worship?"

"Aye," she said, blue eyes flashing. "It is a place where men may worship a cultured and educated woman. Where they can bask in the presence of someone who will be kind to them. Who will treat them well. Where any fantasy can be fulfilled, but also any lonely hours can be made warm and comforting."

He was looking at her with a cocked eyebrow. "Do men pay for sex here?"

"If both the man and the woman are agreeable to such a thing, they do."

"Then it is a whorehouse, no matter how much you try to make it sound respectable."

That was all Desdra could take. This place, and Chester de Long, had saved her life and she hated to see someone speak so callously about it. Perhaps, technically, he was correct, but there was so much more to it.

Her worst nightmare about Chester's nephew had been confirmed.

He wasn't worthy of it.

"How dare you say such things about the women who have a position here," she hissed, slamming her hand on the table. "God pity Chester de Long for leaving this place to you. You, who have only come to judge. Clearly, you only see and hear what you want to, but that is to be expected. You've probably never had a hungry day in your life, have you? Or suffered cold and despair? Of course you haven't. You are a privileged knight from a great family and you've only known that privilege. How dare you judge people who have not had the same good fortune? There are no whores here. Only women who provide a service. Much as you provide a service to your liege. In your terms, I suppose that makes you a whore, too, doesn't it? A whore for bloodlust."

She wasn't shouting, but what she was doing was far more intimidating—calmly growling. Each syllable was rapid and succinct, slashing at him like the blade of the sharpest dagger. Her eyes were swirling with rage, her features tight, and Jareth realized he'd let the wine do the talking. He'd had no tact whatsoever and now he was faced with a very angry woman.

Rightfully so.

He'd said everything that was on his mind and shouldn't have.

"My apologies," he said quietly, suddenly not so drunk. "I do not know why I said any of that. I should not have."

Her eyes were still flashing. She glared at him a moment before returning to her ledger, opening the first one and turning it in his direction.

"You can look these over yourself," she said, cold and stiff. "You do not need me to sit with you while you do. Should you have questions, I will be downstairs in the main reception chamber."

With that, she gathered her skirt and blew past him, heading for the door. Knowing he'd made a mess out of things, he stood up before she could leave.

"Lady Desdra," he said, struggling to focus in spite of his inebriation. "I am not a man who usually speaks as I just did, so please believe me when I say that I am sorry. It's simply that… no one told me about this place until today. I knew Uncle Chester had the manse and the shipping business, but no one told me about this place—and what goes on here. You must understand that I am a knight sworn to our king, Henry, and I have worked my entire life for a strong and noble reputation. Knights simply do not own—forgive me again—trollop houses. It has all come as something of a shock, and that wine you provided early has made me embarrass myself. I hope you will not leave. I have many questions already."

Desdra paused by the door, listening to him with a baleful expression. "*In vino veritas,*" she said quietly. "The wine did not make you say anything you did not want to say. That was your choice."

"You are right," he said honestly. "It *was* my choice. It was foolish."

Her gaze lingered on him for a moment. She didn't know this man, yet she sensed sincerity. But sincerity could be an act. Her guard was up because as far as she was concerned, she was facing the enemy. The man who had inherited Chester's empire didn't appreciate any of it. He didn't respect it. She'd made a promise to protect Chester's legacy and she was going to keep that promise.

But she had to figure out how.

"I will be downstairs," she said. "Look over the ledgers and come to me with questions."

With that, she left the chamber, leaving Jareth feeling just as bad as he possibly could. But he'd be damned if he didn't deserve it.

The day had not gone as planned.

CHAPTER SIX

Ridlaw Manor
Twenty Miles East of Bristol

THE MAN WASN'T bluffing.

He'd seen men like this before—men who turned gambling into a business, and when those who owed debts didn't pay fast enough, they came for their pound of flesh. Now, they had come to him for more than a pound of flesh because, unfortunately, he owed them all that and more.

That was nothing new in his world.

Ciaran le Daire owed the entire world money, it seemed. He couldn't remember when he had actually not been in debt, but certainly, at some point in his life he hadn't owed anyone anything. Maybe in infancy. In any case, it seemed like every action in his adult life had been to either pay a debt or create a debt or try to make money somehow. He got that particular trait from his father, who had inherited Ridlaw from *his* father, as the manor had been in the family for more than one hundred years. Not strangely, it had been purchased from a man who had run up a debt with a French count, a man who wanted his money and wasn't afraid to kill people to get it.

That was how Ridlaw Manor came into the possession of the le Daire family.

Therefore, the manor had seen its share of shady characters coming and going. There was always something happening there, as the townspeople would say. It used to be a nice place in relatively decent repair, but the years had not been kind to it, as the le Daire owners had not seen a need for upkeep. It used to be a place of prosperity, because it had a good deal of land that was used to grow wheat. But le Daire wasn't a farmer and he didn't employ farmers, so a few of the local farm workers had taken to leasing his land so they could at least make a living. They split the crop with Ciaran and he did what he pleased with it, which was usually trade it for drink or sell it for money to gamble.

It was a difficult existence.

It was even more difficult now that Ciaran was staring down a man from Glasgow, a pirate with a nasty streak in him. In addition to his pirate activities, he was also a man who sponsored a traveling game of chance that went all around the south of England, a game that Ciaran had spent a good deal of money on when it had come to Bath. When the money was gone, he'd asked for credit. That had been his mistake.

Now, the creditor had come to collect.

"My father, unfortunately, does not have all of the money." It was Benedict, Ciaran's son, pleading on behalf of his father. "If you will only give us a little more time, I am sure we can pay you to your satisfaction."

The man who had done the threatening shifted his focus to Benedict. There was malevolence behind the dark eyes as he gazed at the man begging on behalf of his father. He called himself King Dagda, though his real name was cause for much speculation among those who knew him. Some said that he had come from Scottish nobility while others said he came from the gutter. Wherever he came from was of little matter, however.

It was what he'd learned while he was there that caused concern.

Torture techniques, among other things, both physical and mental.

No one wanted to be on King Dagda's bad side.

"You *do* understand that your father borrowed money from me," he finally said to Benedict. "He owes me a great deal."

"I know," Benedict said, avoiding his father's pleading gaze. "We are attempting to sell property as we speak. We only need a little more time."

King Dagda seemed interested by the mention of valuables to sell. "What kind of property?"

There really wasn't much, to be truthful, but Benedict didn't want to let on. He wanted King Dagda to believe that they did indeed have things to sell, things that could pay the debt.

"Land, mostly," he said. "If you feel that it would help pay your debt if we were to give them to you, then by all means, you may have it."

As he'd hoped, King Dagda shook his head. "I have no use for grass," he said distastefully. "What else are you selling?"

"Would you take my daughter?"

The question came from Ciaran. King Dagda looked at him with surprise as Benedict closed his eyes in horror.

"Papa, we agreed," Benedict said before King Dagda could respond. "We do not sell Desdra. Not again."

"Not *again*?" King Dagda said, interrupting. He looked between Benedict and Ciaran. "What's this about selling a daughter?"

"My daughter," Ciaran said, a little louder this time. "Desdra is a good worker. She is educated. She can help you with your accounts. She can run your household. She can do anything."

King Dagda frowned. "I do not need a chatelaine," he said. "I need my money."

"And I shall get you your money," Ciaran said. "If you'll not take my daughter in payment, will you take her as collateral until the debt is paid? That has been done before. She is quite valuable."

King Dagda was still frowning. He looked at Benedict. "What is he speaking of?" he said. "What does he mean?"

Benedit sighed heavily. "He means that he used my sister to settle a debt with Chester de Long," he said. "The man owns Aphrodite's Feast in Bristol. Have you heard of it?"

That brought a look of surprise from King Dagda. "Of course I have," he said. "I have visited there, many times. Are you telling me that your sister has a position there?"

"Aye," Benedict said. "She has for three years."

That information fed the possibilities in King Dagda's mind. "Is she a muse?" he said, referring to the general term for the women who had positions at Aphrodite's Feast. "She must be beautiful and accomplished, indeed. Aye, I will take her in payment for the debt. I will take her immediately."

"Wait," Benedict said quickly, holding up his hand in a quelling gesture. "Before we take such drastic steps, please give us time to sell property to pay you what we owe first. My sister is an accomplished woman, as you have said, and should not be used for barter like a mare. I will tell you quite honestly that my father was wrong to do so in the first place. To do it again would be a sin of the greatest magnitude."

King Dagda stared at him a moment before breaking into laughter. "What do I care about a sin?" he said. "It is not as if the church and I are on speaking terms. Nay, lad, I care about money. *My* money. And your father owes me money. I will happily take a woman who has worked at Aphrodite's Feast in payment. She will make my men very happy."

Benedict tried to keep the look of disgust off his face but couldn't quite manage it. "You'll not have my sister," he said, his voice low and threatening. "I will make sure you have your money, but you must give me a fortnight. Return at that time and I will have it for you."

The humor on King Dagda's face faded. "You speak as if you are sure you can get it."

"I am."

King Dagda held his gaze for a moment, contemplating that reply, before finally conceding. "Very well," he said. "But not a fortnight. I'll return in a week. But if you do not have the money, then I will take everything you own, including your sister, and you will have no say in it. Any resistance and I'll kill you and your father. Do you comprehend me?"

"I comprehend."

"Good."

King Dagda began to move toward the door of the chamber, pulling his men with him. They'd been spread out around the sparsely furnished room, one that had once been a solar of lavish means until Ciaran took over. After everything came into his possession, he'd started selling possessions off, a little at a time, to fund his gambling habit. Now, there was nothing left but the house itself and his children. Desdra had already been used for a substantial debt, and Benedict, though a knight, refused to be used by his father as barter.

Pity, Ciaran had once thought.

Benedict could have been worth a lot to him.

But now, it was Benedict trying to protect the last vestiges of his inheritance as his father tried to ruin everything. Only he stood between Ciaran and complete destruction. His gaze tracked King Dagda as the man stood in the doorway, ushering his men through, until he was the only one left standing there. He pointed right at Benedict.

"A week," he said, his tone deadly. "I will see you then."

Benedict simply nodded, watching the man depart. He waited a nominal amount of time for the gang of men to leave the manse, waiting for the sounds of horses moving out in the ward until he turned to his father to speak.

"Again," he growled. "You did it again."

Ciaran had his head down. "And you had no right to take away my ability to bargain," he said. "*I* am your father. *I* am the lord of the manor and you are not in command here."

"I am the only one in command here," Benedict nearly screamed at him. "You are a pathetic excuse for a father, one I am deeply ashamed of, so remember that. Remember that for the rest of your life your son does not respect you and your daughter hates you, you worthless cretin. God, how *worthless!*"

Ciaran wanted to shout at him in return, but that wouldn't get them anywhere. They'd already shouted at one another. For years, they'd shouted at one another. They'd screamed and yelled and berated each other. But it always came down to Ciaran giving in to his gambling urge and Benedict trying to get him out of it. The same old dynamics.

The same old heartache.

"So I am worthless," Ciaran muttered. "If you do not pay that man, I will be dead."

Benedict was so frustrated with his father that all he could do was wave at the man in a sharp gesture. "If it were not for me, you would have been dead a long time ago," he said. "Mayhap we would have been better off. At least Desdra would have been better off. I would have found her a husband who would not sell her off to pay a gambling debt."

Ciaran didn't have a retort for that because it was true. "If I had not used her to pay the debt, I would be dead," he said. "Chester de Long would have sent men after me."

Benedict snorted with the sheer irony of his father's defense. "Chester de Long is not the killing kind," he said. "You're lying about that, too. You lie and you cheat and you gamble and then you blame everyone for your woes. Well, no more. This is going to end. I am going to go to Bristol and talk to Desdra about all of this. Mayhap she has some ideas as to where to come up with the money."

Ciaran simply sat there, in a chair that was cracked, staring at the floor and knowing that the verbal browbeating he was receiving was nothing undeserved. There were times when he hated himself, too, but he couldn't admit it.

"Mayhap she can get the money," he muttered. "No matter what you think of me in sending Desdra to de Long to pay off my debts, he never used her as a muse. He was good to her."

"I know," Benedict said without patience. "And that is the only thing that keeps me from killing you for what you did to her, the knowledge that she's simply a scribe. Unlike you, I have visited her several times in Bristol, and she seems to be relatively content with her lot in life. But it's not right and you know it."

Ciaran wouldn't look at him. "The debt was paid some time ago," he said. "She no longer needs to remain there."

"And she should return here so you can sell her off to King Dagda to pay off yet another debt?" Benedict said, shaking his head. "I will not allow it."

"She is my daughter."

"She is *my* sister."

Ciaran finally lifted his gaze, looking at his son. "So you would rather see King Dagda kill me?" he said. "Is that what you want?"

Benedict wasn't going to let his father put any guilt on him, not when they both knew he was right. "I will get the money somehow," he said. "But I will tell you this now, Ciaran—never again will I pay a debt for you. Never again will you use Desdra as barter. The next debt you incur will be one you must deal with yourself, because I will not do it, and if King Dagda comes to extract his pound of flesh from you because you refuse to pay, I will not stand in his way. And that is a promise."

With that, he left, leaving his father sitting alone and dejected in the cold, stale chamber. Ciaran knew that Benedict was going home, home to the wife he loved and the two small boys he had fathered. Children that he'd never allowed Ciaran to be around. He kept his little family away from Ridlaw Manor and away from the grandfather who had gambled away their legacy. Benedict was going back to that perfect world, back to the fortified stone and timber dwelling that was the only part of his father's property that Ciaran hadn't yet stripped or ruined.

Benedict lived in the hall house in the larger village on the Ridlaw property, basically a home with a public space, or hall, on the ground level where the law could be dispensed and other town business could be conducted, but the second floor had living quarters for Benedict and his family.

While Ciaran sat in his manor home in squalor, doing little

else but gamble and drink, Benedict was the law for the area. He took care of the things his father wouldn't. He was a well-respected and decent fellow, which was why the ambush just outside of the village came as such a horrible shock to everyone. Benedict had no enemies, but on that evening when he traveled away from his father's home after the encounter with King Dagda, Benedict le Daire's life was unceremoniously stolen from him by a few highwaymen on the hunt for someone to rob. Surprisingly enough, it wasn't King Dagda or his men. It was simply a group of random outlaws.

Ciaran, however, didn't hear about his son's death until the following morning.

And then he drank himself into oblivion.

CHAPTER SEVEN

Aphrodite's Feast

THE RIVER WAS green.

Jareth had seen many rivers in his lifetime, and usually the ones closer to the sea turned shades of green because of the silt and sand that the currents brought in. It was a murky river and he was unable to see the bottom as he sat by the river's edge, watching the water amble by.

As it turned out, he had a lot to think about.

He wasn't as drunk as he had been earlier. That strong Spanish wine had gone straight to his head and he'd ended up saying things he wished he hadn't. He couldn't stop himself from thinking it, but he certainly should not have spoken of them to the woman who was trying hard to be kind by orienting him to his inheritance. Clearly, he had insulted her, her colleagues, and pretty much the entire city of Bristol with his questions.

They were a reflection of the confusion he was feeling.

He was still having a difficult time accepting the fact that these enterprises had been in his family for quite some time and his mother had never told him about it. He was going to go with the assumption that she didn't know of the ventures, because anything else wasn't something he wanted to face. He didn't want to face the fact that his mother, the only parent he actually loved, might have been part of something seedy. Or at least had knowledge of something seedy.

In either case, it was an appalling prospect.

Like it or not, however, he found himself now at a cross-roads.

He could continue to resist his inheritance or he could simply accept it. His friends already knew, and the king already knew, so it wasn't as if he could hide this from them. Perhaps the best thing he could do was simply accept what fate had given him and move forward. He paused and turned to look at the great structure of Aphrodite's Feast behind him. It was truly a magnificent building. The artwork, the fine furnishings, and the like made it a most remarkable place. He didn't even need to see the ledgers because he could just tell that the place was rolling in money.

That meant *he* was rolling in money.

But was that money worth his dignity?

That was where he was having problems.

With a sigh, he turned around to face the river again, watching the gentle waters and seeing people on the other side of the riverbank as they went about their business. He was thinking that, perhaps, he needed to go back in and take a look at those ledgers so he could get the complete idea of what he was facing. He could only spend so much time out here in confusion, a state that was not normal for him.

He needed to settle the situation.

"Here you are," Hugh said as he walked up behind him. "We were wondering where you'd gone off to."

Jareth turned to look at the man as he plopped down beside him. "I just needed some time to think," he said, returning his focus to the river. "Today has been… a good deal to comprehend."

Hugh snorted softly. "I can imagine," he said. "Are you still resistant to all of this?"

"Shouldn't I be?"

Hugh grinned. "Nay," he said with soft sincerity. "Jareth, you do not seem to realize what you have here. What are your concerns? Why does this not appeal to you?"

Jareth grunted, looking away. "I told you," he said. "It is shameful to admit I own a brothel. A place where women sell themselves. My God, Hugh, what is honorable about that?"

"So you are only concerned with honor?"

"Wouldn't you be?"

Hugh had to think on that. He wasn't as honor-driven as Jareth was. In fact, he didn't have a huge amount of respect for honor or men who held it in such high regard, because Hugh de Winter lived for himself. He'd had to because he'd spent his entire life in the shadow of his great brother, a man who had earned a stellar reputation as a defender of the Crown. The entire de Winter family had earned that reputation, Hugh's mother included, and Hugh simply wasn't the caliber of knight that his brother was. But he tried. God knows, he tried. And he'd learned long ago to only live for himself, not for the opinion of others.

Jareth hadn't learned that yet.

"You are looking at this all wrong," Hugh said. "Let me explain this to you."

"Explain what?"

"Aphrodite's Feast," Hugh said, throwing a thumb back at

the building. "You need to look at this enterprise for what it is—you are giving women, who would otherwise be destitute, the opportunity to earn a living. Every woman in there has a story. Did you know that? Have you even tried to talk to any of them? Because if you did, I think they would tell you that The Feast has saved their lives."

Jareth looked at him, frowning. "Saved their lives?" he repeated. "How?"

"By giving them the opportunity to feed themselves," Hugh said, emphasizing his answer by poking Jareth in the chest. "You have the opportunity to feed yourself and earn a living by serving Henry. But can a woman do that? Of course not. And what of the women who have lost their husbands? Jareth, you should know that there is a woman at Aphrodite's Feast whose husband was a great knight. He was killed in de Montfort's wars, so she came here to earn money to feed and house her two daughters. She is an elegant, educated woman who can read, and that is how she spends most of her time—reading to men who want to lie there with their eyes closed and listen to her. She can also sing, which she does on occasion, and she is paid handsomely for it. That's *all* she does, if you get my meaning. Now, do you consider that shameful and demeaning?"

Jareth was looking at him with an expression between disbelief and curiosity. "Nay," he admitted. "I suppose not. But how do you know this?"

Hugh was back to grinning. "Because she has read for me," he said. "Sometimes, a man simply wants to spend time with a lovely woman without any expectations. Sometimes I just want a pretty companion to talk to while I eat. Her name is Anosia, and I will bring her to meet you if you wish. You can ask her how she feels about Aphrodite's Feast. Because if you genuinely refuse this inheritance, and it falls into ruin, these women will have no place to go and it will all be your fault."

Jareth was starting to see the situation from a different point of view. Hugh may have been a fool at times, but his advice was sound. Jareth had always considered himself to be open-minded, to try to see all sides before making a judgment, but he realized that he hadn't done that in this situation. He'd been overwhelmed and terrified of the opinion of his friends, and all of them seemed to think this wasn't a dishonorable situation.

That had Jareth second-guessing himself.

"Then send me whomever you wish," he said, looking out over the river again. "I will wait here."

Hugh patted him on the shoulder before standing up and heading back into the building. Jareth sat there, shaking his head, wondering how much further his life would deviate before he could bring it under control again. It occurred to him that he hadn't even seen any of his friends since their arrival—Aidric, Britt, Dirk, Stefan, or Orion. They were all inside Aphrodite's Feast, undoubtedly having a good time. Everyone was having a good time but Jareth.

The whole situation was just so damn confusing.

But it wasn't to Hugh.

He had an opportunity here to do something for his friend, and he intended to do it. Jareth seemed to have opened his mind a little to the possibilities of Aphrodite's Feast, so it was time to strike while the iron was hot. Before Jareth had too much time to think about it again.

Hugh had been to Aphrodite's Feast enough to know the general layout of the place. He knew The Guardians at the door and they knew him, so he was admitted without question. He asked one of the men to fetch Desdra, and a servant was sent on the hunt. Hugh wandered into the feasting room, the one with the mosaic on the floor, where wine and song filled the chamber. Two women were in one corner, and one played the lute while the other sang a haunting melody. Hugh poured himself some wine into a goblet made of expensive rock crystal, but such were the drinking vessels at The Feast.

Only the best for their customers.

As he sipped his wine, the singer finished her song and there was great appreciation for her talent. Hugh knew the woman, named Anosia. He beckoned her over and she came to him eagerly.

"Lord de Winter," she said, smiling. "It is a pleasure to see you again. We've not seen you in a few days."

Hugh smiled in return. "Believe it or not, I do have a position that keeps me busy," he said, watching her laugh. "I know I pretend otherwise, but I truly do have duties to accomplish over at the castle."

"Not too bothersome, I hope?"

"Nay," he said. "The usual things that the garrison commander must attend to. But let us speak of why I summoned you. I would like to ask a favor of you."

"I am honored to serve, my lord."

Hugh pointed in the direction of the river. "The man who inherited all of Chester de Long's possessions is sitting out by the river, wondering what in the world he has inherited," he said. "He does not understand what The Feast is. I have tried to tell him, but he thinks I am mad. May I ask you to go and speak with him? Tell him what The Feast has meant to you. Let him understand it through your eyes."

Anosia nodded. "I am happy to do so," she said. "He's out

by the river, you said?"

Hugh pointed again. "You cannot miss him," he said. "A broad knight with a dark beard. Handsome. His name is Jareth."

Anosia dipped her head in acknowledgment. "I will tell him what I can."

"That would be helpful."

Anosia quit the chamber about the time Desdra entered. When she saw Hugh, she smiled politely and headed in his direction.

"My lord?" she said. "You wished to speak with me?"

Hugh nodded. "I did," he said. "May we go somewhere private?"

She motioned for him to follow, and he did. She took him up a narrow spiral staircase, one that had locking gates at the top and the bottom of it. This was the section of the building where Lord Chester's chamber was and where the lord's solar was, where all of the business was conducted and the money counted, so it was well protected from the rest of the establishment. Desdra led him into the solar, with its neatly stacked ledgers and iron chests that were bolted into the floor.

"How may I be of assistance, my lord?" she asked.

Hugh casually wandered over to the windows that faced the entry and the river beyond. He could still see Jareth sitting out there, now with Anosia talking to him. Hugh wasn't usually so thoughtful of others, but there was something in him that genuinely wanted to help Jareth see the value of what he had inherited. Or maybe he was living vicariously through Jareth, because he certainly wouldn't have the same reservations about inheriting such a place.

He wanted to make Jareth understand that.

"You've met Lord Chester's nephew?" he finally said.

Desdra paused by the big table that contained the ledgers. "I have, my lord."

"What did you think of him?"

She drew in a long, thoughtful breath. "He called this place a brothel," she said. "His opinion of this establishment is not a good one."

Hugh turned to look at her. "That is natural, don't you think?" he said. "The man inherited a place where women take money from men. What else is he supposed to think?"

Her jaw twitched faintly. She was unhappy with the subject matter. Hugh was a good customer and she didn't want to offend him, but she didn't have much of an opinion on his friend.

"If he did not understand what The Feast is, then he could have asked me in detail," she said. "I would have told him everything. But he accused me of being his uncle's concubine, among other things. He did not seem to want to learn about the place. He only wanted to spout his uneducated opinion on it. Sir Hugh, I will be honest with you. My biggest fear was that Lord Chester would bequeath his empire to someone unworthy. I've not seen anything yet from Sir Jareth that would ease my fear."

Hugh held out a hand, suddenly quite serious. "You go too far, lady," he said in a low voice. "Jareth is neither ignorant nor unworthy, I assure you. He is an elite knight, a bodyguard to King Henry. One of only six men who are honored with such a position. He is a veteran of Henry's wars against Simon de Montfort and, I might add, fought with distinction at the Battle of Lewes. I have never met a more just or moral man, so as much as you accused him of being ignorant when it comes to

The Feast, you are ignorant when it comes to Jareth de Leybourne. You do not know what you are talking about, so I suggest you still your tongue until you do."

Properly rebuked, Desdra lowered her gaze. "Forgive me, my lord," she said. "It is only that I am very protective of Lord Chester's legacy. I should not like to see it go to someone who will not take good care of it."

Hugh backed down a little. "I know," he said quietly. "You have always been very diligent with Lord Chester's business matters. I know he was quite dependent on you."

Desdra was still feeling scolded. "As I was dependent on him," she said. "He saved my life. You will forgive me if I am passionate when it comes to protecting him."

Hugh turned to the window, still seeing Jareth and Anosia in conversation. "I realize that," he said. "But in speaking of Jareth's ignorance of The Feast, I am trying to remedy that."

She looked at him then. "How?"

He pointed out the window. "By having Anosia tell Jareth her story," he said. "He needs to understand that this place is far beyond a brothel. It is a place that does good, for many, so he must be told that from the very women whose lives have been saved by Lord Chester. Mayhap someday you will tell him your story, also. It will help him understand what, exactly, he has come into possession of."

Desdra wandered over to the window, seeing Jareth and Anosia on the riverbank. "Anosia has quite a story to tell," she said quietly. "She is very persuasive."

"She is," Hugh said. "Now, I will go downstairs and find more women to send out to speak with Jareth. You will go, too."

She looked at him dubiously. "He will not want to see me, I am certain," she said. "Our exchange earlier was not... pleasant."

"Then this is your chance to smooth things over," Hugh said. "He is not going away, my lady. You would do better to learn to live with him, because butting heads with him will only see you thrown out. I swear to you that he is a good man, a decent man. Give him the chance to show you when he is not full of strong wine."

He had a point. Desdra thought on his request a moment before eventually nodding her head. Slowly, reluctantly, she agreed.

It wasn't as if she had a choice.

Long after Hugh left, Desdra stood at the window, watching the man as a parade of finely dressed women went out to speak to him. The conversation would end and another woman would walk out to the riverbank.

He's a good man.

That statement kept rolling over and over in her head. A good man who had become slightly drunk and had spoken his mind over an unexpected inheritance. Was it the end of the world? Of course not. But Desdra had already been unsettled by the appearance of an unknown nephew enough that she wasn't willing to show any measure of understanding to any statement uttered, and most especially not toward those who earned a living at Aphrodite's Feast.

Perhaps she was partly to blame.

When the fifth woman left Jareth down by the river's edge, Desdra decided it was time to go down herself and tell him what Chester de Long had done for her. Perhaps she'd been too hasty in her judgment.

Perhaps the man deserved another chance.

CHAPTER EIGHT

A FTER HUGH LEFT him, Jareth lost track of time as he watched the river roll by. He saw a few children on the opposite bank, trying to fish and being thwarted by the fact that they only had a piece of twine and some cheese. He could hear them yelling about the cheese. Finally, one of them caught something and they all seemed to be quite excited by that. As he watched them jump up and down on the riverbank, he caught movement out of the corner of his eye.

"My lord?"

A soft female voice spoke, and he turned to see a shockingly elegant woman in silks. She had ribbons in her hair and wore a dress that showed her belly through diaphanous fabric. In fact, she was draped in sheer fabric as part of her clothing, and Jareth stood up, facing the woman who wasn't particularly young, but she *was* exquisite.

"My lady," he said. "Did Hugh send you?"

She nodded, the ribbons in her careful coif fluttering. "He did, my lord," she said. "My name is Anosia. Sir Hugh says that you have questions about The Feast. May I answer them for you?"

Jareth was still surprised over the fact that she didn't look like any prostitute he'd ever seen. "Aye," he said. "You can if you have time. I do not want to keep you from something important."

Anosia shook her head. "Only Sir Hugh, but he said that he will wait," she said, a twinkle in her eye. "He told me that you were more important, but he also told me to tell you not to keep me overly long."

Jareth snorted. "I'll try," he said. His smile faded. "Do you know who I am?"

She nodded without hesitation. "You are Lord Chester's nephew."

"I am," Jareth said. "Aphrodite's Feast now belongs to me."

She smiled. "I am sure you will be a good lord to us all," she said. "Lord Chester was so very good to us. We are grateful to him."

Jareth considered that statement for a moment. "Will you tell me why you are here?" he said. "What I mean to ask is: why is a lovely woman such as yourself not married with children? With a home of your own?"

It was a struggle for her to keep the smile on her face. "But I *was* married, once," she said. "My husband was killed at the Battle of Lewes."

"Ah," Jareth said, subdued. "You are the widow of the knight."

"I am, my lord."

"Who was he?"

She hesitated. "At Aphrodite's Feast, we do not give out names," she said. "We do that to protect our families, but also to create a fantasy world. One where only muses live and men enjoy them."

"You are a muse?"

She nodded. "That is what the women of The Feast are called," she said. "We inspire. We whisper. We laugh and we sing. Can you think of anything better to call us?"

She was smiling as she said it, clearly proud of herself and of her situation. *Every woman here has a story,* Hugh had said.

Jareth wanted to know Anosia's.

"I am unfamiliar with The Feast," he said, using the colloquial term for the business. "I was not even aware of it until quite recently. I was under the impression that this was a brothel, but some people have told me otherwise. *Is* it a brothel?"

Anosia chuckled. "That is like asking if the church houses priests," she said. "Of course it does. But it is so much more than that."

"Will you tell me how this benefits you?"

Anosia nodded, moving to sit on a rock that was a few feet away from him. She was very ladylike in her movements, something that spoke of her education and breeding.

"I do not know where I would be without The Feast," she said. "I am not a unique story here. We all have our reasons. But my reason began when I was born the youngest of many children and, not being a boy, was sent away to foster at four years of age. That is quite young to foster, but my father had his sons, and my mother died soon after my birth, so the decision was made to send me away."

"Where did you go?"

"Prudhoe Castle," she said. "The lady of Prudhoe was kind to me and raised me with her other daughters. My education is the finest, my lord. My family, my real family, are quite important in Norfolk. Through their connections, I met my husband."

"You did not meet him while you were fostering?"

"Nay," she said, shaking her head. "Only when I returned home after. We were married for several years before I gave birth to my first daughter. A few years later, I bore a second daughter. When she was quite young, my husband went to war for Henry against de Montfort. I would tell you that my husband was a knight in a prestigious household, but I will not tell you which one. When he was killed in battle, I was left with two very young children and no means of income."

"But what of your family?" Jareth asked. "Surely you could return to them."

Anosia smiled weakly. "You would think so," she said. "But that was not the case. An older brother is now head of the family and does not wish to be responsible for me, a widow."

"What of your mother's family?"

"Unfortunately not," she said. "I wrote to them, several times, but never received a reply. Either they did not want me or there is no one left."

Jareth understood. "I see," he said. "But what of the Lords of Prudhoe? Could you not return to them?"

She waggled her eyebrows. "The Lady of Prudhoe and her husband have long since passed away," she said. "Their son is the lord now, and although he knows me, he does not want to be burdened with a woman who was once a ward. I do not blame him, of course. I am not his responsibility."

"So you had nowhere to go," Jareth finished quietly.

Anosia shook her head. "Nay," she said. "I had two young daughters and no future. It was terrifying."

"But how did you come to Aphrodite's Feast?" he wanted to know. "Why not become a beguine? You would be taken care of and your daughters would have been educated."

Anosia sighed faintly, considering his question. "I suppose because I do want to marry again," she said. "Once I became a beguine, I would essentially be a nun. I want to live my life, my lord. I want to find joy in it and I want my daughters to find joy in it. I do not want to see them starving in a nunnery, used like animals for labor. That is what would happen to them, you know."

He couldn't disagree with her. He'd heard tales about that, too. "So you came to a brothel?" he said.

Her smile was back. "I never took money and allowed men to bed me, if that is what you are asking," she said. "My husband would not have approved, and, truthfully, I knew I could do something more, something better. A friend of my husband's told me about this place because he had been here before, so he brought me here and I spoke with Lord Chester. I told him my problem and I told him of my background, and he told me that I could be useful here if I did not mind the company of men. So I became Anosia, the weaver of tales, the singer of songs. I make more money in a month than my husband made in an entire year as a knight. I made enough money to have a small home built on the edge of town, where my daughters live with an older woman, the widow of a merchant, who is educating them. They have ponies and dogs and good food to eat. And none of this would be possible without The Feast, my lord. It has saved my life."

It was an eye-opening speech. Jareth believed her. Even with her secrecy about who she was and who she had married, she spoke eloquently and with conviction. It ran so contrary to what he believed about a place like Aphrodite's Feast that it was difficult for him to comprehend it. In fact, he was looking at her rather dubiously as he rubbed his chin.

"And you are not enslaved in any way?" he said. "You are not abused and forced into this life?"

Her smile grew. "Not at all, my lord," she said. "Generations of de Longs have ensured we are free to come and go, free to earn what money we can, and protected from the rabble that sometimes likes to come to these places. That is why we have The Guardians at the door. If any of us get into trouble, they will help us right away."

"And… and you *like* this life?"

Her smile faded. "I loved my husband," she said. "It is difficult to enjoy life without him, but at least his children are not starving. At least I am not starving."

"What about your intention to marry again?"

"When the right man comes along, I will," she said. "But The Feast has made it so I can be discerning. I can choose out of love or affection, not desperation."

Jareth couldn't think of any other questions for her. She had been honest and forthcoming about her experience at Aphrodite's Feast and he was genuinely astonished. It wasn't like any brothel he'd ever heard of. Maybe everyone had been right.

Maybe this was an inheritance to be proud of.

"There is one more thing," he said as a thought occurred to him. "Tell me about Lady Desdra. Is she a muse, too?"

"Nay," Anosia said, shaking her head. "She could be, and she could make a great deal of money if she wished, but her function has been strictly with the ledgers. Lord Chester depended on her. She knows everything about The Feast. Have you spoken to her yet?"

He shook his head. "Nay," he said, but then hesitated. "Well, not much, anyway. If she is not a muse like you, why is she even here, I wonder?"

"A debt," Anosia said.

Jareth's brow furrowed. "What kind of debt?"

"I do not know," Anosia said. "But I do know she is here because of a debt. She is a very bright lass, but had an unfortunate upbringing. I have heard her father was not very kind to her, but I do not know more than that."

Jareth simply nodded. "Thank you for telling me about yourself, Lady Anosia," he said. "I appreciate your candor."

Anosia smiled and stood up from the rock, excusing herself now that she'd accomplished what she'd set out to do. As she headed back toward the building, another young woman was heading toward them. This lass had long, curly black hair and blue eyes. She was quite lovely and quite young. She introduced herself as Melaina, and Jareth listened to a second young woman tell him about her place at Aphrodite's Feast and what it meant to her. Yet one more young woman who seemed to have found a life here, only in Melaina's case, she was indeed a prostitute, but she did it of her own free will. She did it because she liked to be touched—and she wasn't shy about telling him.

Jareth sat for about a half-hour, listening to Melaina speak most happily about her life at Aphrodite's Feast. She loved to dance and sing, and she had a lot of repeat customers. Jareth suspected that it was not only because she was pretty, but she also had a childlike manner about her. She seemed innocent, but she wasn't. She would do anything for money and wasn't the least bit sorry about it. It had made her very rich, and she made sure to show him the jewels she wore on her neck and ears. Jewels she had paid for herself. With a happy farewell, she bounded off, being replaced a short time later by a woman named Limenia.

Limenia was different. She wasn't from England, but from a

sunny land somewhere near the Levant. She had beautiful skin, kissed by the sun, with dark hair and flashing, dark eyes. She was calm by nature, speaking of the great artists from her land of birth and of her own paintings. Evidently she was a painter, and took great pride in telling Jareth that it was she who had painted the murals in the room where the great mosaic floor was. She also painted pictures for men who paid her a good deal of money to recreate their homelands or sweethearts based on their descriptions. Sometimes, she would dine with them and have conversations about her home far away, or their homes far away, but she was an introspective woman who was allowed to create her paintings to her heart's content.

And on the afternoon went.

When the sun began to hang low in the western sky and the boats were brought in from the river, pulled upon the banks, Jareth was still in his spot overlooking the waterway. He'd spoken to eleven women that afternoon, all of them telling him different stories as to why they'd come to Aphrodite's Feast. Quite honestly, he was stunned by what he'd heard. It was nothing that he'd expected after everything he'd been told. These were strong women, women who had made a life for themselves any way they could, but in every case, they'd managed to keep their dignity. Even Melaina, who genuinely seemed to like what she was doing. She wasn't ashamed or embarrassed.

Perhaps if she wasn't, then Jareth shouldn't be, either.

It was the strangest thing he'd ever experienced.

"It is getting dark, my lord. Mayhap you should come inside now."

The soft voice came from behind, and he turned to see Desdra standing behind him. When their eyes met, she forced a smile and he could feel his heart leap.

Just a little.

Just enough.

"In a moment," he said, thinking his reaction to her odd. "I am enjoying the sunset. Will you sit?"

Desdra went to sit on the same rock that the other ladies had sat upon. It was a few feet away from him and he watched her settle down, noticing the sunlight as it played upon her hair. She had the longest hair he'd ever seen, all the way down to her ankles. He thought it was dark, but as the sun glinted off it, he could see red and gold flecks. Coupled with her pale blue eyes, she was truly a stunning woman.

He'd never seen finer.

"I believe that I owe you an apology," he said, looking back to the river, to the sunset. "I was quite rude to you earlier and I am sorry. That is not my usual manner."

"So I am told," she said. When he looked at her curiously, her smile turned genuine. "Sir Hugh and I had a conversation about you."

"Whatever he told you, they are lies."

"He told me good things."

A smile tugged at the corner of his lips. "I should hope so," he said. "He knows my wrath shall be swift."

Desdra sensed humor in his statement. "He does not seem to be the fearful type," she said. "He does, however, seem to be the honest type. He spoke highly of you."

"What did he say?"

"That you are a fine man," she said. "He said that you are an elite knight who serves King Henry."

Jareth nodded faintly. "What else did he tell you about me?"

She shook her head. "Not much beyond that," she said. "But

he did ask me to tell you my story. Why I live at Aphrodite's Feast."

Jareth found himself turning back to the river, watching the serene water as it flowed gently to the sea. It occurred to him that he rather liked the sound of her voice, sort of low and sweet. She was well spoken. He also sensed that she was genuinely trying to make amends for their rough start, when the truth was that he should have been the one trying to make amends. He'd been the rude one, after all. He'd tried to make excuses for his behavior when the truth was that there was no excuse.

He'd behaved like a jackass.

"How long have you been here?" he asked.

"Three years," she replied.

"And the reason you came here?"

Desdra spoke matter-of-factly. "Because my father owed a debt to Lord Chester," she said. "It is no great mystery. There is gambling here at The Feast. There is a lower level where games of chance take place. My father loves games of chance, so he was a regular visitor here until he incurred a debt he could no longer pay. Therefore, he gave me over to Lord Chester to work off the debt."

It wasn't a new story. Jareth had seen, and heard, of things like that before, but he was rather surprised that Desdra didn't seem distressed by it.

"I see," he said. "And... this does not trouble you?"

Desdra shook her head immediately. "Nay," she said. "The debt was repaid in full last year, but I remained because I like it here. Lord Chester was very good to me and I am grateful to him. I will remain here until you ask me to leave, my lord, but know that I am good with sums and I ensure everything about

Aphrodite's Feast runs smoothly. I would like to offer my services to you, to ensure everything remains as it should."

He nodded. "Of course I should like you to remain if you want to," he said. "I know nothing about this business. And it seems to me that a great many people depend on it."

"That is true," Desdra said. "The Feast is far more than what you see or what you've been told. We also provide alms to the poor, and twice a week, we provide sustenance for them. We feed them."

Jareth was listening intently. "Fascinating," he said. "And this is a usual occurrence?"

Desdra nodded. "The Feast has been helping the poor for over twenty years, so I am told," she said. "Lord Chester's mother started it. She was appalled by the hungry children in Bristol and decided to do something about it. You should know that she did not approve of her husband's family's endeavors, but she sought to make good out of them. And she did."

Lord Chester's mother. That was Jareth's grandmother. He didn't know the woman because she had died before he was born, but his mother always spoke fondly of her.

"You speak of Lady Adelie de Leybourne," he said. "I am the son of Lord Chester's younger sister, so Lady Adelie was my grandmother."

Desdra nodded. "I knew you were his nephew, but I did not know the relationships," she said. "He never really spoke of his family."

Jareth shrugged. "It is unfortunate that our family was not close," he said. "Not only is my family not close—I do not speak to my father or older brother—but my mother's family was not very close, either. It's sad, really. Families are supposed to be loving to each other, or so I've been told, but that is not my experience."

"Nor mine," Desdra said with regret. "My mother died long ago and my father saw me as nothing more than a burden, except when he realized he could use me as collateral for debts. I do have an older brother, whom I adore, but I do not see him much."

Jareth was watching her as she spoke, watching the dimples in each cheek as her mouth moved. "What does your brother think about your serving here?" he asked softly.

She tried to smile, but there wasn't much joy to it. "He comes every few months and tries to convince me to come home with him," she said. "At least, he used to come, but he's not come for a while. When he realized that I was far happier here than at home, he stopped trying. I know he only wants the best for me, but he's a little like you—he sees the brothel. Not what this place truly means to me and many others."

Jareth could understand that. "I suppose you cannot blame him," he said. "He does not want his sister living at such a place. I can understand that."

"I know," she said. "But I told him what I have told you— The Feast does so much good for this community. It is so much more than what you and my brother think it is."

"So I have come to see," Jareth said. "I have had several women tell me their personal stories this afternoon, including you, so I have been given much to think on."

"What will you do?"

"About what?"

"Will you accept your inheritance? Or will you decide you do not wish to be associated with us?"

His eyes crinkled with mirth. "I will need more information before I can make that decision," he said. "I hope you will help me with that."

She nodded. "However I can, my lord."

"Good," he said. "Now, you can start by showing me where I may find some food. I need more of those cheese tarts."

Desdra quickly stood up from the rock. "Come inside," she said. "There is food in the main reception room. There's always food there, but if you do not find anything you like, tell me and I shall tell the cook to make you whatever you wish."

Jareth stood up, moving to follow her, but her hair was so long that it got caught on a rough part of the rock. Instinctively, he reached out to free it, feeling those silken strands in his hand before she even realized her hair had been caught. When she felt it and turned around, she caught him with her hair in his hands.

"It was caught," he said, feeling foolish as he quickly released it. "I did not mean to be bold."

She merely smiled, though it was done as if she wasn't sure what else to do. As if his action had caught her off guard. "Thank you for your concern," she said, smoothing her hair down. "It was kind."

"Your hair is very long."

She kept smoothing it. "It is," she agreed. "I have never cut it."

"You shouldn't. A woman's hair is her crown."

"I have a very long crown."

Jareth didn't know how to respond to that because he'd already been caught touching her hair. He didn't want to sound like he was complimenting her hair because he didn't want her to think that he might actually think her hair was lovely.

He did, but he didn't want *her* to know that.

Silently, he followed her back into the building where two Guardians stood at the door. Truthfully, they were ridiculously large men, fearsome, and Jareth paused to look at them as he came inside. They gazed back at him steadily, knowing who he was. Everyone knew who he was. Jareth found himself inspecting both of them, looking at the weapons they carried at their side.

"That is a fine weapon," he said to the man on the right. "Where did you train?"

"Blackchurch, my lord."

Jareth looked at him in astonishment. The Blackchurch Guild was the premier training guild for warriors in the world. After a knight completed his regular training, years of it, sometimes they would continue on to Blackchurch and hope they could pass all of the rigorous program.

It was like no other training guild in the world.

Blackchurch was an equal-opportunity establishment—men who had never had a day of training in their lives could also participate as long as they passed the entry tests, and there were a litany of them. Big, strong men straight off a farm could train at Blackchurch for a better life, providing they passed every single course with every single trainer. One failure and they were expelled. Some men would make it up to the final course only to fail at something, and then they were out.

It happened more often than not.

But those were the strict standards that Blackchurch functioned by. When a man graduated Blackchurch, he was literally perfect, and that made Blackchurch warriors the most highly coveted anywhere. After five years of intense training, by the best knights and warriors in the world, they could command a very high price. Blackchurch-trained warriors served kings and princes and powerful warlords.

Jareth had never heard of one serving at a brothel.

"*You* are a Blackchurch-trained warrior?" he said incredulously.

The man nodded. "I am, my lord."

That only seemed to confuse Jareth further. "Forgive me, but why are you not serving with a great army somewhere?" he asked. "Why are you here?"

The man smiled faintly. "Because Lord Chester pays me twice as much as a king could," he said. "I have a large family to support, my lord. It is true that I am highly trained, but I do not do this for the love of battle. I do it for the love of money."

Jareth couldn't fault the man his honesty. "What is your background?"

The man chuckled. "You will be disappointed, my lord."

"Why?"

"Because I am a blacksmith's son."

Jareth shook his head. "I am not disappointed," he said. "I am deeply impressed. What is your name?"

"I am called Heracles, my lord," he said. Then he gestured to the other man. "This is Orpheus. He is also Blackchurch trained, though he only made it to the third year."

Jareth looked at the other man, who was very tall and very big, with fists the size of a man's head. He had dark hair and eyes, and skin that had been kissed by the sun. Jareth looked him over before speaking.

"You look strong enough," he said. "Why did you only make it to the third year?"

"I cannot swim, my lord."

"What does that have to do with it?"

The man was factual in his reply. "There is a segment that requires men to know how to fight upon the sea, my lord," he said. "It requires a man to know how to swim to shore should his vessel be scuttled. I am not a swimmer and could not pass the test."

Jareth shrugged. "I am not entirely sure even I could do that," he said. "Are all of The Guardians Blackchurch trained?"

Orpheus shook his head. "Nay, my lord," he said. "Heracles and I are. The others are simply well-trained knights."

"Sworn knights?"

"Sworn to the House of de Long," Desdra put in. She'd been listening to the conversation, and when he looked at her, she stepped forward to stand next to him. "In fact, all of The Guardians are sworn to the House of de Long. They are now sworn to you, as the heir."

That hadn't occurred to Jareth. He now had eight sworn knights at his disposal, and the idea wasn't a bad one. Rather pleasing, actually. "Interesting," he muttered, looking between Heracles and Orpheus. "I assume you already know who I am?"

Both men nodded. "We do, my lord," Heracles said.

"Do you know whom I serve?"

Heracles shook his head. "Only that you are now our liege, as Lord Chester's nephew."

Jareth thought he should probably enlighten him so the word would get around and they didn't think some privileged fool had been lucky enough to have the de Long legacy fall into his lap.

"I am a member of a group known as the Guard of Six," he said. "We are the personal guards of King Henry. I serve the king directly and my home is Westminster Palace. As for my background, I come from the House of de Leybourne. We are the direct descendants of King Mark of Cornwall. I trained at Corfe Castle and Warwick Castle, and I served as a master knight, a trainer, at Warwick before I served Henry. I have seen years of battle, including nearly every battle between Henry and Simon de Montfort that was fought. More importantly, I survived. That makes me an elite knight, highly trained and experienced, and quite worthy to be your liege. Am I clear?"

Both men nodded. "You are, my lord," they said in unison.

"Excellent," Jareth said. "Now, do The Guardians have a leader?"

"His name is Zeus," Desdra said. "He usually sleeps during the afternoon because he is up all night and into the morning. I shall introduce you to him when he rises."

Jareth glanced at her. "Good," he said. "I should like to meet him, though I probably saw him when I entered."

"He was at the door when you arrived."

Jareth didn't remember much about the men at the door when he arrived because he'd been so agitated, but he didn't say so. He simply let her think that he'd seen Zeus.

"I look forward to meeting Zeus formally," he said. "And these names—they are not your real names, are they?"

The two men shook their heads. "Like everyone else who serves at The Feast, the assumed names protect our families," Heracles said. "They are meant for anonymity."

"I understand," Jareth said. "But if you are to serve me, I will know your given names at some point."

"Understood, my lord."

With the situation clear to both of them, Jareth headed into the chamber with the feast mosaic on the floor. A woman was playing the lute in the corner as another woman, Melaina, danced gracefully. There was a table full of food and the rich smells lured Jareth inside.

All around the chamber he could see Aidric, Britt, Dirk, Stefan, Hugh, and Orion, spread out among silk cushions and soft taper light. Orion was quite drunk and had three women around him. The big blond knight had something magnetic about him, something that drew women to him wherever he went, and Aphrodite's Feast was no exception. He was laughing and drinking, telling very bad jokes, as others were trying to listen to the music. Jareth caught Aidric's attention and the man rolled his eyes.

That was usual where Orion was concerned.

"Well?" Jareth said to Aidric and Britt, the closest to him. "What do you think of this place?"

Knowing Jareth's reluctance toward the situation, Aidric was careful to answer. "It's a remarkable establishment," he said honestly. "More importantly, what do *you* think?"

Jareth was standing near the food. It was an incredible spread and he let his gaze drift over it, looking at the suckling pig, the castle made from marzipan, and other delights. Things that he'd only seen at feasts at Westminster, but here they were, tucked away in this decadent place in Bristol.

From the start, he'd been told that Aphrodite's Feast was like nothing he'd ever seen before. Nothing he'd ever experienced before.

He was starting to believe them.

And that was exactly what he told Aidric.

CHAPTER NINE

WELL, HE WASN'T *so* bad.

It was sunrise over Bristol as Desdra stood in the solar that overlooked the entry and the river beyond. She was facing west, so the sky was still a little dark, but fingers of light were beginning to touch the landscape as if to shake the world from its slumber. There was a chill in the air and a servant had stoked the fire in the hearth, so it was beginning to warm up as Desdra watched the river with a cup of hot brew made from herbs and flowers steeped in hot water in her hand. There was mint and honey in there, along with the distinct flavor of rosehips and the rind of lemons. It was a delicious drink that she had every morning to start her day.

And a new day had indeed dawned.

There was a new lord of The Feast. Desdra had spent the entire night thinking about him, hoping that this situation would, indeed, work out for all concerned. Truthfully, she hadn't been sure when she'd first met him. She still wasn't completely sure. But he'd redeemed himself somewhat as the night went on and the drink he'd suffered from had faded. Hugh had told her that Jareth was a good man, so she was at least willing to keep an open mind about him. It wasn't like she had any choice.

She wanted to keep her position.

That was the truth of it. Jareth de Leybourne was as handsome a man as she'd ever seen, and given where she worked, she'd seen plenty. But there was something about Jareth that spoke of power and intelligence. She liked that. He was a follower of the king, but around his men, he seemed to be a leader as well. He projected the confidence of command, something Chester never had. Chester had been congenial, sometimes firm in his decisions and sometimes not, but Jareth had no weakness about him. Not like Chester had.

Jareth seemed to be a man who knew what he wanted.

And she was sure he was able to get it.

That meant someone new to manage the business, should he so desire it.

That was most definitely not what Desdra wanted. Were he to relieve her of her position, her only choice would either be to become one of the muses or return to her father, and returning to her father was not an option. She found herself well remembering that time three years ago when her father had told her of her fate. She was to go to a place in Bristol, he said, a place where women had positions and serviced men, and Desdra thought that her father had consigned her to being a prostitute for the rest of her life.

She remembered the horror of that moment.

But it was strange how that moment had turned into something that changed her life. Her father had brought her to Bristol, to the beautiful old building that housed Aphrodite's Feast. He had accompanied her inside, where they had been met by Chester, who proceeded to explain how long it would take to work off Ciaran's debt.

Only eighteen months, she had been told, but she feared those eighteen months were going to be the worst of her life. Initially, becoming a prostitute hadn't been completely out of the realm of possibility because, belonging to Chester as she did, he could have had her do anything he wanted. Only after Ciaran left and she and Chester had been discussing her education did the old man think that, perhaps, it might be worth her taking a look at the ledgers. Desdra explained that she had always been very good with sums, and once she took a look at Chester's accounts, she could see how badly mishandled they had been, probably for many years.

As Chester had explained to her, he'd had a man who had worked for his grandfather tend to his accounts, but he caught the man stealing from him and had ordered The Guardians to throw him in the river. That left him without anybody to handle his accounts, and, truth be told, Chester was not very good with money or with organization. And that was how Desdra found her place at Aphrodite's Feast. If she was going to have to work off her father's debt, then it was best that she use her strengths, one of which happened to be her mind. She had a very good one.

That was how Aphrodite's Feast had become her home, a home she didn't want to leave. That meant she was going to have to show exceptional obedience toward Jareth. Even though he'd asked her to remain, she didn't want to give him any reason to dismiss her. She hoped a night's sleep and a new day hadn't changed his mind about keeping her on. Finishing up her hot drink, she went to the big table in the solar where she spent most of her days tending to the accounts, and she began to go over some inventories that had been delivered the previous week.

And that was how Jareth found her.

"Are you always tending to your duties so early?" he asked.

Startled by the sound of his voice, Desdra looked up from her ledgers to see him standing in the doorway. The last time she'd seen him had been the night before, in the feasting room, where he'd settled in with his friends for conversation and drinking. He hadn't even noticed when she left. But here he was this morning, up early and dressed in a long-sleeved tunic and breeches. Not the armor he'd had on the day before. She got a good look at the size of the man's shoulders.

Something impressive, indeed.

He was impressive.

"I'm afraid I do, my lord," she said, trying not to pay attention to the size of his arms or hands or the way the tunic strained over his broad chest. "There is always work to be done, so I try to start early to ensure it is all taken care of by the end of the day."

He came into the chamber, his gaze moving between her and the ledgers in front of her. "What are you tending to?"

She gestured to the ledger in front of her. "Food purchases," she said. "We receive deliveries daily, so I do the tally every day."

"Who keeps a record of your stores?"

"The cook," she said, pulling out another ledger that was carefully marked. "But I double-check everything to ensure we are not stolen from."

He glanced at the ledgers before looking at her, a smile playing on his lips. "Something tells me that you know everything there is to know about this place," he said. "Am I correct?"

She smiled modestly. "It is my duty to know."

"That makes you indispensable. You do realize that, don't you?"

She shrugged. "I hope I will always do my duty well."

He snorted. "As do I," he said. "You'll have to tell me all of it if this place is to belong to me. I should like to know what you know."

She watched him as he yawned and scratched his head. "Have you decided if this place is worthy of you, then?"

He looked at her, still scratching his head. "I am not too proud to admit that yesterday was quite an eye-opening experience," he said. "Hearing from you and Anosia and Melaina and the other women made me see this place as something… different."

"Different than what you expected?"

He nodded. "Aye," he said honestly. His focus lingered on her for a moment before he continued. "I am very sorry for what I said to you yesterday. I know I have apologized already, but I will do it again. I was rude, and that has riddled me with guilt since it happened. I have asked you to stay and you have graciously agreed, so I hope that in the dawn of a new day, you and I can start again. I hope we can always be pleasant with one another. Yesterday was simply… a rough day."

He seemed both embarrassed and remorseful about it, which made Desdra feel better about her security there. Her fears that he might have changed his mind were alleviated for the moment. In fact, she felt encouraged.

"It was a difficult day for all of us," she said. "And with everything that happened, I've not yet had the opportunity to convey my condolences on the passing of your uncle. I am sorry, my lord. He was a good man."

Jareth held up a hand to thank her. "Truthfully, I've not seen him in many years," he said. "He was my mother's older brother, as I mentioned, but he and my father never got on. I think, for that reason, I simply did not see him much when I was younger, and when I was older, the only time I saw him was when he came to London, but that stopped a few years back."

"I know," Desdra said. "His health was not good the last two years of his life. He did not travel any longer. In fact, he did not travel to London the entire time I have been here."

Jareth nodded. "I thought it might be something like that," he said. "But he sent no word to me about it, so I was unaware."

"And I was unaware of you until he dictated the missive that you received, the one that brought you here," she said. "He never really spoke of his family. You mentioned that he did not get on with your father, so mayhap that is why."

Jareth thought on the fraught relationship that his father and Chester had endured. "Did Uncle Chester ever speak of my mother?" he asked.

She shrugged. "Once or twice," she said. "At least, I think it was your mother. Did he have any other sisters?"

"Nay."

"Then it must have been your mother."

"What did he say?"

Desdra had to think for a moment. "He spoke of how sweet she was as a child," she said. "Little comments like that. He said she loved the water. She loved to swim."

Jareth smiled faintly. "She did," he said. "She was a firm believer that cold water was good for your blood. She would jump into a cold river and splash around. She would try to get my brother and I do it, too, but we wouldn't."

"Lord Chester mentioned that you had a brother," she said.

"He called him the heir."

"He is."

A mischievous expression crossed her features. "He told me to tell you that you should not give your brother anything."

Jareth chuckled. "I do not think that will be an issue."

"You and your brother are not on good terms?"

Jareth's smile faded. "Not particularly," he said. "He inherited everything when my father died a few years ago and I've not heard from him since that time, probably because he thinks I will want a piece of his inheritance. Or money. Or something. Jasper is the suspicious type. He thinks everyone is out for what he has."

Desdra looked at the ledgers on the table. "I think you have more than he does," she said. "In fact, I am certain of it. No one in England, save the king and mayhap a few very wealthy families, has as much as you do. Chances are that he will want some of *yours*."

"Is that so?" he said, interested. "How much do I have?"

She looked at a pile of ledgers and pulled forth one bound in wood with iron edges. It actually had a lock on it, and she pulled forth a small key from the chatelaine she bore on a belt around her waist. It was the name for a collection of keys that chatelaines or housekeepers usually had, keys to every door or lock within their domain. Curiously, Jareth watched as she unlocked the small iron lock on the book and then opened it.

"That is an interesting ledger," he said. "What's in it?"

She was carefully turning the pages. "This is an accounting of every penny your family has made since your ancestor bought his first cog and decided to bring goods from France."

He peered at the very old, very thick book. "How long ago was that?"

She looked at him. "Don't you know?"

He shook his head. "Lady, I had no knowledge of any of this until I received my uncle's missive," he said frankly. "I did not even know about The Feast until yesterday, so in answer to your question, I know nothing about his establishment. This is my mother's side of the family and she simply never spoke of it. Any of it."

She smiled at him. "Then let me be the first to tell you," she said. "And the only reason I know the story is because Lord Chester told me, but his grandfather six times over was the one who bought the first boat. He had a little merchant stall in the city and he evidently married into a family of merchants, so he went into business with his wife's father, I was told. His name was Damien de Long and he was very enterprising. He's the one who purchased this building, or at least what it used to be, and built Aphrodite's Feast around it. The other things came after that."

His brow furrowed. "What 'other things'?"

She looked back to the ledger. "Would you like an accounting of it all?"

"You may as well."

She began to flip through some of the pages. "In addition to Aphrodite's Feast, you also own Redcliffe Manor," she said, reading from the ledger. "Additionally, there is a very large merchant stall on the Street of the Merchants, run by a man named Marston, that is very lucrative. It is the most popular merchant stall in the entire shire."

"Marston?" Jareth repeated. "Who is that?"

She answered without hesitation. "Some say he was Lord Chester's lover for many years," she said. "If he was, that relationship was over before I came. Marston is a lovely man and quite devoted to Lord Chester. He manages the stall quite ably."

"Is he trustworthy?"

"Extremely."

That made Jareth feel better. "I will go and meet the man," he said. "Does he know about me?"

"He does."

"Is that a full accounting?"

"Nay," she said, shaking her head. "You also own eight cogs that bring goods to and from France. You have two cogs arriving in the next day or two, and you will have to be there to meet them and take an accounting of the goods. The captains know that Lord Chester has died, so we do not want anyone taking advantage of the situation."

"Stealing?"

She shrugged. "Possibly," she said. "The captains are all good men, but a couple of them must be watched."

"How are they paid?"

"A percentage of the goods they have brought," she said. "I will do the sums for you, but you will pay them. And stress that their loyalty will be rewarded. You're big enough, and frightening enough, that they will not want to cheat you."

He cocked an eyebrow. "Smart," he said. "Is that all? The cogs and the stall?"

"Not yet," she said. "Along with the cogs, you also own two properties toward the mouth of the River Avon. Two castles, on either side of the river, that guard the waterway from the pirates that like to roam the Bristol Channel from time to time. Portbury Castle is the larger of the two, commanded by a man who served your grandfather. The other, Long Cross Castle, is on the north side of the river and is a small garrison. Just a tower, really. Between the two of them, there are about four hundred soldiers."

She was still looking at the ledger when she realized Jareth hadn't said anything. When she finally looked up at him, he had the oddest expression on his face. Something between surprise and awe.

"What?" she said, concerned. "What is it?"

He shook his head. Then he laughed softly. "I have two castles."

"You do."

"And four hundred soldiers?"

"Aye."

He let out a grunt of disbelief, but he was also chuckling, which made a strange combination. "God's Bones," he muttered. "Is *that* all?"

"Nay," she said, looking to her ledger again. "There are also twenty-three properties in and around Bristol that all produce income. Lord Chester owns the land where seventeen farmers plow and plant, but the properties in town are residences and buildings. He also owns the town hall and the land it sits upon."

An astonishing situation only grew more astonishing. "The income everything draws must be… substantial," he said.

Desdra nodded. "You asked how much money you have, and I shall give you the figures," she said. "With all of the enterprises your uncle possessed, and the accumulation of wealth over generations of your family, everything totals to around twelve thousand pounds a year. The total amount in your coffers, not including the value of the buildings owned, is a little over eight hundred and eight thousand pounds."

She heard a thump. Startled, she looked up to see Jareth sitting in a chair, though he was listing heavily to the right. He sat so fast that he'd nearly missed the chair and had to put out a hand to brace himself against the table so he wouldn't fall over. He was staring at her in utter shock.

"Would you say that again?" he said, sounding breathless.

Desdra nodded, looking back at the ledger. "You have eight hundred and eight thousand pounds in your coffers," she said. "The money is split up, of course. It is not all in one place. Some is at Redcliffe, some is here, and the rest is spread out between the gold- and silversmiths that surround The Feast. Did you notice we are located on the Avenue of the Jews?"

Jareth had his hand over his mouth, looking at her with an odd expression that bordered on awe. "I did," he said.

"That is because they are all holders of your money," she said. "They protect it, exchange it, but it is there if you need it. It is too great an amount to keep in one place."

Jareth still had his hand over his mouth, nodding quickly. "I realize that," he said. "But an amount like that... I am not entirely certain I am comfortable with it being spread around."

Desdra looked at him thoughtfully. "Then you could have it distributed between The Feast and Redcliffe," she said. "Lord Chester did that for years before he gave some over to the Jews. He had an excellent relationship with them. They are very trustworthy."

Jareth didn't want to talk about his uncle's business relationships. He was still lightheaded from having heard just how much money there was in the de Long coffers. He'd never heard of anyone other than kings and God himself having that amount of money, so hearing that *he* was now in possession of it was a distinct shock.

He needed to get out and clear his head.

"Thank you for telling me all of this, my lady," he said,

rising from the chair but still feeling woozy. "We can discuss the storage of the money at another time. I must think on it. I will speak with you later."

Desdra could see that he was somewhat dazed. "I realize this is a good deal of information," she said. "I am sorry if I was indelicate about telling you everything."

He looked at her. "There was nothing indelicate at all," he said. "I asked the question and you gave me an answer. I feel better knowing my empire is in such capable hands. But I must truly think on this for a while. Go about your business and I will come to you later."

She stood up as he headed for the door. "I have been looking at these accounts for the better part of three years," she said. "I forget how shocking the amount is. But it is true, all of it."

He paused by the door, leaning on the frame. "I believe you," he said. Then he smiled weakly. "You are correct—it is a bit of a shock."

He turned to leave, but she stopped him again. "There is something you should know," she said, coming out from behind the table. "Lord Chester was very good to me. He saved my life and I swore to repay him the only way I know how—by protecting his legacy. I am not a member of your family, but I feel as if Chester is the only family I have, and I am very loyal to him. Other than Lord Chester, I am the only one who knows how much money the House of de Long has. I am the only one who knows where it all is. I... I swore that if the nephew of Chester de Long was unworthy of his legacy and only wanted to spend his money recklessly, I would not tell him where it all was. I was going to lie about it. But with you... I can see that you are worthy of the legacy."

"Oh?" he said. "And just how would you know that?"

She shrugged. "Because you listened," she said softly. "The women who went to speak with you yesterday… you *listened* to them. You let them use their voices and their minds and tell you what this place has meant to them. Only a man of character would have done that, like it mattered. Like the *women* mattered. Even if your friend had not told me that you were a good man, your actions yesterday afternoon alone would have told me that. Lord Chester would have been pleased."

A smile crept over his lips. "Thank you, my lady," he said. "I can understand your concern and I am glad that it has been alleviated. As for my uncle, I can see your devotion to him. I am sorry that I suggested that it might have been anything else."

She waved him off. "I suppose given what Aphrodite's Feast is, that was understandable," she said. "But I only looked at Lord Chester like a father. My own father is a caddish man, selfish in every way. Lord Chester was the first man who showed me that not all men are like that. Other than my brother, he was the only man who was ever kind to me."

Jareth's smile grew. "Then I hope in some small way, I can show you that also," he said. "Now, I really must get some fresh air before I faint like a weakling. I will speak with you later."

Desdra let him go. She'd said what she needed to say, hopefully enough to prove to him that she was necessary here. And she would remain here for as long as he would allow it. Feeling somewhat relieved, she returned to her ledgers as the sun rose and day broke. She could hear the shouts from the street below, from people going about their business.

It promised to be a normal day.

"Des?" There came a knock at the door. "May I have a moment of your time?"

Desdra looked up from her ledger to see Anosia standing in

the open doorway. She waved the woman in.

"Of course," she said. "How are you feeling today? Better?"

Anosia came in, smiling. She was wearing a beautiful green garment, with green stones around her neck and gold earrings. Her hair was lavishly done, with ribbons and curls, and she smelled of roses. She looked like any other fine lady in a fine home as she took a seat at the table.

"I'm perfectly healthy," she said. "That little sniffle I had a few days ago never became any worse. Of course, the physic made me eat pickled lemons and had me drink hot apple cider, but it did the trick. I am cured."

"Good," Desdra said. "Do you have a full day scheduled?"

At Aphrodite's Feast, the women kept their own client schedules. Most brothels had a single woman who managed the women who worked there, but not at The Feast. Each woman was like an independent business, and they had to pay the house half of everything they took in on a daily basis. To keep them honest, Zeus, the head of The Guardians, kept track of the men in and out and what services were rendered. Anosia produced her silk purse, one that matched her dress, and put a large handful of coins on the tabletop.

"That is from yesterday," she said. "I will bring you my ledger later. I wrote everything down from yesterday in it."

Desdra took the coins off the table and put them into a basket that was on the shelf behind her. "I will count it later," she said. "Bring up your ledger and I'll match it against Zeus'."

"Shall I fetch it from him?"

"Nay," Desdra said. "There is no immediate need for it. I have not yet received the accounting from everyone, so I will wait to go over everything all at once. Now, let us speak on something more pleasant. You spoke with Lord Chester's nephew yesterday? What did he say?"

The subject shifted to Jareth, and Anosia nodded to the question. "I spoke to him," she said. "Truly, Des, I do not know what I was expecting of our new lord, but a very handsome knight was not among my thoughts."

"He said that you told him your story," Desdra said. "How did he respond?"

Anosia shrugged. "Kindly, I suppose," she said. "He said he was at the Battle of Lewes. That is where my husband was killed. I wonder if he knew him but am afraid to ask. We are not supposed to reveal our true identities here."

"But he is your new lord," Desdra said. "He has a right to know who you truly are. You should ask him."

Anosia thought on that a moment. There was distress in her eyes as she sat back in her chair, averting her gaze.

"I wonder if I even want to know," she said quietly. "That was seven years ago. Seven years since I last saw my love. When I was informed of his death, I was only told that he died in battle, not how he died. I never spoke to anyone who was with him. When his body was delivered to me, I did not ask questions. He was dead and knowing the circumstances would not bring him back. But I find that the more time passes, the more curious I am about it. Like a door that has been left open, not quite closed. Not quite satisfied."

Desdra could see the pain in the woman's expression. "Mayhap you will want to know someday," she said. "Mayhap you will have the courage to ask, because I hope that open door does not remain open and you are forever wondering."

Anosia nodded wearily. "I know," she said. "But anytime I hear of the Battle of Lewes, it is almost as if I am hearing the news again. My belly feels strange. I feel sick."

"Then it is not time for you to need answers yet," Desdra said. "What did you think of Sir Jareth when you spoke with him?"

Anosia lifted her shoulders. "He seemed kind enough, I suppose," she said. "He seemed interested in what I had to say. But those men he brought with him—it has been a long time since I have seen a collection of knights like that."

"What do you mean?"

"Elite, I suppose," Anosia replied. "You can tell they are well trained, from good families. And one of them—he says his name is Orion—has been quite persistent. You asked me about my schedule today. He *is* my schedule."

Desdra looked at her strangely. "What do you mean?"

"I mean that he has already paid for nearly the entire day," Anosia said. "All of my time. He says he only wishes to play chess. I am very good at it. I hope he knows what he is asking."

Desdra chuckled. "He shall soon find out."

"Indeed."

They shared a giggle before Desdra picked up her quill again. "Will you please ensure that the morning meal has been set out?" she said, returning to her ledgers. "And ask Zeus to bring me his accounts if you see him."

Anosia stood up, preparing to face the day ahead. "I shall," she said. Then she paused. "God's Bones. Today is the day following the Sabbath."

"It is."

"The Pope visits today."

Desdra looked up from her ledger. "It is his usual day," she said. "Did you not send word to him about Sir Orion?"

Anosia shook her head. "Nay," she said. "I will do it now and tell him he must come later today. I cannot entertain him when he comes midday as he usually does."

The Pope was the name they used for a local priest who thought he was being clever by wearing alternate clothing and a mask when he visited. His real name was Father Ignacio Joseph, and he was one of the priests over at the cathedral that Chester had built. He was also a man who lived a secret life, one with a love of women and, some said, a secret family. But he paid well and he was kind to Anosia and another woman named Limenia, who were his favorites. All he ever asked Anosia to do was sing for him and sometimes dance, but Limenia would remove her clothing and dance for him. He seemed to like that a great deal. He also paid her very well simply to touch her while she stood still. He liked to touch her breasts, her buttocks, running his hands over her smooth skin, but he never made any attempt to bed her.

All the man wanted to do was touch.

It was simple enough for Limenia to take his money and let him.

"You could send him word and tell him that only Limenia is available," Desdra said. "That way, he will not be disappointed if at least one of you is accessible today."

Anosia nodded in agreement as she moved for the door. But she paused before leaving completely.

"Speaking to Sir Jareth yesterday about my life here was an interesting experience," she said. "What I mean is that I simply do not speak of my life here, to anyone, so speaking of it makes me realize how fortunate I am, I suppose. We *do* have a good life here, Des. I suppose we need to be reminded of that once in a while."

Desdra simply smiled at her, nodding, as Anosia quit the chamber. Outside, the gulls were beginning to circle, calling to one another, officially signaling the start of the day. It wouldn't have been a normal day at all if some of them hadn't gathered on her windowsill, looking for food or just being genuinely annoying. Chester used to throw things at them or make countless trips to the windows to chase them away, but back they would come. She wondered if the birds knew Chester was gone and were trying to be bold now about claiming those ledges like some men claimed countries. The thought made her grin.

We do have a good life here, Anosia had said.

Desdra couldn't agree more.

Hopefully, it was going to get better.

CHAPTER TEN

HE CALLED HIMSELF **Zeus.**

Of course, it wasn't his real name. His real name involved a very recognizable family name, something he'd hidden from for many years, ever since he had sided with Simon de Montfort and his family had sided with the king. His father had distinctly told him he never wanted to see him again and, in fact, seemed to wish his son dead.

That was what the war with de Montfort had done. It had separated families and friends and had left the country nearly bankrupt. It was only seven years ago, but the effects were quite lasting. That included a Kenilworth-trained knight who was currently serving in a brothel. It would have been shameful had it not been so lucrative.

And that was what Zeus wanted at this point in time. If he couldn't serve in a prestigious household, at least he could make some money. He was too old to start over again and too set in his ways to change. Serving at Aphrodite's Feast wasn't so bad, after all. He had six highly trained men to command, and that included two who had been Blackchurch trained. The group of men under him were no slouches, and they made a fortune doing what they did, which mostly included screening the men who entered, looking for female companionship, and disposing of those who didn't behave properly. Oddly enough, and given the fact that Aphrodite's Feast exchanged copious amounts of money on any given day, they'd never had a genuine threat.

That was saying something.

There were hordes of pirates on the west coast of England and Wales, but they never seemed to bother the de Long holdings. In fact, Zeus knew with certainty that a few pirates had visited them as clients over the years, indulging in the good food and fine company. Perhaps there was some respect for a place like Aphrodite's Feast that kept them from trying to sack it, but even if they tried, the building was quite fortified and designed to keep marauders out. There were no windows on the lower floor and the only doors were heavily fortified with iron. Even if they burned the wood, the iron would remain.

If, by some miracle, an enemy managed to make it inside, all of the stairwells had iron grates. Every chamber had a door that was largely the same as the entry door—iron and wood. Each chamber could function as a cell or a fortress, depending on how an enemy entered, so the idea of greedy pirates trying to roust the place didn't concern Zeus or The Guardians in the least.

But one thing did concern him.

A new lord.

He hadn't met the man yet because he'd been taking his usual sleep period when Chester de Long's nephew and heir arrived with a stable of studly knights behind him. By the time he rose, the new lord and his men were sequestered in the feasting room and didn't want to be interrupted. He'd remained up, all night, as was usual, but somehow he never came into contact with Lord Jareth, as he'd been told that was the man's name. He was one of Henry's elite knights and, quite frankly, Zeus was fairly certain he'd fought against the man in any number of battles with de Montfort. He already had to deal with Anosia, whose husband had been killed at Lewes, and now he was going to have to face a liege who had also fought for the king's cause.

He hoped he wouldn't be in search of a new position at some point.

As the day began to dawn, Zeus and his guardians, with the exception of the two who had been on guard duty throughout the night, went about opening the facility for the day. Windows were uncovered and the entry door was unlocked. Zeus could see a farmer coming in from the main avenue, a man who delivered their meat to them, and he sent a Guardian by the name of Castor down to the kitchens to supervise the delivery with the cook. Whenever money changed hands, The Guardians were present. Everyone kept ledgers for checks and balances to ensure everyone remained honest. He'd just sent Castor away when he heard someone coming down the stairwell.

A big man he didn't recognize emerged.

Since there were sleeping chambers above that were sometimes used by guests, it wasn't unusual to see unfamiliar people. The man who came off the stairs was quite big, muscular, with dark hair and hazel eyes. A faint beard embraced his jaw. He had the look of a knight about him, so Zeus made that assumption.

"My lord," he greeted the man. "Are you with the new lord's party?"

The man nodded. "Who are you?"

"Zeus, my lord."

That seemed to bring some recognition to the man's features. "Ah," he said. "The leader of The Guardians. I was beginning to wonder when we would meet."

"And you are, my lord?"

"Sir Jareth de Leybourne. I am Chester's nephew."

That brought recognition from Zeus, and perhaps a hasty salutation. "Welcome to Aphrodite's Feast, my lord," he said pleasantly. "I apologize that I was not on duty when you arrived yesterday. I have the night watch, and most of the day, so I just happened to be sleeping when you arrived."

Jareth nodded. "I know," he said. "I spoke to a couple of your men—Heracles and Orpheus. They explained where you were."

"Good," Zeus said. "Is there anything I can tell you? Would you like me to show you about?"

"Lady Desdra already did," Jareth said. "When I spoke to your men, they told me a little about their backgrounds, and since we are to work closely together from now on, I will tell you what I told them—I am a member of a group known as the Guard of Six. We are the personal guards of King Henry. I serve the king directly and my home is Westminster Palace. My mother was Chester's younger sister, but my father is from the House of de Leybourne. We are the direct descendants of King Mark of Cornwall. I trained at Corfe Castle and Warwick Castle, and I served as a master trainer at Warwick before I served Henry. I have seen years of battle, including the wars between Henry and Simon de Montfort. That makes me an elite knight, highly trained and experienced, and quite worthy as your liege. Better you should know at the start who, and what, I am. Do you have any questions?"

Zeus shook his head. "Nay, my lord," he said. "Thank you

for telling me."

Jareth nodded. "I should like to meet all of The Guardians at some point soon, so can you please arrange a time for everyone to gather?" he said. "I am going to be here for the foreseeable future, so any time should be convenient. You arrange it and I will attend."

"Very good, my lord."

"Thank you," Jareth said. "Now, have you seen any strange men wandering around here this morning?"

Zeus pointed toward the feasting room. "There are a few I do not recognize in there," he said. "There are still others down by the river, I think."

Jareth strained to look from the front door, down toward the river, but he couldn't see much. "I'll find them," he said. "By the way, I've brought five knights with me. They are all part of Henry's guard. And Hugh de Winter has been lurking around here, too."

"Aye, my lord."

With that, Jareth headed into the chilly morning in search of some of his friends. Zeus watched him as he headed outside, making his way across the road and over toward the riverbank. On the avenue, the gold- and silversmiths were starting to open their stalls, all of them with heavily armed men to protect their valuable wares. It seemed like just another normal morning, and one he had to admit he was glad to see. The new liege didn't seem like an arrogant ass, after all. That was a good start.

Little did he know just how sour that morning was about to turn.

 CB

IT HAD BEEN a long time since he'd been to Bristol.

Ciaran arrived in town as the sun cleared the eastern horizon and began its ascent. He'd left Ridlaw in the middle of the night, riding beneath a moon that sat low in the sky and provided a silvery glow by which to travel. It had been cold and damp, and he hated travel, but this was necessary.

He needed to see his daughter.

His life had been one big mess since the death of his son. Benedict had always played the fatherly role, which sounded strange, but given that Ciaran had no real desire to be a parent to either of his children, Benedict had stepped into a necessary role. Ciaran was well aware that Benedict and Desdra were close, and he well remembered when Benedict had nearly killed him for giving Desdra over to Chester de Long. Ciaran had always resented his son for the fact that the man tried to parent him, and while he was naturally melancholy that his son had been murdered, he wasn't devastated by it. That meant there was no one around to make him feel guilty about the life he led.

And there was no one standing between him and Desdra.

The outskirts of Bristol were busy at this time in the morning as the farmers either headed out to their fields or were bringing in cartloads of produce to sell. Bristol had a market every seventh day, and it'd had a royal license for one for many years, so farmers heading into town weren't going to sell their wares at market, but rather door to door, with private clients that they had sold to for years.

The fish market, however, was a different story. Because Bristol was so close to the sea, fishermen went out every morning and returned shortly thereafter to sell their daily catches. The fishmongers were alive and well that morning as Ciaran entered the city. He thought the whole city smelled like the ocean, anyway, and it certainly smelled like fish down by the river. In fact, that was where he was going—to the river—because that was where Aphrodite's Feast was, where he assumed his daughter was.

And he was prepared to do battle with her.

He left his horse at a livery downriver from The Feast, mostly because he wanted to walk the rest of the way so he wouldn't be obvious riding on horseback. A man on foot was often overlooked in a big city, whereas a horse could draw attention. The streets were still fairly empty at this hour as he approached Aphrodite's Feast from the east. The way the building was constructed had it facing the river, but there was a big bend in the river just to the east of it, so the rear of the building was exposed to the road that ran along the river.

Ciaran found himself looking up at that enormous, gray-stoned building.

As he drew near, he could see some men gathered down on the riverbank. He assumed they were customers of The Feast and paid them no mind. There was a short walkway off the road and then the stairs that led to the elaborate entry door, a great stone arch with a door that God himself could not penetrate. There were two men standing at the door, big men with weapons, and Ciaran was prepared for them. He knew who they were, as he'd been to Aphrodite's Feast several times, usually to gamble but sometimes to seek female companionship. This time, it was different. He paused before entering, speaking to the man on the left.

"I have come to see Desdra le Daire," he said. "I am her father. Will you send for her, please?"

The man didn't reply. He looked to another man, standing a few feet away in the foyer, and this man stepped forward. He'd heard Ciaran's request.

And he recognized him.

"Le Daire," he greeted Ciaran. "Do you remember me?"

Ciaran found himself facing a big man with dark, curly hair. "Zeus," he said. "I never forget a face. You're still here?"

"I am."

"Is my daughter?"

"She is."

"Then tell her I have come to see her."

"Is she expecting you?"

"She is not."

Zeus' gaze lingered on him a moment, a haughty gaze, for he was well aware of Ciaran le Daire and his gambling debts. They all knew that Desdra was there because of those debts, because of a father who paid for his weakness with his own flesh and blood.

"I will fetch her," Zeus said after a moment. "You may wait in the reception room."

He was indicating the chamber to the right of the entry. There was a fire in it, comfortable chairs, but no food. That was in the feasting room with the mosaic on the floor. Knowing this, Ciaran ignored Zeus' invitation and went into the feasting room, where a couple of men were finding sustenance for the morning. There was a warm, mulled drink of apple juice mixed with wine as well as a half-dozen dishes that were being kept in warm pots.

As Ciaran picked over the food and demanded wine from a nearby servant, Zeus headed up the stairs to the solar where Desdra was. She was seated at the table and carefully writing in one of the ledgers. It seemed that she was always there, always writing in those ledgers.

He cleared his throat softly.

"Desdra?" he said quietly. "Are you terribly busy?"

Desdra looked over her shoulder at the man who, during the course of her residency at The Feast, had tried to court her more than once. She liked him very much, but she simply wasn't interested in anything romantic with him, much to his disappointment. But to Zeus' credit, he was always professional and courteous with her, even when she'd broken his heart repeatedly.

"Simply going over accounts," she said. "Why? Do you require something?"

Zeus stepped into the chamber. "Nay," he said, shaking his head. "I've come to tell you that your father has arrived. He has asked to see you."

The calm expression vanished from her face and she looked at Zeus in surprise. "My… my *father*?" she gasped. "Here?"

"Aye," he said. "He said that you did not know he was coming."

She shook her head. "Nay," she said, struggling with her shock. "I did not. I have not heard from him in almost a year."

"Well, he's here now."

"Did he say what he wanted?"

Zeus shook his head. "Nay," he said. "He simply asked me to fetch you. Do you want me to bring him up here?"

Desdra took a deep breath, forcing herself to calm. The unexpected arrival of her father had her rattled more than she cared to admit. Although she knew he was still alive, she had been hoping he'd forget about her and go on with his life.

"Aye, bring him up here," she said after a moment. "I do not want anyone seeing him. And I do not want anyone hearing him, though when you bring him up here, please have someone on the stair landing outside the door in case I need assistance. I do not trust my father, sorry to say. Not knowing why he is here, I cannot vouch for my own safety."

Zeus knew that. Having seen Ciaran at The Feast over the years, there had been a few occasions when they'd been forced to either subdue the man or escort him out because of his violent tendencies.

"Have no fear," he said. "I will stand on the landing myself."

"Thank you," she said, though it was clear she was unhappy about the situation. "Show him in. Let's see what he wants this time."

Zeus simply waggled his eyebrows in sympathy before heading out. When he was gone, Desdra sighed sharply and moved away from the table, over to the hearth and its comfortable chairs. Her father's appearance was a distinct shock, but not too unexpected in hindsight. He'd been known to come around from time to time, but, as she'd said, she hadn't seen him in nearly a year.

A lot could happen in a year.

So she waited.

Ciaran wasn't long in coming. Zeus escorted him up the stairs, but once he hit the landing, he bolted inside the solar, forcing Desdra up from her chair. Her father was moving so quickly that she immediately looked around for a weapon. She wasn't entirely certain that she wasn't going to have to beat the man away, so she went to stand behind the chair as he approached.

As if that chair could protect her.

"Daughter," he greeted her, looking far older and more haggard than she'd ever seen him. "Am I not welcome?"

Desdra didn't move. She merely nodded. "You are welcome," she said evenly. "But why are you here?"

Ciaran had his arms open as if he was going to hug his daughter, but it was clear that she didn't want that. He ended up lowering his arms and looking around for wine.

"I can see things are as they usually are between us," he said, irritated. "At least offer me some drink. I am thirsty."

Warily, Desdra moved out from behind the chair and over to a small table that contained the warmed cider she'd been drinking. "All I have is this warmed drink," she said. "There is wine in it, but it is watered. Do you want it?"

Ciaran made a face of disgust. "Nay," he said. "Send for wine. I'll not drink that sewage."

Already, his visit was off to an unpleasant start. Desdra went over to the entry door and called to the nearest servant, sending the woman for wine. She also rolled her eyes at Zeus, who was standing at the top of the stairs. As he fought off a grin, she dutifully returned to her father, who had taken a seat by this time and was warming himself at the fire.

"Well?" Desdra said. "Why did you come?"

Ciaran glanced at his daughter, his hands out in front of the fire. "I came to tell you that your brother is dead," he said. "Killed by outlaws as he traveled home about a few days ago."

Desdra gasped. "Benedict is dead?"

"That's what I said."

He was so cold, so unfeeling. That was not news Desdra had been expecting and, in fact, he'd nearly smacked her over the head with it in the most insensitive way possible. She immediately burst into tears.

"Benedict," she sobbed into her hand. "My sweet brother."

Ciaran eyed her, annoyed. "Aye, it is tragic and all that," he said impatiently. "But now I have a problem. That is why I have come to you."

His attitude enraged her. "A *problem*?" she said. "I'd say you do, indeed, have a problem. Your son is dead!"

"He is," he said. "My weeping like a woman will not bring him back."

Desdra couldn't believe what she was hearing. "How can you be so callous?" she said. "Your son has been killed. You could show some grief or sorrow. You could show something for his memory."

Ciaran sighed sharply. "Stop carrying on so," he told her. "I have come to you with a problem. Benedict is no longer here, so you must help me. I have no one else to turn to."

Desdra was becoming increasingly angry at him. "Why do you not care about your own son's death?" she demanded, wiping the tears from her face. "Why are you so cold?"

"I told you," Ciaran said as if she had asked a stupid question. "Crying copious amounts of tears will not bring him back. He was traveling home from Ridlaw and was felled by outlaws, who stole his purse and left him on the road. He was found by someone from his village, who went to tell his wife. She buried him. That is the end of it."

Desdra had stopped openly weeping and just stood there, staring at him in disbelief. "You are a vile creature," she spat. "Get out of here. I do not want to talk to you."

She started to march toward the door, no doubt to summon someone to escort him out, but he leapt to his feet and grabbed her by the arm before she could get away.

"It does not matter what you want," he growled. "Sit down. You and I have much to discuss."

She glared at him. "If you do not let go of me, I will scream and Zeus will come in here and throw you from the window."

Ciaran wasn't pleased with her disobedience, but he let her

go. "Chase me away and you will never know peace," he said in a low voice. "By the rights of God and the law, I am still in control of your destiny, so I would remember that if I were you. All I have to do is go to the local magistrate, tell him of your disobedience, and you will be forced to comply."

She stepped back from him. "Comply with what?"

He looked at her before giving a wry snort. It was humorless. "Sit down and I will tell you."

With a sharp sigh, Desdra moved away from him and sat down in front of the hearth. She made sure to be within reach of the iron poker in case her father got any wild ideas. He wasn't beyond violence and she didn't trust him.

Not in the least.

"Well?" she demanded. "What do you want?"

Ciaran sat down in the chair opposite her. "I will be brief," he said. "You have been here at Aphrodite's Feast for three years, have you not?"

"You know I have."

"My debt to Chester de Long was paid within a year and a half."

"I know."

"But you refused to come home."

"For good reason."

"Did Chester pay you for the months you served him and did his accounts?"

Desdra paused. "Why do you ask?"

"Answer my question," Ciaran said. "And if you think not to, I will go to Chester directly and ask him. If he refuses, I will find that magistrate and tell him that Chester has imprisoned you and charge him with abduction. Need I go on?"

That gave Desdra pause. She didn't want her father to know

that Chester was dead, mostly because it would give him a reason to demand she come home. No Chester, no more debt, and there was literally no reason for her to be here. She didn't want to give him that ammunition against her.

"He paid me wages that were commensurate with my duties," she said. "He did not cheat me if that is what you are asking."

"How much money do you have?"

She frowned. "I will not tell you anything more until you tell me why you are asking these questions," she said, but even as the words came forth, it occurred to her why. She already knew. "Wait… I know what this is about. You need money."

"If you already know that, then tell me how much you have."

"I will not pay your debts, Ciaran."

She never called the man Father or Papa, always Ciaran because that was the kind of relationship they had. He wasn't a father to her, merely the man who'd helped give her life. But Ciaran didn't like her attitude and he leaned forward, glaring menacingly.

"You will give me your money," he said. "It belongs to me. You are a woman without a husband, meaning any money you have is mine. Women cannot have their own money."

"And yet I do. You cannot have it."

He was prepared to explode at her but thought better of it. Somewhere in the past year or so, she'd grown up. There was some bravery there. Or hardness. He couldn't decide which, but one thing was for certain.

He couldn't frighten her into compliance.

Therefore, he had to be clever.

"I am in trouble, daughter," he said, hoping to appeal to her compassion. "A very bad man wants money from me. Benedict tried to appease the man and, for all I know, it was that man who killed your brother. He will do the same to me if I do not pay him what is owed."

As he'd hoped, the mention of Benedict drew a reaction. "Who is this man?" she asked. "Do you believe he killed Benedict?"

Ciaran nodded. "It is possible," he said. "Benedict was trying to help me negotiate a way to pay the man when he was killed. I will pay you back in time, but I need the money now or my life is forfeit."

Desdra was frowning at him. "You have done things like this my entire life," she said. "You spend money you do not have and expect others to pay your debts. That is how I ended up here. *I* paid your debt to Lord Chester. Now you want me to pay another debt."

Ciaran was struggling not to become angry. He did much better when people were obedient to him. Desdra's defiance was something new, and he didn't like it.

"Then let me speak to Chester," he said. "The man is wealthy—mayhap he will loan me the money and keep you on in repayment. Where is he?"

Desdra shook her head and stood up. "I cannot help you," she said. "You should leave."

Ciaran stood too. "I will not leave until I have an agreement," he said. "Let me speak with Chester."

"Nay," Desdra said. "Get out. Go back home and take your punishment from this man, whoever he is. You deserve it."

Ciaran's patience snapped. He was on her in a flash, grabbing her by the arm again and squeezing. "Listen to me," he hissed. "You will do as I say. Either give me your money or fetch Chester. Mayhap he thinks you are worth something and will give me what I want. You can stay here and work off the debt. You can rot for all I care. But you will do as I say."

Desdra's features were tight with anger. "Let me *go*."

"Not until you do as I say."

Enraged, she tried to yank her arm out of his grasp. "Let me go or I'll scream!"

Ciaran's other hand shot out and he grabbed her around the neck. "I'll snap your throat before help can arrive."

Desdra went into panic mode. Lashing out a foot, she caught him in the groin, causing him to lose his hold. But she pulled away from him so hard that she ended up falling back over the chair. Ciaran charged at her but she pealed off a scream, enough so that Zeus appeared in the doorway. When he saw Ciaran standing over her and Desdra on the ground, he launched himself into the chamber and grabbed Ciaran before the man could run off. He had him by the back of the neck, shoving him out of the chamber as Desdra picked herself up. She could hear her father shouting and cursing all the way down the stairs.

Rubbing her neck, she rushed over to the window in time to see Zeus literally throwing her father out of the entry door. Ciaran sprawled on the dirt, furious at his treatment, demanding to see Chester, but Zeus and two other Guardians were there, unmoving sentinels as he tried to get back in and impervious to his demands. Ciaran tried to push past them, several times, and he ended up being knocked back on his arse.

The activity got the attention of the knights by the river. They were only across the road and it wasn't difficult to hear Ciaran shouting his demands. They headed in the direction of the commotion, just in time to see Zeus toss Ciaran on his arse again. It was the fourth time. As the seven of them, Hugh included, began to head toward the brawl, Ciaran picked himself up one last time and saw the incoming knights. Thinking they were reinforcements coming in to assist The Guardians, he had to fight back his indignation in lieu of self-preservation. He brushed himself off and quickly headed down the road toward the east, in the direction of the livery where he'd left his horse. He was practically running, knowing he couldn't survive an attack by ten big men. Even he wasn't that stupid.

But he was wounded.

Pride only, but wounded just the same.

And he would have his revenge.

CHAPTER ELEVEN

"**L**ADY ANOSIA?"

Anosia looked up from the harp she had been fussing with only to see Orion standing in the doorway. She was in a smaller chamber off the feasting hall, a demilune-shaped room with windows that faced the river and the road, one that was smaller and more intimate for things like conversation or games or even music. Anosia did much of her entertaining in this chamber, and even now, she was trying to tune her small harp so she could practice a new song that she'd purchased from a merchant in town, but Orion's appearance had her thinking she might have an audience for her practice.

Truthfully, she wasn't surprised. The man had stuck to her like flies on honey since nearly the moment he arrived. He was young, perhaps ten years younger than she was, but very handsome and well mannered. She didn't want to encourage him, but it was nice to have someone good-looking and articulate around. So often that was not the case. He'd paid for the full day with her today, and he was a little early, but it seemed that their time was about to start.

Truthfully, she didn't mind.

"Sir Orion," she said, smiling at the debonair knight. "Good morn to you."

"And to you," he said. "May I come in?"

"Of course," she said, indicating a chair nearby. "Please sit. I was just tuning my harp, but the cold morning is hard on the strings. They do not want to tune."

"Oh?" he said, taking a seat. "I heard you plucking the strings and it does not sound bad to me, but then again, I know nothing of music, so do not trust my opinion."

Anosia laughed softly. "Thank you for the warning."

"Are you going to sing something?"

She nodded, indicating a piece of vellum that was affixed to a piece of wood. "There is a merchant in town who has musical instruments and sometimes he has music," she said. "He has just returned from Paris and said a man who played the citole sold him this song, so let me see if I can play it."

Orion partially came out of his seat to see what she was indicating. It looked like a bunch of stroke marks with words beneath them. "And that is music?"

"It is, for the most part."

"You can read it?"

She nodded. "A little," she said. "I was taught to read it as a child where I fostered because the lady of the house was very fond of music and wanted all of her wards to learn how to sing and play a harp."

He sat back in his chair, watching her fumble with the strings. "My training was somewhat different."

She smiled. "I can imagine it was," she said. "Knights are not usually taught singing, although I have known some that were. I suppose it depends on where you fostered."

"True," he said. "I fostered at Kenilworth."

"Ah. With the master knights."

"Indeed," he said. "Would it be too much to ask where you fostered?"

She plucked the string, listening to the note. "Prudhoe Castle."

"And they trained you in music?"

She grinned. "Of course," she said. "Why so shocked?"

He shrugged. "Because it's a battle castle," he said. "They are not known for their arts and music."

She finished plucking the string, having reached a note that was satisfactory. "With their male fosters, mayhap," she said. "But female wards are trained in the great arts. A truly refined woman knows many things, and the Lady of Prudhoe was determined we should be proficient in it all."

"And you clearly learned your lessons," he said. "Is that where you met your husband? Prudhoe?"

Her smile faded. "I explained the rules to you yesterday, my lord," she said. "My name is Anosia. Someone told you that I am a widow, but beyond that, we do not speak of our past or our families. I am what you see—a muse for your entertainment and nothing more."

Orion knew that. It was Aidric who had told him about Anosia, and he had heard it from Jareth, who had spoken to Anosia yesterday when she explained the value of a life at Aphrodite's Feast for women with no other choices in life. He knew that she had been married to a knight who had perished at the Battle of Lewes, and he further knew that she had two small daughters. But that was really it. From his own observations, he knew that she was an elegant creature, beautiful and poised, and in his opinion, she had no business being in a place like this. A woman like that was meant to be married to a powerful lord and cherished.

"You are far more, lady," he said quietly. "I knew that when I first saw you. You are far too fine for a place like this. You would make a wife a man could be proud of."

She smiled, genuinely, at the soft flattery. "I was, once," she said. "It is kind of you to say so. Now, would you like to hear my new song? I am only practicing, but I think I can produce a worthy sound."

"You could not do anything else," Orion said, sitting back in his chair. "Go ahead. I would like to hear you."

With a modest, if not somewhat flirtatious, glance at him, she cleared her throat and began to strum the strings of the harp.

Underneath the moonlight, shadows begin to fall,
Whispers of thy heartbeat echo through the hall.
A love so passionate, burning like a flame,
But in the darkest moments, nothing feels the same.

She abruptly came to a halt, staring at the words, but just as quickly she began playing the notes again, gently strumming the harp. But no singing. Orion found himself watching her face as she read the music, seeing what looked like distress on her features. But she continued to play, very skillfully, until the song was finished. When it was over, she looked at Orion, smiling wanly.

"It is only practice, after all," she said. "I will become more proficient the more I play it."

"It is beautiful," he murmured. "But why did you stop singing the words?"

She struggled to keep the smile on her face and finally gave up. "Those are words of pain, not of joy," she said. "I do not wish to sing of pain."

"Because you've had pain of your own?"

"Mayhap."

He sat forward, resting his elbows on his knees as he gazed steadily at her. "Do you never talk about yourself at all?" he asked. "Or do you truly feel like you're nothing more than the furniture?"

Her brow furrowed. "Clearly, I am more than the furniture," she said. "But there is safety in anonymity."

"I understand," he said. "But you… you're not like the other women in this place."

"And you've been around enough to know that?"

He shrugged. "I am a knight," he said. "I am trained to observe. I have seen the young woman who only wants men in her bed. I've seen another young woman who talks to the food she eats and recites the most detailed poetry without the benefit of reading words before her. And then there's you."

"So there is."

"Is that all you want out of life?"

"You ask many questions, my lord."

"That is because you intrigue me."

Anosia wasn't sure what to say to that. She'd had nosy clients before, but Orion was coming on strong. She knew he was an elite knight, undoubtedly from a good family, but that didn't give him the authority to know everything about her. As she struggled to come up with yet another refusal to allow the man into her personal world, Heracles was suddenly at the door of the chamber.

His gaze sought her out.

"Anosia," he said quietly, "Lord Ellersby is here."

Anosia immediately stood up. "Thank you," she said. "I will come."

Orion stood up, too. "Why?" he said. "Where are you going?"

Anosia paused. "Lord Ellersby has come to listen to me read the journal his dead wife kept," she said. "He wants to hear it in my voice. It reminds him of her."

Orion scowled. "Ridiculous," he said. "I paid for the entire day with you."

Anosia cocked an eyebrow. "But you are early," she said. "It will not take me long to read to him, and then we will have the rest of the day uninterrupted."

She started to leave the room, but he caught up with her, blocking her way. "I will pay you double what he will," he said. "I want to hear more of the song. I want to talk to you."

Anosia stood her ground. "Lord Ellersby has a session with me every week at this time," she said. "I told you yesterday that our time would start midmorning because I will not tell an old man that I will not read to him simply because you want to talk. I will see you afterward if you still wish it, Sir Orion, but for now, Lord Ellersby calls."

With that, she pushed past him, out into the feasting room and on into the foyer, where a very old man with a bound book in his hand was waiting for her. Anosia greeted him sweetly as Orion watched and proceeded to escort him into the reception chamber. Far away from Orion and his demands.

And he knew it.

But he also knew he'd see her later.

Dejected, he went to break his fast with Aidric and Britt, who were in the feasting chamber, devouring an egg dish. As Orion sat down beside them, he was already plotting the rest of the day with Anosia.

This time, there would be no more old men to interrupt them.

Or so he hoped.

℣

IT HAD BEEN an eventful morning.

Jareth was sitting in the solar with Aidric, both of them going over the ledgers that Desdra so carefully kept, analyzing the details of what, exactly, Jareth had inherited. Aidric had a mind for sums, so Jareth wanted the man's help in deciphering everything. He would have asked for Desdra's help, but she'd made her loyalties clear the night before when she spoke of her devotion to Chester, so the truth was that Jareth wanted someone with an unbiased point of view to help him review everything. Not that Desdra wouldn't tell him the truth about the empire he now found himself in command of, but he couldn't be entirely sure she wouldn't omit something out of loyalty to Chester. Even though she had told Jareth she felt him a worthy heir, he wanted the opinion of someone who had no stake in this.

There was also the fact that Desdra had had a run-in with her father that morning. Zeus had told him all about it when Jareth saw The Guardians running a man out of The Feast. There had been some shouting going on, so there was clearly a conflict, and Zeus had told him what happened afterward. Desdra was well, he assured him, so no harm had come to her.

But Ciaran le Daire was a man to be watched.

Ciaran was the one who had used his very own daughter to pay off the debt to Chester, which, in turn, ended up being the best thing that could have happened to her. But he was back for some reason and had evidently tried to abuse his own daughter, which brought Zeus and The Guardians to her rescue. Jared had tried to speak to Desdra after that, simply to ask if she was well, but she was so upset that she went to her chamber and shut the door. She didn't want to speak to anyone. Therefore, Jareth had left her alone and retreated to the solar to busy himself by inspecting the ledgers.

But his mind continued to linger on her.

It was odd how he felt that the chamber, though it was technically his, seemed to belong to her somehow. Her imprint was all over it, from the careful writing in the ledgers to the very furnishings around them. It was a woman's chamber even if that hadn't been the intent. About two hours into the audit, it was clear that this was something that was going to take more than just a day. Not only were there ledgers stacked on the table, but there were a dozen bookshelves that were positively stuffed with well-organized accounts.

Desdra had organized them by month and by year, so it was easy to go through them one at a time and get a picture of the fiscal health of Aphrodite's Feast as well as the entire de Long empire. Every property had its own ledgers, and that included the farms and the other dwellings that the de Long family owned. By midafternoon, they had at least isolated the ledgers for every property, and both Jareth and Aidric counted twenty-nine different ventures.

It was nearing sunset when they heard a door open and close out on the landing. There were two other chambers out there, plus a small corridor that ran to the back of the building where another set of fortified stairs led down to the kitchen and a small array of servant rooms. Jareth was studying a ledger from last year pertaining to Portbury Castle when he caught movement in the doorway of the solar. Looking up, he saw Desdra standing in the opening.

"Lady Desdra," he said, setting the ledger down. "I hope you do not mind that I've been going over the ledgers without you."

She stepped into the chamber, smiling weakly. "Of course not," she said. "They are your ledgers now, after all. You are welcome to look as much as you wish."

He smiled at her, seeing how pale she appeared. He wasn't sure if he should simply gloss over the fact that her father had tried to get physical with her earlier in the day, but the truth was that it really wasn't his business. He'd only known the woman a day, so he wasn't going to insert himself into her world more than he already had. But he had to admit that he was concerned for her. Given her pale face, it was a natural reaction.

"Thank you," he said. "I do have a few questions, but they can wait. I'm sure you have other things to do."

She shook her head. "Nothing terribly pressing," she said. "It is the day I usually tally money spent on things like food and fuel for the fires. Things necessary to ensure The Feast runs smoothly. But I can certainly answer a few questions."

"I have a question, my lady," Aidric said from his position over near the hearth. He had been sitting in the same chair Ciaran had sat in only hours before, and Desdra hadn't noticed him. She gasped in surprise when he sat up, poking his head over the chair. "My apologies if I startled you."

She giggled at her own foolishness. "The back of that chair is so high that I did not see you, my lord," she said.

"This is Sir Aidric St. John," Jareth said. "He is part of the House of St. John in Cumbria. His father is a great warlord and Aidric is part of the Guard of Six. He is also one of the most educated men I know, so he has been helping me decipher the ledgers so I understand what I am looking at. Aidric, this is Lady Desdra le Daire, a woman who appears to have single-handedly maintained this empire."

Desdra smiled modestly at the accolade. "It has been my honor," she said, but her focus fixed on Aidric. "You said you had a question for me, my lord?"

Aidric nodded, picking up one of the ledgers he had spread out on the chair next to him. "Aye," he said. "I understand that de Long had eight cogs for shipping?"

"That is correct."

"But I see that he owns five other smaller vessels," Aidric pointed out. "Fishing boats?"

Desdra nodded. "Aye," she said. "You will note that the ledger in question only deals with those boats. He had them brought over from Calais about two years ago after a bad bit of weather moved through here and destroyed several fishing vessels. Lord Chester bought them so the fishermen would not lose their livelihoods. They are his boats, but the fishermen use them and maintain them, and pay us a portion of their daily catch."

"Ah," Aidric said. "That was my question—who owned the boats."

"Sir Jareth does."

A smile tugged at Aidric's mouth as he glanced at Jareth before turning back to his ledgers. "Excellent," he said. "Well done, Uncle Chester, for giving the fishermen boats for their livelihoods."

Jareth chuckled at the man's tribute to his generous uncle before returning his attention to Desdra. "Have you eaten yet?" he asked. "Would you like for me to send for food?"

Desdra was shaking her head even as he offered. "Nay, but I thank you," she said. "Truthfully, I was simply going to finish up my work from this morning, but I do not wish to impose upon you. I shall leave you to your inquiries."

"Please do not leave," Jareth said. "If you feel strong enough to answer more questions, I beg you to stay. And also because I've been looking at Aidric's ugly face all day and your shining presence would be most welcome."

Aidric, who was quite handsome, shrugged. "I agree she is better to look at than I am," he said. "But I will admit that I am becoming rather hungry, so I will take my leave at this time. Jareth, do you want me to send something up to you?"

Jareth nodded. "Please," he said. "Enough for us both."

Aidric nodded, ignoring Desdra's soft refusals. Once he left the room, Jareth sat back down at the table and pulled forth the ledger he had been reviewing. He pulled out a stool for Desdra, indicating for her to sit, and she did so slowly.

"Did you have specific questions of me?" she asked. "Truly, I do not need to be here if you'd rather be alone. This is your solar now and I do not wish to intrude."

"You are not intruding," Jareth said, focused on the ledger. He flipped a page, casually. "Is your father a regular visitor here?"

Desdra drew in a long, slow breath. The subject of her father had come up, expectedly so, but she wasn't eager to discuss him. "Nay," she said. "I've not seen him in a year. You saw him being chased out. And before you ask me, he did not hurt me. He tried, but Zeus prevented it."

"This is the same father who used you to pay his gambling debt?"

"The same."

Jareth looked up from the ledger. "Then it seems to me that you can never return home," he said. "You must stay here forever. I will ensure that you are always fairly treated, and I will further ensure that your father is never allowed within these walls again."

Desdra smiled weakly. Just as quickly, the tears came and she tried not to be obvious about wiping them away, but Jareth saw her. It was hard to miss.

"That was not meant to make you weep," he said. "It was meant to give you comfort. When you told me how, and why, you had come to Aphrodite's Feast, you never mentioned that your father was brutal toward you."

She was looking at her lap, flicking away tears when they started to trail down her cheeks. "I have only just met you, my lord," she said. "There has not been time for me to tell you my entire family history."

"True," Jareth said. "Can we expect your father back anytime soon, then?"

She shook her head. "Probably not," she said. "At least, I hope not. May… may I return to my duties now, please?"

Jareth sighed. She genuinely had no intention of allowing him to know her any more than she already had, and that bothered him. It shouldn't. He shouldn't have cared. But he didn't like the thought of someone roughing up this lovely, bright woman, even if the man doing the roughing up was her father.

But there was also something in him that understood her situation, very well.

"I know we do not know one another, my lady," he said quietly. "I know I am virtually a stranger to you. But I have inherited something I never expected to inherit and you are the one person who knows everything about it, inside and out, so by virtue of that fact, we will be working closely together as I become accustomed to the workings of this empire. It would make it more pleasant for us both if we knew each other a little. Trust has to start somewhere."

She wiped at her cheeks and looked at him. "That is true," she said. "I am not trying to be evasive. It is simply that my relationship with my father is a complicated one. Complicated and unpleasant. The only good thing he ever did for me was give me over to Lord Chester to pay off the debt he owed him."

"You mentioned that that debt was paid."

"It is," she said. "That was one of the reasons my father came here today. He knows the debt is paid and he further assumes, rightly so, that Lord Chester has been paying wages for managing his ledgers. He wanted to know how much money I have because he evidently has another gambling debt to pay off."

Jareth grunted in disapproval. "So he was here with a purpose."

She nodded. "Aye," she said. "He also came to tell me that my brother was murdered. In my whole life, my brother is the only person who has ever been truly kind to me. That is why I retreated to my chamber when my father left. I simply needed some time to come to terms with Benedict's death."

Jareth began to feel sorry for her. "You have my sympathies, my lady," he said. "News such as that is never easy to bear."

"Nay, it is not."

"May I ask what happened?"

She shrugged, thought she was starting to tear up again. "My father said that he was set upon by outlaws who intended to rob him," she said. "Killed by outlaws, he said. But he was just so cold about it, as if Benedict was not his son, just some stranger he had no ties to. It is heartbreaking to think that Benedict tried so hard to take care of a man who gave him such disregard. As if he was not his father."

"The same way he treats you."

"That is very true," Desdra agreed. "A man like that should not have children."

Jareth couldn't disagree with her. "In my experience, men like that are the way they are for a reason," he said. "A horrible childhood, mayhap the actions of others. Sometimes it is a way to defend one's feelings."

But Desdra shook her head. "Not Ciaran," she said. "He was the same way with my mother. I was young when she died giving birth to a son, who also died, but I remember my father hardly caring. He sent her body home to her parents and demanded money in return for the loss of his wife. I was very young, but I still remember him becoming angry when they refused to pay him."

Jareth thought the man sounded like a detestable creature. "That is unfortunate," he said. "I'm sorry you had to endure such callousness."

She nodded, accepting his sympathies, wiping at the tears that were still trickling. "Benedict wasn't like my father in the least," she said. "He was compassionate and kind. My father drifted between hating him and depending on him. When he sent me to Lord Chester in payment of the debt, I thought Benedict was going to kill him. He was furious. But in the end, there was nothing he could do. My father had every legal right to make those decisions for me."

Jareth could only imagine how a loving brother might have felt over the destiny of a helpless sister. "But you stayed in contact with your brother over the years?" he said.

"I did," Desdra said. "In fact, he came here to visit me about three months ago. He said that he'd been in negotiations with the Earl of Lincoln. He had been offered a position with him."

"Oh?" Jareth said. "John de Lacy? I know him well. Did your brother assume the position, then?"

Desdra shrugged. "I do not know," she said. "I only know he was offered the position. I do not know if he actually accepted it. Knowing my father, he surely gave my brother a good deal of grief over even considering it, but the truth is that even though my father is titled, there is no money. Benedict would inherit an empty title and no money, so he was trying to make his own fortune. I cannot blame him."

"Nor I," Jareth said. "My lady, would you like me to write to de Lacy and find out if your brother had indeed accepted the position? Mayhap there are wages owed. I can clarify the situation if you wish, and if there is money involved, I can have it sent to you directly."

Desdra looked at him with some surprise. "That is very kind," she said. "Benedict was married, however. Any money should go to his widow."

"Would you like me to contact de Lacy about it?"

"I am not sure," she said hesitantly. "Truthfully, I am more concerned for his widow. She is a sweet woman, and since I know my father will not take care of her, I feel as if I should. I will write to her and ask her if she is returning to her family. If not, Aphrodite's Feast was made for someone like her, because she can earn money so she and her children will not starve."

"Would you like me to send a few of my men out to her home to see to her situation?"

She looked at him for a moment, puzzlement in her expression, as if she wanted to say something but wasn't sure how to go about it. When she spoke, it was haltingly.

"Forgive me, but… but why should you want to do anything for me?" she said. "I am not your responsibility. Your offer is kind, but I would feel very odd accepting."

He cocked an eyebrow. "You're wrong," he said. "About your not being my responsibility, that is. You serve here, at The Feast, and you are indispensable. Surely Uncle Chester thought so, also, and your loyalty to my uncle affords you privileges when it comes to me. I am more than willing to help someone who has been so devoted to my uncle."

She broke into a grin, shyly. "You are most kind to offer," she said. "I will think on it, I promise."

He smiled in return. "Good," he said. "Now, will you eat something with me? Aidric was supposed to have something sent up, but it is not here yet and I am famished. Will you show me the kitchens? I can get my own food."

Her smile turned genuine and she stood up. "That is not necessary," she said. "I can fetch it for you."

"You are not a servant."

"Neither are you."

His expression suggested that he saw her point. "True," he said. "But let's go down to the kitchens, regardless. There were some good things there yesterday. Mayhap there are more good things to eat today."

Desdra began to head from the chamber with Jareth following. "We can certainly find out," she said. "Did you speak with the cook yesterday?"

Jareth shook his head. "I was still trying to reconcile this place in my mind," he said. "So, nay, I did not speak with him at all."

"He's an interesting man," she said. "He used to be a priest."

"A priest who is now a cook?"

She giggled. "And a very good one," she said. "A terrible priest, but a wonderful cook."

Jareth liked seeing her smile. Given the day she'd experienced, he was glad that she seemed to be feeling better. Perhaps he'd contributed to that, just a little.

He hoped so.

The cook, who, Jareth discovered, was named Gustave, didn't look like either a priest or a cook. Jareth hadn't noticed him much yesterday, but today, he did. The man looked like an ancient Roman wrestler, with a shiny, shaved head, muscular arms, and a beard that was long and braided. He seemed pleased that Jareth made the effort to visit him again and gave him a bowl of stew with cream and salt, peas, and cured meat in it. It was positively delicious. Jareth and Desdra ended up sitting at a table in the kitchen, stuffing themselves with the rich stew, and listening to Gustave tell adventurous tales about his life as a priest.

Jareth was fairly certain most of it was fabrication, especially when Gustave explained how he once saved an entire village from an old church that had collapsed on them, but Gustave told the stories so well that he didn't care. More and more, he was starting to agree with what everyone in the know had told him.

Aphrodite's Feast wasn't *just* a brothel.

It was more than he could have imagined.

CHAPTER TWELVE

Ridlaw Manor

"**A**S I TOLD you when you arrived home from Bristol a few days ago, the fact that your son was killed does not interest me. What does concern me is my money."

The words came from King Dagda. They weren't spoken, but growled. Like a preying beast, King Dagda had uttered those words, the same words he'd been uttering since Ciaran returned from Bristol and walked straight into an ambush, only now King Dagda seemed to be tired of uttering them. He'd spent a few hours knocking Ciaran around and stolen his horse as part of the debt owed, but there was literally nothing else of value in the manor, so his frustration was getting the better of him.

But no one was more frustrated than Ciaran.

The beating he'd taken the first two hours of King Dagda's visit had rendered him nearly unable to talk. He'd had six teeth knocked out, and a broken one in his mouth was slicing into his cheek. He'd told King Dagda about Benedict's unfortunate death, but that hadn't made an impact. Ciaran had been trying to use Benedict's death to hold off King Dagda's demands or, at the very least, delay them, but that hadn't happened. It still wasn't happening.

King Dagda wanted his money and he wanted it now.

That put Ciaran in a bind.

He was going to have to get creative.

"Listen to me," he said, mouth damaged, one eye swollen shut. "I have a way we can all be satisfied, but it will take an effort from both of us. I know where I can get my hands on the money."

King Dagda looked at him in doubt. "Then why did you not say this from the beginning?" he said. "Why tell me stories of your son's untimely death and blame a dead man for your troubles?"

Ciaran didn't want to say what he was thinking. He had genuinely been hoping that King Dagda might give him a reprieve with Benedict's death, but the Scottish pirate had no intention of doing so. "You never gave me the chance," he said. "All you wanted to do was beat me. How am I to speak when you knock my teeth out?"

King Dagda went over to him and pinched Ciaran's face between his thumb and forefinger, forcing him to look up and open his mouth so he could see the damage caused by his men. He clucked his tongue sadly.

"The lads have knocked you around a bit," he agreed. "But you could have stopped them. All you had to tell me was that you have a way to get me my money."

Ciaran wasn't going to argue the fact that when King Dagda's men were in full swing, it would have taken more than words to stop their assault. "I do have a way," Ciaran said firmly. "I told you about my daughter, the one who serves at Aphrodite's Feast."

King Dagda sat down on a chair opposite him. "I remember."

Ciaran leaned toward the man as if he was about to relay a great secret. "What I did not tell you is that she handles the ledgers," he said. "She has access to the money at Aphrodite's Feast."

That bit of information had King Dagda's interest. "She is a treasurer?"

Ciaran nodded eagerly. "She knows where it all is," he said. "If I can get to her, I can convince her to part with some of it. But I will need your help to accomplish this."

King Dagda frowned. "What do you want me to do?" he said. "I have been to The Feast, you know. There's a young woman there who reminds me of my wife when she was young, only she's sweeter and prettier than my Joanne. I want to *keep* attending The Feast, if you understand my meaning. Attacking it will ensure that I will never return again."

"Nay, not attack it," Ciaran said, shaking his head. He was trying desperately to come up with a plan on the spot, anything to keep them from beating him again. Thinking fast on his feet had never been a strong suit, but he had to try. "I… I need a distraction to pull The Guardians away from The Feast. Can you do that? Create a fire or roust the town. Something that will have them leaving their posts. I just need the chance to get in and get out without being seen."

King Dagda considered the request. He looked at his men, who really didn't have much input into his decision, but he wanted to see what they thought. He could tell by the looks on their faces.

What he saw wasn't exactly positive.

"If this is another delay, Ciaran, I'm afraid it will not end well," he said.

Ciaran shook his head quickly. "It is no delay, I assure you," he said. "My daughter really does manage the accounts. She has access to the money, I swear it. But you must help me by getting The Guardians away."

"Why?"

"Because if I am to take the money, don't you think they will stop me?"

He had a point. King Dagda looked at his men again, one of whom shrugged. No one seemed to have an opinion one way or the other, so King Dagda sighed heavily with indecision.

"I'm not sure what I can do," he said. "If I take my ships up the river to get their attention, they could trap me. That would put me and my lads in danger."

Ciaran was very nearly pleading with the man. "Then what about at the mouth of the river?" he said. "It's well known that there's an outpost there, a castle. What if you were to harass the castle? That would bring the men from Bristol."

King Dagda grunted, shaking his head. "I know that castle," he said. "Portbury. There are soldiers out there. There would be no reason for The Guardians to come and help."

"There would be if *you* sent a missive from the castle, asking for their assistance," Ciaran said. "Send a missive to The Feast begging for help. Once the Guardians arrive, you can flee out to sea. That will give me time to get into The Feast, get the money, and get out."

That was a viable plan, or at least viable enough. King Dagda really did want his money, and a dead Ciaran wouldn't give him any, so he was trying to put the fear of God into the man enough so that he would pay his debt. Given he had very little, it seemed that stealing from The Feast might be the only chance for King Dagda to really get his money. But he still wasn't completely satisfied.

"If I do this," he said pointedly, "then I'll need more money than simply what you owe me."

Ciaran furrowed his brow, thinking the man was going to try to trick him somehow. "What do you mean?" he said. "We agreed on how much I owe you. Do you think to change that now?"

King Dagda shook his head. "Nay," he said. "But if you are to steal from their coffers, you'll have the opportunity to take more than your share. In addition to what you owe me, I want half of everything else you can get your hands on."

Ciaran didn't like that in the least. "But—!"

King Dagda cut him off. "*I* am the one risking my ship and my lads by attacking a castle," he said. "*I* must be compensated or I'll not do it."

Ciaran was stuck. King Dagda was a greedy man, but he didn't get where he was in life without being a little greedy. A little conniving. In that respect, he and Ciaran were cut from the same cloth, only Ciaran's cloth was a little more frayed. He knew he had no choice at this point.

If he wanted the money, he was going to have to compromise.

"Very well," he said. "But if I am forced to fight any of The Guardians because you were not sufficient enough to draw them away, even with a forged note from the garrison, then I shall take some of your share. I am risking a great deal, you know. You will have your ship to flee in. I will have nothing, since you've taken my horse."

King Dagda stared at him a moment, menacingly, before breaking down into soft laughter. "You may have your horse returned to you for this," he said. "I should not expect you, of all people, to try to run. The Guardians would catch you and fillet your bones."

"And it will be your fault if you do not give me my horse."

King Dagda's smile faded. "I told you I would," he said. "But push me too far, little man, and we'll see who shall fillet your bones. Am I understood?"

Ciaran hated being chastised like a child. He hated it when other men had dominion over him. "I know what I must do, and betraying you is not one of those things," he said, avoiding agreeing with the man. "How long will it take you to reach the mouth of the river?"

King Dagda shrugged. "We are anchored to the south," he said. "There is a little inlet near St. Thomas Head, and I pay the man well to hide my ships at the base of the cliffs below his house. It will take me at least a day or two to reach the ships and two or three days to sail to the mouth of the river. I would say that we shall be able to send the missive to The Guardians by the seventh day, so be prepared to move when you see them depart. *If* they depart. If they are the only protection for The Feast, I cannot imagine that all of them will go. Some may remain behind. You must be prepared for that."

Ciaran nodded. "I will," he said. "Have faith that I shall get your money and then some."

"And if you do not?"

Ciaran looked at him, his dark eyes a maelstrom of malevolence and determination. "My daughter will cooperate or there will be… consequences," he said. "Desdra will do as she is told. And you shall have your money."

King Dagda could match Ciaran's malevolence and then some.

"I'd better."

Ciaran didn't doubt it for a moment. The stakes, this time, would be his life… or his daughter's.

God help Desdra if she resisted him.

CHAPTER THIRTEEN

A week later

"I WISH YOU would have let me bring the carriage for you," Jareth said. "It would have been much more comfortable."

A week after his arrival at Aphrodite's Feast, Jareth was finally heading out to Portbury Castle to inspect his property, but he'd brought along an entourage that included the entire Guard of Six, Hugh, and Desdra. Since the day her father had been chased from The Feast, Jareth and Desdra had been inseparable, but only because circumstances dictated so. They'd gone over account after account. Desdra had indoctrinated Jareth into the world of his mother's family, something not even Chester had ever done. She knew the details as if they were her own family, and there were times when Jareth saw a flash of longing in her features, as if she wished they were.

It made for an interesting few days.

But something else had made for an interesting few days. Jareth had never been strongly attracted to a woman in his life, mostly because he was very selective about the women he spent his time with. They had to be intelligent and they had to be pleasing to look at, and in London he could find one or the other, but rarely both. Compounding the problem was the fact that he hardly had time to hunt for such a woman if he were so inclined. But here in Bristol, he'd found all of those qualities in Desdra.

After the first couple of days, spending nearly every waking hour with her, he'd started to feel something more than politeness toward her. Days three and four and five crept upon him and he realized that not only had he spent most of his time with her, but he'd also eaten every meal with her. When he awoke in the morning, he was eager to see her, even if it was only to go over more ledgers. It didn't even matter what they did, only that he did it with her.

It was the strangest thing he'd ever experienced.

He wasn't the only one who was noticing how much time he spent with her. His friends were noticing, too, and by the expressions on their faces, they approved. Whenever Jareth was with them, he spent half the time denying that he was fond of her or that there was anything going on between them and the other half speaking about the things she'd educated him on. The more he denied his fondness of her, the more they teased him about it, and the angrier he became.

It was a vicious cycle.

Even as he was quite possibly becoming more interested in Desdra, Aidric told him that Orion was becoming quite attached to the widow of the knight who had been killed at the Battle of Lewes. Jareth knew who Anosia was because she had been the very first lady who had told him the story of her association with Aphrodite's Feast. That elegant woman seemed out of place at what was essentially a brothel. But several days after his arrival, not even Jareth could call it a brothel any longer.

He'd seen the light.

Today, as they made their way to Portbury, the knights were mounted and in full armor while Desdra, astride a sturdy gray palfrey, was only protected by the traveling clothes she wore, dark green in color, woolen and durable. She looked like a queen with her magnificent hair in a braid that was longer than the horse's tail. It had rained the night before, so the road was muddy and all of the horses were filthy up to their bellies from the slop that had been kicked around, hence the reason for Jareth's statement.

I wish you would have let me bring the carriage for you.

Desdra wouldn't hear of it.

"Completely unnecessary, my lord," she said. "Although I appreciate your kind offer, I would rather ride. It is not often I have the chance to do so like this."

Jareth wasn't pleased that she had denied him, yet again, and made a face to reflect that displeasure. "Stubborn wench," he muttered.

"What did you say?"

He fought off a grin. That was the kind of relationship they'd developed as of late, where he could insult her and get away with it. Truth be told, she'd done plenty of insulting herself, and he'd found it the most charming thing about her.

"I said that you would have been more comfortable on… on a bench," he said, feigning innocence in his dastardly comment. "You know, the bench of the carriage. Sitting on it. A bench."

Her eyes were narrowed as she looked at him. "A bench?" she asked.

"Aye, a bench."

She was well aware that wasn't what he'd said. So was everyone else. She looked at Aidric, at Britt, riding closest to her.

"Is that what you two heard?" she asked. "That I would be more comfortable on a bench?"

Aidric and Britt were part of the game. "I think so," Aidric said. "But I actually thought he said fence."

"Fence?"

"Aye."

"That I would be more comfortable on a fence?"

"I think he said dense," Britt said. He was usually a man without humor, so his comment was surprising. "He said you were dense."

"He did, did he?" Desdra said in outrage, her head snapping to Jareth. "Did you say I was dense?"

Jareth found himself scrambling as his entire group of friends snorted at his predicament. "I said no such thing," he insisted firmly. "Britt has hearing like de Lohr. He cannot hear a damn thing."

"What's that?" Stefan said from behind Jareth. "Do I hear my name taken in vain?"

"Oh, do shut up," Jareth said. "No one is talking to you."

"*I* am taking to him," Desdra said, slowing her horse so she came in alongside Stefan. "Well? You were closest to him. Did he say that I was dense?"

Stefan shook his head. "He called you a wench."

The entire group burst into laughter except for Jareth. He rolled his eyes and shook a fist at Stefan, but Desdra was onto him. She had a riding crop in her hand because the palfrey sometimes needed a little encouragement, so she took the crop and slapped the big rump of Jareth's warhorse. The animal would have bolted had Jareth not been strong enough to hold him back. But the animal was quite excited, and Desdra smacked the crop against her hand, making the sharp and smacking sound again, and the animal began to dance and kick a little.

Jareth had a hell of a time holding it steady.

Everyone thought it was hilarious.

"That is punishment for your slander," Desdra called after him as he struggled with his horse. "Let that be a lesson to you."

"A lesson for what?" he said, grunting as he brought the horse under control. "A lesson in the wickedness that strikes a woman when it suits her? A lesson in how truly awful you are? Pray, tell me what lesson I am to learn."

Desdra fought off a grin. "A lesson that you should always be polite to a woman who is smarter than you are," she said. "Otherwise, your life will be misery."

"It is already misery," he grumbled. "With you, it could be nothing else."

"What's that you say?" she said, pretending to cock an ear in his direction. "That you're not miserable enough? I'll see what I can do about that."

Next to Desdra, Stefan laughed in support. He was always in support if it put Jareth in a bad light. But riding at the head of the column, Orion groaned loudly.

"Christ, de Leybourne," he said. "Kiss the woman already. Stop with all of this foolish flirting and get on with it!"

Jareth was trying to move his horse forward, to get to Orion, but the animal was still skittish. Without hesitation, Desdra spurred her little horse forward, got in behind Orion, and whacked his horse right on its big rump.

The horse bucked and jumped right off the road.

The laughter was loud and long as Orion struggled with his young, butter-colored stallion. That gave Desdra an idea, and she moved through the column, smacking any horse rump she came close to. Stefan was spared because he was her ally, and Dirk backed away when he saw what she was doing, but it made for utter hilarity as they plodded along the road toward Portbury Castle. Or not so much hilarity for those wrestling with startled warhorses, but Desdra and Stefan got a good laugh out of it.

Until Jareth came up behind her and snatched her right off her palfrey.

Before Desdra realized it, she was across Jareth's thighs, her backside completely exposed, and he brought a gloved hand down on the general area of her buttocks. She was wearing such heavy clothing, however, that it made more noise than it actually hurt, but Desdra howled.

"Fiend!" she yelled. He smacked her again, listening to the laughter of the men around him. "Vile creature! Put me down this instant!"

"Why?" Jareth said, grinning. "You thought it was very humorous to spank horses. Why is it not humorous to spank you?"

He whacked her again, not hard, but enough to make a loud sound, and she crowed with displeasure. Jareth laughed, especially when Stefan managed to make it up beside him and spank her himself. They had a fine time laughing at Desdra, sprawled across Jareth's thighs with nowhere to go.

But this was how their relationship had developed.

And he loved every minute of it.

"Apologize," he told her steadily. "Apologize for smacking my horse and for causing mayhem. Do it and I may be merciful."

Desdra refused. She was hanging by his left leg, and as he lectured her and demanded apologies, she carefully pushed aside the mail coat and began to pull his breeches out of his boot. The boots were snug, so it took a bit of doing, but she managed to get the bottom of his breeches out of the boot, exposing the flesh of his leg. As hard as she could, she pinched him, and the man nearly sent her flying.

"Yow!" he boomed, pushing her pinching fingers away. "That bloody well hurt!"

More laughter in the group. The antics were hilarious. She wouldn't back down and neither would he. But Jareth sought to punish her, albeit good-naturedly, and began to spin his horse around in circles as she screamed.

Of course, he had hold of her so she wouldn't fall off. In all things, he would keep her safe, even when he was trying to scare her. Somehow, the jokes, the repartee, the bonding was under his skin as if it had always been there. Moments like this were moments he'd never shared with anyone else, but there was no possible way he could tell her that. Or even express it.

But he was having the time of his life, unexpectedly so.

As he bounced Desdra around, he realized that she was trying to slither off. She was pulling on his saddle cinch, trying to gain leverage so she could fall headfirst to the ground. He stopped the horse and grasped the back of her bodice, pulling her upright, or at least somewhat upright. The moment he did so, she grabbed him around the throat with both hands and started squeezing. Not hard enough to actually do any damage, but more as an outlet for what he'd just done to her.

"No mercy," she grunted, shaking him back and forth as much as she could. "Do you hear me? No mercy for you. Apologize for calling me a wench!"

He put up his hands in surrender as she pretended to choke him. "*Mea culpa,*" he said, eyes twinkling. "My apologies, lass."

"Tell me that you did not mean it."

"I did not mean it."

"I am not convinced!"

"I swear, I did not mean it. Have pity, my lady."

She stopped squeezing, stopped shaking, and gazed into his eyes. They were incredibly close to one another, probably more than they should be, but they both just sat there and grinned at one another. God, it was wonderful. The warmth, the friendship, all of it wonderful. Jareth had the urge to kiss her, an urge he'd had frequently over the past few days, but as always, he refrained. He was afraid to. Afraid of what would happen.

Afraid he'd lose his soul to this fiery slip of a woman.

But that was his last coherent thought before chaos descended.

Jareth heard the noise before he ever felt the blow. A high-pitched sound, and he knew exactly what it was. Putting a big, gloved hand on Desdra's head, he suddenly shoved her down just as an arrow slammed into his left shoulder, right where she had been sitting. The blow from the projectile was a heavy one and knocked him sideways. He was still holding on to Desdra, however, and she fell with him. He hit the ground first with her on top of him, cushioning the fall.

Arrows were flying everywhere.

The Six, along with Hugh, were spurred into action. Stefan and Aidric were the closest to Jareth, and they leapt from their horses to drag him to safety while Hugh, Britt, Dirk, and Orion headed toward the source of the projectiles—only to run headlong into a small group of outlaws just inside the tree line. As Aidric and Stefan dragged Jareth into the safety of the trees, with Desdra helping them as much as she could, they could hear the sounds of battle.

"Go," Jareth said, irritable and in pain. "Go and help the others. I will hold for now."

They weren't listening. They were both inspecting the arrow, noting that the tip was protruding from the other side of Jareth's body. They could feel it through his mail.

"Damn," Aidric said, realizing it was worse than they'd thought. "Jareth, it goes all the way through, but I do not think it hit anything vital. Can you breathe?"

As Jareth nodded, Stefan was trying to pull the mail and fabric away from the wound site. "We need boiled linen and medicaments for this, things we do not have here," he said. Then he looked to Desdra. "How far are we from the castle?"

Desdra was pale with sorrow. She was also a little sick because she'd never seen a man with an arrow in his body and, unfortunately, her first happened to be Jareth. It was an effort not to become physically ill.

"Not far," she said. "Over the next rise, we will be able to see it."

"Then we must ride for it and ride fast," Stefan said, returning his attention to Jareth. "Can you ride?"

Jareth nodded. "Get me on my feet," he said, grunting. "I can make it to the castle."

They pulled him up, carefully, making sure he was steady before Stefan ran off to grab his horse. Desdra's palfrey was nowhere to be seen, so Stefan brought the horse back into the shelter of the trees. Once they helped Jareth to mount, Stefan lifted Desdra up behind him. Her arms went around his torso, holding on tightly, as Jareth spurred his horse up to the road. As a short but brutal fight went on behind him, he headed to Portbury Castle at a gallop.

CHAPTER FOURTEEN

Portbury Castle

I T WAS GOING to take all of them to get the arrow out.

When the projectile entered, it had broken on his shoulder blade. They'd figured that out by the angle of the shaft and angle of the tip. They were different. Orion, for all of his annoying habits, was actually a very skilled healer, something he'd trained for when he fostered at Kenilworth. His mother had been a healer and it was something he'd learned as a child, and the master knights of Kenilworth had recognized that, so they permitted him to train with the physician at Kenilworth who took care of the knights. Therefore, there was no one more qualified to remove the arrow than Orion.

But he didn't like the looks of it.

"Very well," he said after thoroughly examining the injury. "This is going to take all of us. I believe the arrow is broken, so it may not come out cleanly. Aidric, ask the soldiers about a local physic. He will have medicines that I do not. Fetch him immediately. Meanwhile, Dirk and Britt—bring me scalding hot water and any rags that have been boiled clean. If they haven't been, then do it immediately. Boil them for at least a quarter of an hour and do not let them touch anything when you remove them from the pot. Bring them to me immediately."

As the three knights fled, Orion turned to Hugh, who had been hovering anxiously. "I will need your help," he said, catching Stefan's eye as well. "Both of you. This arrow is bent, which means we cannot take it out in one piece. The shaft will have to be pulled out of his chest, but the head will have to come out of his back. And we must do it in a way that ensures no wood or debris is left behind."

As Stefan and Hugh nodded seriously, Jareth smiled weakly at Orion. "When did you become the serious physic?" he said.

Orion was focused on the entry wound. "I've always been."

"How did I not know this?"

"You never asked."

There seemed to be a rebuke in that answer, but it wasn't untrue. No, Jareth had never asked him about his background. All he knew was that Henry wanted him to be part of the Six, so he was. And he was as annoying as hell. They'd spend so much time being vexed by his irritating personality that it never occurred to Jareth that they may have had something to do with it.

It wasn't like they'd really welcomed Orion into the group.

But at this moment, it was as if something had changed between them.

"You are right," Jareth said after a moment. "I never asked. I apologize."

Orion didn't answer right away. He was still trying to gauge the angle of the arrow as compared to the angle of the head.

"My mother was a healer," he finally said. "I fostered at Kenilworth and the master knights like for their trainees to have a specialty. With some, it is weapons, with others, it's tactics or strategy. My specialty was healing."

"Kenilworth," Jareth said. "That is impressive. Your family must be prestigious."

"It is," Orion said. "The House of Payton-Forrester has always served the lords of Beverly Castle, in the north. They are allied with the House of de Wolfe and the Earls of Teviot."

"Knights?"

"Aye."

"No titled lords?"

"Nay."

"Interesting," Jareth said. "There are plenty of prestigious houses who have sons that do not warrant admission to Kenilworth. If your father is merely a knight, you have to earn an appointment like that."

"I was a legacy."

Jareth knew what that meant. "I see," he said. "Then your father trained at Kenilworth."

Orion stopped poking at the wound and looked him in the eye. "Since you are the only one of the Guard of Six who has ever bothered to ask me about myself, I will tell you," he said. "I know that the lot of you think I'm aggravating. I know you think I'm an arrogant dolt who only thinks of himself, who annoys you to the point of tears. Did you ever stop to wonder why, Jareth? Because Henry has acquired me and has decided I need to fit into his Guard of Six, only the six of you are so tight, like brothers, that there isn't room for anyone else. So—I become annoying because it is the only way anyone pays any attention to me."

Jareth could hear the disappointment in the man's voice. Truthfully, he was coming to feel like a cad. This was the most conversation he'd ever had with Orion, here in a critical moment, and it had taken an unexpected turn.

"I am sorry about that," he said. "It is true that we are all very close. We are called the Guard of Six, not the Guard of Seven or Eight. We have been a unit for a very long time. We are like brothers. But nothing lasts forever. Torran and Kent have moved to other stages of their life. The truth is that the Six has fractured somewhat. We must be more mindful of men like you who have been assigned to our group. I am sorry we have not been more welcoming."

Orion shrugged. "But you have been to Stefan," he said, looking at the big knight a few feet away. "I know why. He's a de Lohr and there is no finer family in England. You accept him because of his father and grandfather and great-grandfather. He is a legacy knight. But me… I come from the small house of Payton-Forrester. My background is not so prestigious, or so you think."

"We accept Stefan because we have fought with him and his family before," Jareth said. "I am willing to apologize for our failings, but not all of our actions are failures. Stefan was already part of us when he officially became part of the Six. But you…"

"You had not fought with me before."

"Nay, we had not."

Before Jareth could reply, Dirk and Britt came back into the chamber with servants behind them. Two of the servants were lugging big iron pots of steaming water while three others had neatly rolled rags. Boiled rags. Given that this was an outpost, someone knew something about the value of boiled rags when tending wounds, so there was a supply.

Orion had everything set upon a table next to where Jareth was sitting.

"Excellent," he said. "I also need wine. Lots of it."

One of the servants went running. Orion fingered the rags and tested the temperature of the water when Aidric suddenly appeared.

"I'm told the closest physic is in Bristol," he told Orion. "I'll send one of the men back to town for him."

But Orion shook his head. "Do not trouble yourself," he said. "I have what I need to remove the arrow, and then we'll simply send Jareth back to Aphrodite's Feast to recuperate. You can send for the physic from there."

He was the man with the plan. That normally annoying, always-egotistical knight was taking control of the situation and men were listening. It was a surprising natural air of command that they hadn't seen from him before. It was a side he'd never shown. When the servant brought back two big earthenware bottles of wine, Orion got down to work.

"My lady," he said to Desdra, "please leave the chamber. You will not want to see this."

Desdra, who had been sitting next to Jareth the entire time, even through his conversation with Orion, appeared surprised by the request, but she didn't argue. She'd never been around a wounded man in her life, so she didn't know what mystical, terrible things were going to happen to heal Jareth from the arrow jutting out of his shoulder. She didn't feel qualified to stay.

"As you wish," she said. "I… I will be just on the other side of the door if you need anything. Anything at all."

Jareth watched her go, warmth in his eyes. "It will take a moment," he said. "I am sorry to have spoiled your morning."

She smiled weakly as she reached the door. "And I am sorry your ride led to a near-death experience," she said. "I will wait until you are ready."

He lifted his right hand and waved at her. She waved back. The door closed and every man in the room looked at Jareth with a grin.

"God's Bones, Jareth," Aidric said. "Orion was right. Kiss that woman already. Marry her already. What are you waiting for?"

Jareth scowled. "If you do not shut your lips, I am going to get out of this chair and throttle you," he said. "All of you. A woman is a delicate creature, and if your foolishness scares her away, I will hunt each and every one of you down and make you pay in the most painful way possible."

Britt started laughing, but Dirk had to tell Stefan what Jareth had just said, shouting it so loudly that Desdra undoubtedly heard it on the other side of the door. When Jareth realized that, he closed his eyes and hung his head as his friends had a good time at his expense.

"Please," he muttered to Orion. "Just leave the arrow there. Let it kill me, for surely, it would end my humiliation."

Orion was grinning. "It would take too long," he said, but quickly sobered up. "Stefan, get in behind him and hold him. Do not let him move. Aidric, grab the shaft. I must go to his back and remove the head. Everyone else, hold him down. He cannot move."

While everyone took position, Jareth tried not to tense up, knowing what was coming. But knowing Desdra was on the opposite side of the door would keep him quiet. He wouldn't want her to hear his pain and become frightened. Or, worse still, think he was weak.

"You know it was only by a sheer miracle that this arrow did not strike Desdra," he said as Aidric took hold of the shaft.

"Did you kill those who did this?"

Aidric nodded. "They did not seem very organized," he said. "The garrison commander says that they are fools who live in the trees and set upon those they think are easy prey. Why they should attack seven heavily armed knights is beyond my comprehension. But they attacked and paid the price. No one walked out alive."

"You have the bodies?"

"Eleven of them and counting."

"Good," Jareth said, grunting in pain as Orion took a sharp dagger and cut the wound where the arrowhead was barely protruding. "Get this over with. Be quick about it."

Orion tried. He truly did. But the arrow shaft came out in pieces and he was forced to dig for a big chunk that had come off in Jareth's shoulder. Fortunately, the projectile had missed anything vital, and once he dug out the piece of wood that made the arrow whole, and a piece of cloth that had been torn from Jareth's tunic, he doused the wound repeatedly with wine and let it bleed heavily to wash out any further impurities before binding it tightly with the boiled linen.

Through the entire event, Jareth never uttered a sound.

When it was over, they moved an exhausted Jareth to a chamber with a bed in it belonging to the garrison commander. It was messy and smelly, but the bed was a good one. Desdra headed off to the kitchens to find Jareth something to eat as Orion and Stefan and Aidric carefully settled him in the bed.

"Now," Orion said, "you must rest. You can stay here for a couple of days, time enough for the wounds to heal over a little and for you to regain some strength, before we move back to The Feast. How do you feel?"

Jareth eyed him. "Like you dug pieces of wood out of my

back," he said. "I've had arrow wounds before. That one was not simple."

Orion shook his head. "It was not," he admitted. "If the piece of wood had not remained in you, it would have been much easier for us both. As it was, it was more complicated than I had anticipated. I am sorry for that."

Jareth laid his head back on the pillow. "You could not have known," he said. "But there is more chance of poison getting into my blood now."

Orion nodded faintly. "Time will tell," he said quietly. "I cleaned it out heavily with the wine, but sometimes that does not work. We can only pray for the best outcome."

That was the truth. Given how Orion had been forced to dig into his back to find the wood, it was very possible that Jareth would end up with a fever, but they would have to wait and see. For now, the situation was stable and Jareth could begin healing.

All thanks to that annoying, arrogant knight.

And Jareth knew it. He watched Orion as the man tightened up his bandages. "Orion," he said hesitantly. "Your care has been exemplary. And for the conversation we had, I appreciate that it must have been difficult to tell me, but know that after this, I will do better where you are concerned. We all will."

A wry smile crossed Orion's lips. "You mean that I have earned my way into the group by digging wood out of your shoulder."

"You have shown a side to you that we did not know," Jareth said. "You've been something of a buffoon up until this moment. Now, we know differently."

It was a fair statement, one Orion couldn't disagree with. With a simple nod, he excused himself, leaving Jareth lying flat on his back, surrounded by the remainder of the Six.

"What was that about?" Aidric asked, moving over to the bed to check the bandages. "What was difficult for him to tell you?"

Jareth sighed faintly. "He confessed that not one of us has really been kind to him since Henry decided he was to be part of the Six," he said. "He feels that we have such a tight group that there is no room for anyone else, and the only reason he's been irritating is because it is the only time we notice him."

Aidric's brow furrowed. "That is not true."

"Truly?" Jareth grunted. "Think about it. Have we ever truly embraced him like a brother? Like someone who belongs? I do not think so. I do not think he was wrong."

Aidric was forced to reflect on that, remembering Orion since he became part of the Six and the interactions they'd had with him. Had they ever gotten to know him? Probably not. The man had been such an arrogant boor that Aidric, personally, hadn't really tried to befriend him. He was simply there and they accepted that.

Perhaps there was a grain of truth to what Jareth said.

"Then we shall have to examine our behavior and make amends," Aidric said. "Especially since he used his skill on your shoulder. I think we owe him something for that."

Jareth reflected on that. "His opinion was that a man wasn't truly accepted into the Six unless he proved himself," he said. "I think he just did."

Aidric gave him a lopsided grin. "I will agree," he said. "He performed admirably."

"He did."

That was about all Jareth could manage at this point. He closed his eyes after he spoke, clearly exhausted from the injury, and Aidric took it as a hint.

"Rest," he told him. "We are going to check the woods in the area to see if there are any more outlaws. I shall speak with the garrison commander on the matter, and any other security matters he might have. Do you wish to speak with him as well when you are feeling better?"

Jareth peeped an eye open. "Let me sleep tonight," he said. "I will speak with the man on the morrow."

"I will bring him to you when you are ready," Aidric said. "We'll come back later to see how you are faring."

Jareth simply lifted a hand in acknowledgment. As Aidric, Stefan, Dirk, and Britt headed out, Desdra headed in. She was carrying a tray with a cup and bowl and a few other things on it. Behind her was a servant carrying a heavy coverlet, and she had the woman put it on the bed while she set the tray down. As the servant scurried out, Desdra shook the folds out of the coverlet and draped it over Jareth.

"There," she said. "This should keep you comfortable. I've brought some stew for you. You should probably eat something."

He just lay there, looking up at her. That magnificent woman with the marvelous hair. After a moment, he held out his right hand.

"Come," he said softly. "Sit next to me. I must tell you something."

Desdra complied, thinking he was going to share something important with her. "Of course," she said. "Are you in pain? I do not have anything here, but Lord Chester kept something for pain that was quite effective. He called it the healing flower. It is back at The Feast."

Jareth shook his head. "I am not in any real pain at the

moment," he said. "But I wanted to commend you for your actions today. It was a serious situation that could have gone badly, but you kept your head. That was very helpful and I appreciate it."

A faint flush crept into her cheeks. "To be truthful, I was scared to death," she admitted. "But I was scared for you."

"Me? Why?"

She eyed him, exasperated. "Because an arrow had pierced you," she said, stating the obvious. "I thought it might kill you."

A smile tugged at his lips. "And you were afraid for me?"

"Of course I was."

"What would you do if I died?"

She scowled. "That is a terrible question."

He laughed softly. "Why?" he said. "Just tell me that you would miss me. That is all I wish to hear."

An expression of confusion rippled across her face and she pulled her hand from his. He watched, his smile fading, as she stood up and turned for the food.

"You should eat this while it is hot," she said. "I cannot vouch for the meat in it, but I am told it is mutton. They tried to give me some kind of fish pie that smelled very strongly, so I refused it. Do you like fish?"

"Desdra," he said slowly, "why can you not tell me that you would miss me should I die?"

She had the bowl in her hand. When she spoke, her back was to him and her head lowered. "It is a silly question."

"Mayhap so, but answer it. Please."

She sighed sharply. "What do you want me to say?"

"The truth."

She considered that. Her head came up and she looked at the wall, anything but him. "I suppose..." she began, stopped, and then started again. "I suppose, if you must know, that I have never had a friend like you."

"Oh? What would you miss about our friendship?"

She shrugged. "I would miss our conversations," she said. "The way you like to tease me. You have become a great friend, Jareth, and I am very grateful."

That was as close as she could come to a confession and he didn't push her. She was being braver than he was in even voicing such a thing. Their relationship had come about so organically that it wasn't something to be fleshed out or discussed. It simply *was*. Therefore, he was careful with his next question.

"But you do not want me to be more than a friend?" he said. "If you do not think me attractive or a potential suitor, you need only say it once. I will never bring it up again."

She still wouldn't look at him. "That is a strange thing to say."

"Why?"

She grunted irritably. "This is not suitable conversation, Jareth," she said, grabbing the bowl and standing up. "Now, do you want some nourishment or not? You really should eat something. You have been through a great ordeal."

"Nay, I do not want to eat," he said. "I want to know why this is unsuitable conversation."

"Because it is."

"That is not an answer."

"It is the only answer you will receive."

She came over to the bed with the bowl of stew, but he turned his head away. He wouldn't look at her and he most certainly refused to eat. Realizing that, Desdra pursed her lips irritably and sat down next to the bed, still holding the bowl.

She watched his profile for a moment before speaking.

"Any woman would be very fortunate to have you as a suitor," she said quietly. "But let us be completely honest with one another. When you asked me that question, you did not mean *suitor*."

He turned to look at her, brow furrowed. "I didn't?"

"Nay," she said. Then she took a deep breath to summon her courage. "Jareth, I am glad to be your friend. I am happy to tell you everything I know about the de Long empire so that you know it, too, like I do. I have enjoyed our time together. But I will not become your concubine."

His eyes widened. "Concubine?" he repeated. "Is *that* what you think I meant?"

"You once accused me of being Lord Chester's concubine," she said. "If you want to know the truth, Lord Chester was the father I wish I'd had. He was kind and patient and he treated me with respect. You, too, have been kind and patient and have treated me with respect, and we have had good conversations. You make me laugh. But do not think my laughter or my respect for you means you can take advantage of the situation. If you try, know that I will leave The Feast and commit myself to a nunnery before I will become anything… unseemly. Am I making myself clear?"

He was trying desperately not to smile because she'd been as brave and unwavering as he'd ever seen her in that neat little speech. She was absolutely serious.

"You are very clear," he said. "May I make myself clear also?"

"If you must."

He cocked an eyebrow. "It was never my intention to make you my concubine," he said. "*Ever.*"

"Is that the truth?"

"With God as my witness. I would not want you as my concubine."

Now she was looking the least bit embarrassed. "I see," she said. "Then I am sorry to have made assumptions. Given what you said to me the first day we met, I… I simply wanted to be clear."

"I understand," he said. "And I will be clear now. I said that I would not want you as my concubine because you are too fine a lady for that. But I would want you as my wife. I should like to court you if you will consider it."

Her face ran the gamut of emotion—surprise, disbelief, shock, and finally confusion. "Me?" she managed to say.

"You."

"That is impossible."

"Why?"

"Because… because my father is a very minor lord," she said as if explaining the obvious. "You are an elite knight. You serve the king. You require a wife with a higher standing."

He snorted. "I require nothing of the kind," he said. "You are worth a dozen of those perfumed females. I've been around them my entire life and I've never met one I was inclined to court. Please, Desdra… say you'll think on it. I would be grateful."

Desdra didn't know what to say, at least not right away. She was elated, but also cautious. *Very* cautious. Did she want to be courted by a man as glorious as Jareth? A man she'd admired from nearly the start? A man she'd found more comfort, and more warmth, from than anyone in her entire life? It wasn't a difficult question to answer. Of course she would be delighted to have the man court her.

But there was the little matter of her father.

"If you are genuine, then I will think on it," she said softly. "But you must think on it, too. You know of my family situation, and it is not a good one. You must understand just how dastardly and conniving my father is."

"I've dealt with men like that before," he said. "You needn't worry."

She shook her head. "You do not understand," she said. "My father is a gambler, as you know. If you and I were to… well, to marry, he would use that as collateral for his gambling exploits. He would tell people that his daughter was married to the lord of Aphrodite's Feast and they would give him endless credit, which he could not pay. In order to save your reputation, you would have to pay it. Do you understand that?"

She sounded like she was pleading with him by the time she was finished, but Jareth was unmoved. "I would deal with him appropriately," he said evenly. "It would be a small price to pay for marrying the most wonderful woman who has ever walked this earth."

It was a sweet thing to say. Desdra was trying not to be distracted by it because she was genuinely concerned that he didn't understand just what it meant to court her. Ciaran would try to exploit it by any means necessary. But it was difficult to keep the smile off her face as she set the stew down and went back over to the bed, pulling the coverlet to his shoulder.

"Enough of that," she said softly, a glimmer of warmth in her eye. "This arrow wound has made you mad. You must sleep now and rest. I will come back in a short while to make sure you do not require anything."

Jareth let her fuss with the coverlet, watching her face as she did so. He muttered under his breath.

"I will see you in my dreams," he whispered.

Desdra didn't quite hear him. "What was that?"

He started struggling as if it was difficult for him to speak any louder, so she leaned closer. And closer. When she came close enough, he quickly grasped her face with his right hand and kissed her gently on the lips.

"I said that I will see you in my dreams," he said, loud enough for her to hear. "Thank you for tending me so carefully."

The stolen kiss startled her, but then she grinned broadly. "You are incorrigible," she said, stepping away from the bed. "Behave yourself and go to sleep."

He just smiled at her, a triumphant sort of expression, and she simply shook her head and left the chamber. Shutting the door behind her, Desdra paused a moment, leaning back against the door as she touched her lips as if to feel the imprint he'd left upon them.

Imprint, indeed.

Perhaps something good had come out of the trip to Portbury after all.

CHAPTER FIFTEEN

H E WAS A pirate, after all.

The traveling game of chance was purely a side business, but over the years, King Dagda's main source of income was, in fact, that game of chance. It was always done in secret and usually at a tavern in a larger town, and there was a network of them all throughout Cornwall, Somerset, and Dorset. He mostly stayed to the southwest area of England because he knew every inch of the coastline, every cove, and every cliff. He knew where he could hide and he knew where he could run.

The problem was that there were many pirates in the western portion of England, Wales, and Scotland. It tended to make for crowded seas at times. Given that he was from Scotland, the English and the Irish pirates had a particular hate for him, so it was challenging to do business in the southwest of England at all. When it came to the western coast of Cornwall, he had to pay tribute to a band of nasty pirates who controlled that area known as Triton's Hellions. They took his money and looked the other way when he docked his ships along that stretch of coastline. Some of the pirates from Triton's Hellions even joined in his game of chance if they had the inclination to. King Dagda welcomed them all because he didn't discriminate when it came to money. As long as it was valid and he could hoard it or spend it, he was a happy man.

The journey to his ships at Saint Thomas Head had taken longer than he had anticipated. Rain had moved in periodically, making the roads nearly impassable in some places, so he and his seven men had been forced to ride through muddy meadows, over farmers' fields, and any other way they could to keep their forward momentum going. He hadn't even made it to the coast by the seventh day, as he had told Ciaran, so he hoped the man wouldn't move too quickly in anticipation of The Guardians being removed from their post. Ciaran was the nervous sort, so King Dagda wouldn't have been surprised if the man had simply gone on with his plan to enter Aphrodite's Feast in spite of the fact that The Guardians were still there.

King Dagda was starting to think that this entire undertaking was foolish.

He and his men had stayed in a small village the night before his anticipated arrival to the cove at St. Thomas Head. The town itself was seedy, populated by seamen looking for jobs, pirates, and other outlaws looking for victims. No decent person would visit the village that sometimes went by the name Yatton, or Yattey. King Dagda and his men had two small chambers between them at the tavern that was missing half its roof. Fortunately, they were in the roofed section.

But it was raining again, or at least misty, on that night as a weather system moved through. King Dagda was in a chamber with his second-in-command, a man who called himself Neith, sharing a pitcher of cheap wine between them. King Dagda's real name was Finnegan MacGann, but no one would be fearful of anyone named Finnegan. Hence the name King Dagda.

He even made his mother call him that.

"Are we truly going to lay siege to a castle?" Neith asked, swirling his cup and watching the dregs settle by candlelight. "We've only got one war engine and I'm not sure it'll be stable on deck. It hasn't been in the past."

King Dagda knew what he was talking about. "We have the cannon we took from the Portuguese," he said. "We simply need to balance the wheels better. But we only have two cannonballs and I'm not entirely sure we would not kill ourselves trying to launch them."

Neith grinned. "The last time we did it, it nearly blew half the crew over the side of the boat."

King Dagda snorted. "True. I'm not sure how we can lay siege to a castle without a reliable cannon," he said, his smile fading. "It is not as if we have a large army, and the outpost at Portbury has a few hundred men guarding it. In fact, I've been thinking."

"What about?"

"About the fact that I've lost my patience with Ciaran le Daire."

Neith nodded in agreement. "I was wondering how long it was going to take," he said. "You must face facts—he's been trying to put us off ever since we first went to his home to collect the debt. He's put you off again and again and you've let him."

King Dagda grunted. "I know it," he said. "But this plan with his daughter and Aphrodite's Feast… It will never work. The more I think on it, the more I realize that Ciaran simply said those things to delay the inevitable."

"Then what will you do?"

King Dagda waggled his eyebrows in resignation. "Go back to Ridlaw and take it from him," he said. "The man has the property, the only thing he has of value. We take it from him and throw him out to the mercy of the elements. He has no army to defend the manse, so I will take it in payment for the debt."

Neith liked that idea. "You could sell it."

"And I shall," King Dagda said. "Mayhap. I might like a base here in England. We can make Ridlaw the permanent place for the game of chance."

"A gambling hall!"

"Exactly."

Neith clapped his hands together. "We will make more money than ever before if the game has a permanent residence," he said. "Men will come from all over England."

"And Wales."

"And Wales!"

King Dagda chuckled at Neith's enthusiasm. "Mayhap we can bring in some women to please our guests," he said. "Ridlaw will be lawless with decadence."

Neith poured them more wine. That was a plan he could get behind. Now they had a scheme to secure repayment for le Daire's debt once and for all that didn't involve Portbury Castle or Aphrodite's Feast. King Dagda was, if nothing else, a realist.

He was going to get his money.

At least, he planned to, but fate had something else in mind for him.

Sometimes, the best laid plans of men were circumvented by things beyond their control. In the case of King Dagda and his men, providence was about to intervene. The next morning, as the mist hung low to the ground and the land was damp with moisture and salt, King Dagda's group set out for the short ride to St. Thomas Head, where his two ships were moored. They felt a great deal of comfort as the ships became clear in the mist, looking strong and fearsome. *Home,* King Dagda thought. He was finally home. Nothing seemed amiss until he boarded.

Then chaos reigned.

During King Dagda's absence, it seemed, a group of French pirates, who raided the coast of Cornwall and Devon from time to time, had attacked the two Scottish cogs. Since there were twice as many of them as there were of the Scottish crew, they made short work of the lads from Glasgow. When King Dagda returned, they made short work of him, too. Over the side he went, into the churning water, with his throat cut as the French stole the ships and headed off into the fog.

And that was the end of Finnegan MacGann.

As simple as that, King Dagda the pirate was no more.

CHAPTER SIXTEEN

Aphrodite's Feast

NOW, THINGS WERE a little different.

A few days after Jareth's injury, he and the rest of his men, and Desdra, were back at Aphrodite's Feast. Orion and Aidric managed to put Jareth to bed in one of the many chambers, but it was a chamber that Desdra could quickly get to because she seemed to be doing the majority of the nursing when it came to Jareth's shoulder.

Orion simply supervised.

It was so strange the way things had suddenly taken a turn once Orion settled down and competently tended Jareth's injury. The buzz among the Six was that Orion was like a different man. He was no longer the arrogant buffoon, but a competent physic. Adric and Britt and Dirk had made more of an effort after that to speak with him or show him courtesy. In the days spent at Portbury Castle, they had shared several meals together and included Orion in the conversation more than they ever had.

And he had participated.

Even Stefan, with his bad hearing, had made more of an

effort, and out of all of them, he was the one who had the most contentious relationship with Orion. But even he knew what the man had done for Jareth. He, too, saw something more beyond the conceited fool he'd been butting heads with.

Since the travel time from Portbury Castle to Bristol was just a few hours, they'd waited until the fog had mostly lifted before heading back. Jareth was feeling stronger, though he couldn't use his left arm, so he rode in the center of the group all the way back to the city. He hated that they were treating him differently, as if he was a weakling, but even he knew that he wouldn't be much good if they got into a skirmish. The outlaws that had attacked them had been killed, though there was no guarantee there weren't more of them out there. Once they came within range of Bristol, they were relatively safe.

Jareth never thought he could consider any town other than London home, but he felt comforted when the outskirts of Bristol came into view. It felt like home because Desdra lived there, because Aphrodite's Feast belonged to him, and a whole host of other reasons. It was the first time since being notified of his inheritance that he felt like this was his destiny.

Perhaps he really *was* home.

For the first time in his life.

There was more camaraderie when Orion and Aidric put him to bed in one of the chambers used by the muses. It was very well appointed, as it was meant to impress paying clients, and once he settled in, Desdra went about having the servants bring him food and drink. His appetite was good and he seemed to be healing well, even if he was very sore from the procedure Orion had put him through.

But he was on the mend and that was all that mattered.

"Well?" Orion said as Desdra fussed over the pillows in the

bed. "Is there anything else you need?"

There were too many pillows behind him, but Jareth wasn't going to say anything, not when Desdra was trying so hard to make him comfortable. "Probably not," he said. "But I do want to know when you intend to take these bandages off."

Orion cocked an eyebrow. "You've had them on for three days," he pointed out. "Unless you are a miraculous healer, they will probably be on just a little longer than three days."

He said it sarcastically, which, in the past, would have irritated Jareth. But this time, he could see a glimmer of humor in Orion's eyes and he surrendered to the man's skill. In fact, they ended up grinning at one another.

There was a new understanding there.

"Very well," Jareth said begrudgingly. "But just know that I am not happy about this."

"I know," Orion said. "But behave yourself or I'll leave them on longer than necessary just to teach you a lesson."

"What lesson is that?"

"Never argue with your physic."

Jareth chuckled, distracted because Desdra was trying to put another pillow behind him. With Jareth in danger of being swallowed by too many pillows and a woman determined to make him comfortable, Orion slipped out of the chamber.

There was someone he wanted to see.

In fact, he'd been away from her longer than he would have liked. Taking the mural stairs down to the reception chamber, which was where the stairs to the wing meant for clients was located, Orion went in search of a certain elegant woman who was consuming his thoughts both day and night. He thought it rather odd, because he'd known beautiful women before. Plenty of them. But he'd never known one to keep his attention as

Anosia did. In fact, he was wrestling with overwhelming jealousy because he knew very well what her job was. He knew she was here to entertain men with her singing and dancing.

But, God, he hated that she had to.

There were a few chambers on the entry level of The Feast used for entertaining. Along with the reception hall, and the feasting room, there was also a type of solar because it contained tables, chairs, and valuable books. It even had live flower bushes planted in pots, watered by the many servants that kept Aphrodite's Feast. There were stairs in this chamber that led underground, to vaults that had once been part of the Roman temple from centuries past. It was here that the gambling games were held, run by a man named Eros who also, strangely enough, managed the grounds of Aphrodite's Feast to make sure everything was in working order.

Orion knew that the gambling had been halted in the wake of Lord Chester's death, so the vaults underneath were cold and dark these days. Men came daily to an entrance off the solar, the gambling entrance, to see if the games had resumed, but one of The Guardians always sent them away disappointed. It was into this empty solar that Orion found his way as he hunted for Anosia, and he was about to head into the vaults simply to see if she might be down there, but he was precluded from that part of his investigation when he spied a dark, well-coiffed head sitting in the garden just beyond the gambling entrance. It was a beautiful outdoor space, with flowers and a yew tree, and he quickly made his way over to the doorway.

But Anosia wasn't alone.

Two young girls were with her.

As Orion watched, the young girls, possibly around ten or twelve years of age, were plucking fruit from a small quince tree. They both had dark hair, and resembled each other, but mostly, they resembled Anosia. Orion suspected their identities. Never one to shrink back when he wanted something, he stepped into the garden and cleared his throat softly.

"My lady?" he said politely. "It seems that you have pleasant company today."

Anosia had been watching her girls, and his voice startled her. But she stood up, smiling at him as he came out into the garden.

"My lord," she greeted him pleasantly. "How was Portbury?"

Orion shook his head. "Eventful," he said. "We were set upon by outlaws as we approached the castle and Jareth took an arrow to the shoulder. We have brought him back to rest."

Anosia grew quite serious. "How terrible," she said sincerely. "Is the injury severe?"

"Not too severe," Orion said. "It has been three days and he's yet to develop a fever, which is a good sign. I would say that if he remains without fever for another day or two, he should be completely fine."

Anosia nodded, greatly concerned. "That would be a blessing," she said. "You seem to know something of healing?"

Orion nodded back. "I have been trained in the healing arts," he said. "My mother was a healer. It must be in my blood."

Anosia smiled, but she was prevented from replying when the two young girls ran up to her, their hands full of yellow fruit.

"Mama!" the younger one cried. "May we take this home and cook it? We can put it in a pie!"

Anosia smiled. "Of course you may," she said. Realizing

that she should probably make introductions, she put her arms around the girls and faced Orion. "My lord, these are my daughters, Anora and Emrys. Girls, this is Sir Orion Payton-Forrester. He is a knight for the king."

"A knight?" the oldest girl, Anora, piped up. She looked at Orion with big, curious eyes. "My father was a knight. He fought for Simon de Montfort."

That didn't come as a surprise to Orion. In fact, he'd suspected it might be something like that, since Anosia was so guarded with him. But he smiled at the young lady.

"Is that so?" he said. "I am sure he was a fine knight."

"Anora, enough," Anosia whispered sternly. "Go with Louise now. She will take you home and you can cook your fruit."

It was then that Orion noticed an older woman standing over by the garden gate with a Guardian standing next to her. The girls ran to the old woman, who was escorted out by the Guardian. When they were gone, Anosia turned to Orion.

"Anora will chatter until you wish you did not have ears," she said, smiling weakly. "She does not realize that sometimes, she says too much."

Orion nodded faintly, but his gaze upon her was intense. "So your husband perished at Lewes fighting for de Montfort," he said. "I am sorry, my lady. I mean that."

Anosia averted her gaze, unable to look him in the eye. "That is in the past," she said. "He made his choices and they cost him in the end."

"The same could be said about all of us," Orion said. "I have made my choices, as have you. But you are fortunate enough that a place like The Feast existed."

Anosia nodded firmly. "So many war widows did not have

this opportunity," she said. "But some did and they are here, working in the kitchens or as servants. Lord Chester did not turn a woman in need away, but he was always particular about the women he allowed as muses."

"I do not blame him," he said. "If muses entertain men, they must have that skill set and the beauty to match, as you do. Not everyone will look like you. Or sound like you. Or move like you."

It was turning into a compliment, and Anosia smiled modestly, lowering her gaze. "There is an old saying," she said. "Beauty is in the eye of the beholder."

He snorted softly. "I am not the only one who thinks you are beautiful," he said. "Others have thought so. The old man who comes every seventh day so that you can read his wife's letters to him thinks so. Do not underestimate yourself, lady. You are formidable."

She laughed softly. "I am simply trying to feed my children and house them," she said. Then she paused before glancing up at him. "Shall I tell you what I did today?"

"Please."

She wasn't particularly forthcoming with what she wanted to say. Instead, she cast him a somewhat alluring glance and headed into the vacant solar.

Orion followed.

"A man came to see me today," she said as they moved toward a bench and table in a cozy corner of the room. "He has been here before. He likes to have me read the Bible to him, and I have done so a few times. Today, he came and wanted me to not only read to him, but dance for him as well. He is a wealthy merchant from Flanders, and he pays a great deal, but I sent him away."

"Why?"

Anosia shook her head. "I did not understand it myself at first," she said. "But it seems to revolve around you."

He frowned. "Me?" he said. "Why?"

They had come to the nook with the stone bench and the heavy oaken table. She paused to face him.

"Because all I can think about is how you chased away the old man who wanted me to read his dead wife's letters," she said. "I am afraid of what you might do to a man if you know I have entertained him."

She had a point. Orion wasn't even sure what to say to that. He pursed his lips and looked away, wondering if his obsession with her was turning into something else.

Jealousy?

Probably. But she was an enigma to him, this woman who hid behind a name that meant "unholy" in the Greek language. Aye, he knew that. He was an educated man and he knew quite a bit. He was probably the smartest man in the room anywhere he went, yet he was obsessing over this woman, so much so that she felt the need to decline work that would bring her a good deal of money, all because she feared his reaction.

But *why* did she fear his reaction?

Was it possible that she was obsessing over him, too?

"I never said that I was going to do anything to a man you entertained," he said. "As for the man you were supposed to read to, all I did was tell him to go away. You and I were having a conversation and I did not want to end it, so I offered to double the wage he would have paid you for your time. I've never done anything to threaten you or those around you."

Anosia watched him as he spoke, the way he wouldn't look at her. He was trying to deny her perception of his behavior toward her, but they both knew she was right.

"Orion," she said softly, in a tone that sent shivers down his spine, "this is how I make my living. You, as a knight, earn wages from the king. We *all* have to earn our wages, and since I have no husband, it is especially difficult for me to earn money. I cannot have you impeding my ability to feed my children."

"I never intended to."

"Good," she said. "Because I will be entertaining later this afternoon and I shall not send him away."

His jaw twitched faintly. "I have not asked you to."

"Thank you," she said. "I am glad we are clear on the subject."

He nodded, unable to look at her, and she started to walk away. But he stopped her.

"Anosia," he said hoarsely. "May I ask you how much you make every month? Does it vary from month to month?"

She paused, thinking on his question. "I am not certain that is your business."

"I know," he said, finally lifting his eyes to look at her. "You do not have to tell me exactly. If you can just give me an estimate. Please?"

She thought a moment. "I can earn anywhere from ninety to one hundred and ten pounds a year," she said. "One year, I earned one hundred and twenty. My husband earned seventy pounds a year from the Earl of... Let us say that he earned seventy pounds a year. I must give at least twenty percent to Lord Chester, leaving me with about what my husband made every year. It is enough to feed my children and provide them with a nice home. They want for nothing."

Orion looked at her, fully. "If I paid you eighty pounds a year to stop working here, would you consider it?" he said, sounding as if he were pleading. "If I begged you to marry me, would you? I know it is foolish, but I cannot stomach the thought of you dancing for the coins they throw you, or reading to old men who simply want to look at your lips and think lascivious thoughts, or appreciate your heaving breasts as you breathe. They do not respect you for the right reasons, Anosia. I know that is not your name and I hate calling you that, but you have given me nothing else."

She looked at him in shock. "Oh… Orion," she finally breathed. "You should not say such things. You will hate yourself for doing so."

He shook his head, his jaw tense with emotion. "I will not," he said. "I mean every word. Please… may I at least know your real name?"

She made her way back to him. Taking him by the hand, she led him over to the stone bench that was built into the window-sill. She sat him down, standing next to him as she gazed down upon his sad, lowered head.

"Now," she said calmly, "what is this all about? You behave as if I am the only woman you have ever spoken to in your entire life, and I know that is not true."

He was looking at the floor, at her feet. But she was standing so close that he reached out to take her hand, her soft fingers in his big, rough mitt. She tried to pull away but he held her hand tightly.

"Is there nothing about me you find attractive?" he finally asked. "Is there nothing I can say that interests you in the least? Or must I face the fact that you do not find anything redeemable about me?"

She smiled faintly because the man was beginning to wallow in self-pity. "Of course I find you attractive," she said. "You are a glorious example of a man, finer than anything I have ever seen. But…"

He looked up at her. "But *what*?"

"But you are a knight for the king," she said. "You come from a fine family who, I am certain, are expecting you to make an advantageous marriage. How do you think they will react when you tell them that you found your wife at Aphrodite's Feast, entertaining men?"

"Do you let them bed you?"

Her warm expression faded. "That is truly none of your affair."

"Does that mean you have something to be ashamed of?"

"I have done nothing to be ashamed of."

"Then you do not let them bed you."

"As I said, that is none of your affair."

Orion was verging on losing control. He was holding her hand, positioned close to her, and she was being evasive with him. He was doing what he'd accused old men of doing—watching her lips as she spoke, wondering what it would be like to kiss those lips. He was obsessing over a woman he hadn't even kissed, which was ridiculous, but he couldn't get her out of his head. Without anything to say to her, because she was right and he knew it, he simply lifted her hand to his lips and kissed it warmly, gently, and sweetly.

"I am sorry," he whispered, his mouth against her flesh. "Forgive me. But there is something about you I cannot put out of my mind, no matter how much I try to. I am an honorable man, Anosia. My intentions are true. But if you would rather stay here and entertain men for money, then clearly, you prefer that over an honorable marriage. I have no recourse for that. I am sorry if I have angered you. That was not my intention."

With that, he stood up, towering over her as he kissed her hand again and gazed deeply into her eyes. It was such an intimate moment, full of power and promise if Anosia would only relent. It was clear, as she gazed up at him, that her willpower was wavering. Perhaps everything was wavering.

Perhaps she just couldn't resist him anymore.

Something in her snapped.

Before Anosia realized it, she stood up and wrapped her arms around Orion's head, pulling his mouth down to hers. Orion responded instantly to her, engaging in a heated kiss as tongues plunged deep. He was so surprised that he ended up stumbling back into the wall with his big arms around her as if to never let her go. Anosia had her arms around his neck, trapping him against her, and when she suckled his tongue, Orion nearly went out of his mind. With a growl, he picked her up and set her on the table next to the bench.

Anosia was not a maiden. She was a woman, with woman's needs that had been pent up for years since the death of her husband. Even with those needs, she'd never accepted money for sex. That simply wasn't her way. But now that she had Orion in her arms, things were changing.

Now, she was on fire.

She took on the dominant role. She had to. Anosia wrapped her legs around his hips, skirts and all, holding him tightly as they furiously kissed. She allowed his hands to roam, and he went from holding her tightly to stroking her arms, eventually moving to her thighs. When she didn't stop him, he grew bolder and moved to her buttocks, using them as leverage to pull her body up against his. Her legs were parted and his body was wedged in between them even though they were fully clothed.

Orion sincerely wished, at that moment, that they were not. He'd never been more obsessed with a woman in his life. He gently suckled the tender skin of her neck and shoulders and began to pull back the neckline of her garment. He needed more skin to feast on. He was able to pull the fabric off her right shoulder, baring her skin, as his lips devoured her tender flesh. He could hear her gasping with pleasure, her hands on his head, her face in his hair. He made no move to touch her breasts, but he continued to pull her bodice off her shoulder, exposing the swell of her right breast.

Still, she didn't stop him.

Orion hadn't been with a woman in a while. He simply hadn't had the time. Now, he had a woman who occupied his every waking moment in his hands and he was addicted to her. If she wasn't going to stop him, he was going to explore her, and the bodice was pulled down, down. When the fabric resisted, he reached behind her and untied the laces that were secured on the side of the garment.

The dress fell away.

Orion had his mouth on her cleavage now, investigating that lush, beautiful body. Anosia cried out softly as his mouth clamped over a tender nipple. She began to pull at his breeches, trying to undress him, and Orion went right along with her. He wanted her as badly as she wanted him, not stopping to think about the consequences of his actions or the fact that they were in a public room. He didn't care. All he knew was that he wanted her so badly that he couldn't stop himself from pulling her bodice down around her waist to expose both of her full, luscious breasts.

Mouth on her succulent nipple, he flipped up her skirts without any resistance whatsoever. She was still working on his breeches and he had her skirts up about the time she pulled loose his ties. When his breeches fell to mid-thigh, he positioned himself at her threshold and thrust into her, big and hard. Anosia stifled her cries of pleasure as she bit into his chest, her teeth in his flesh. It only served to inflame him, and he pulled her closer, spanking her on both butt cheeks, which excited her to the point of madness. She was exquisitely tight and hot, and he thrust repeatedly as her legs tightened and drew him in deeper.

In his heart and mind, things were beginning to get serious.

Anosia was nearly incoherent in her passion, feeling every move with the greatest of pleasure. He was so big, and thrusting himself so deeply, that the pleasure-pain of it was quickly driving her toward climax. He was a spectacular form of a man that she had never seen equaled, and nothing had ever felt so right. Certainly, she'd loved her husband and relations with him had been magical. But not like this.

Never like this.

This was beyond her wildest dreams.

Orion's thrusting grew harder, firmer, and he rubbed his pelvis against her every time he plunged deep. It was moving and beautiful and powerful, and after one particularly deep thrust, he felt her release around him as gasps of rapture escaped her lips. Still, he continued to thrust into her, feeling another climax a few moments later. But it was too much for him to endure without joining her. His own release was fast approaching.

Orion tried to pull out, but her legs were wrapped around him. He ended up spilling himself half in, half out of her delicious body, feeling every last twitch and spasm with more pleasure than he'd ever experienced. Even after he was spent, he thrust his semi-arousal into her again and kept moving. Normally, he was far more cautious about where he put his seed, but with Anosia, he hadn't been as careful as he should have been. Perhaps that was because coupling with her seemed like the most natural thing in the world.

With her arms around him was where he was meant to be.

His body still joined to hers, Orion opened his eyes to look at her. In the soft light of a nearby window, she looked like something surreal. Her bodice was down around her waist and her skirts were up to her pelvis, her legs open to receive him. The sight of it was enough to cause him to heat up again. Gently, he bent over, kissing her shoulder, the tops of her breasts, before taking a nipple in his mouth again and suckling tenderly.

"Nay," she breathed, putting a hand over her breast to stop him. "No more. Someone is going to see us. We must stop."

He knew she was right. They'd already pushed the limits of privacy and he didn't want anyone walking in on them.

"You are correct, of course," he said huskily, kissing her one last time before releasing her. He started to help her pull up her bodice. "We must make sure you look presentable. I would hate The Guardians to think I molested you somehow."

She grinned as she pulled her bodice up and pushed down her skirts. "Unless I ask for help, they will not interfere," she said. Then she eyed him coyly. "You did not see me asking for help."

"I did not ask for help, either."

She laughed softly. "Trust me, my bonny lad," she said, "you do not need any help whatsoever. You knew what you were doing."

He smiled weakly, pulling his hands away from her as she

finished dressing. "I… I hope you do not think every word from me, and every situation, was to get to this moment," he said. "What I mean to say is that although I do not regret what happened, it was impulsive. It was not planned. It was never my intention that we should… do this. It simply happened."

He was trying very hard to tactfully tell her that he hadn't charmed her simply to get her into bed. Anosia watched the usually confident knight struggle through his sentence before smiling.

"Who is to say that *I* did not orchestrate this?" she said. "Mayhap I wanted to get you into *my* bed."

He looked stunned. "Did you?"

She laughed softly. "You fell like a hapless tree," she said. "I cut your base and over you went. Right into my hands."

He wasn't sure if she was joking or not, so he started to laugh. "You are too much of a lady to do such a thing," he said. "It could not be."

She cocked a devilish eyebrow. "You think so, do you?" she said. "Well, you can just keep thinking that. But I know one thing for certain."

"What is that?"

"It was worth every moment."

A smile spread across his face.

He happened to think so, too.

CHAPTER SEVENTEEN

H E HAD A fever.

Jareth knew that from the moment he awoke. Since their return from Portbury yesterday, he'd slept the rest of the day and all night, only to awaken because his eyeballs felt hot. He knew that was a sure sign of a fever.

His heart sank.

Sometimes it took time for poison to develop after a wound. He'd had enough of them to know. When he fought for King Henry against Simon de Montfort, he'd received a sword slice to his foot, of all places, and the poison didn't develop for four or five days. It had been mild, thankfully, and the physic had worked hard to ensure he didn't lose his foot. He didn't, and it had healed perfectly, but now he was dealing with a wound to his body that might not be so easy to clean out. He didn't look forward to the moment when, and if, a physic had to clean the poison out of the wound. That could be incredibly painful.

Perhaps he wasn't healing as well as he'd hoped.

It was early morning. He could tell from the angle of the sun. Never being one to lie around in bed, not even when he was sick or injured, Jareth struggled to sit up. It was difficult because of the pain in his shoulder and back, and also the fact that his left arm and shoulder were still bound. He managed to make it into a sitting position, swinging his legs over the side of the bed. He was just about to attempt to stand up when the door opened and Desdra appeared.

"Absolutely *not*," she said, immediately setting down the tray in her hand. Quickly, she made her way to the bed. "You will lie back down this instant. How dare you try to cavort while I am not here."

He smiled weakly. "I can hardly call this cavorting," he said. "But I must attend to some business."

"What business?"

He gave her a wry expression. "Do you need to know every single detail about my affairs?"

"When it involves you getting out of bed, I do."

"Why is that?"

"Because you asked to court me, and that means I have a say in such matters."

His eyes widened for a moment before he broke down into soft laughter. "God's Bones, is that what courting means?" he said. "I had no idea."

"It's true."

He sighed sharply. "Then if you must know, I feel the need to relieve myself," he said. "Unless you want to hold my hand whilst I accomplish this, I can do it on my own."

She wasn't shocked in the least by his rather personal need. "Then I shall escort you to the garderobe," she said. "I shall wait for you to finish and escort you back to bed."

He snorted at her determination. He could see that she wasn't going to be talked out of it. "Very well," he said. "If you must."

"I must."

"You're rather demanding, aren't you?"

Her reply was to reach down and take him by his good arm, pulling him off the bed as he tried to stand. He was a little woozy, but not too terribly. She gripped his arm with both hands, holding him tightly, as they began to slowly make their way from the chamber. The corridor outside was lit by both tapers, having burned low over the night, and streams of sunlight coming through.

"It's misty this morning," he said, having spied the fog through a window. "Is it always like that this time of year?"

Desdra nodded. "Mostly," she said. "It rolls in from the sea. Sometimes it lingers for weeks at a time."

"London can do that also," Jareth said. "Have you ever been to London?"

"Nay," Desdra said. "I should like to see it someday, though."

"I will take you," he said, looking at her with a glimmer in his eye. "I shall take you to every fine place London has to offer. I shall introduce you to the finest people."

She smiled in return, somewhat bashfully. "Do you have your own house in London?"

He shook his head. "Nay," he said. "I live at Westminster. But when we marry, I shall buy you any house you like."

"We are already marrying? I thought we were just courting."

He cocked an eyebrow. "What do you think courting is?" he said. "It is the prelude to the feast—it is still part of the feast, just not the main portion of it."

She chuckled. "You certainly have a way with words," she said. "So eloquent."

"I can speak the goodest of anyone you know."

That set her off laughing with his made-up word. They had reached the door that led to the garderobe by that time, and she let him go in alone. He handled himself well, as she had expected, and at least hadn't fallen down the hole that dumped into a small channel that led to the river. They'd had one or two drunken clients do that. But not Jareth. He made it out of the garderobe alive and Desdra took him on a small walk around the floor, just to stretch his legs, before it was back to bed for him again. Then, and only then, did she notice his fever.

It all happened quite innocently. She had only been holding his arm, which was wrapped in a tunic, all the way to the garderobe and back, but when he went to sit on the bed, she grasped his hands to help him.

His palms were on fire.

That made her touch his face to see if he had a fever and, indeed, he had a raging one going. There was no outward indication that he had a fever because he wasn't pale or clammy. He looked normal.

But he wasn't.

"How long have you had this fever?" she demanded, forcing him to lie down.

He went down easily because even the walk to the garderobe had been exhausting. "I think I woke up with it," he said. "It is not bad. I've had these before. It will pass."

Desdra wasn't taking any chances. She rushed to the chamber door and sent a servant to fetch Orion, who was undoubtedly with Anosia, somewhere. Those two had become inseparable. Once she sent the servant for Orion, she sent another one for cold water and rags.

"Desdra?" Jareth said from the bed. "Desdra, love, you

needn't go through such trouble. This will pass, I promise. It is just a little fever. That happens when things pierce the body. It is the body's way of reacting to it."

"Be quiet," she said sternly. "Any fever must be taken seriously."

He grunted, a smile playing on his lips, knowing there would be no discouraging her. When the water and rags came, she forced him to remove his tunic so she could bathe his skin and cool him down, something he was most agreeable to. With her tender touch, he was actually enjoying it quite a bit, and when she came to his neck and head, she was close enough that he could steal a kiss or two from her. He watched her flush bright red when it did it, and he laughed.

It felt good to laugh.

Jareth was quite enjoying the attention as Desdra fussed over him. But Orion arrived and spoiled it all, sending for a physic because he thought the fever was worse than Jareth was letting on. That nearly sent Desdra into a panic, but the physic used by The Feast arrived shortly thereafter and forced Jareth to drink a concoction of willow bark powder and a tea brewed from mold found on bread, something that had been brought back from the crusades to the Levant. It was a medicine that helped heal injuries and fever, but it tasted like death.

That was when Jareth stopped enjoying the fact that people were fussing over him, but worse still, both the physic and Orion decided that it was the wound at Jareth's back causing the problem and it needed to be cleaned out. It was one of the more painful things Jareth had ever endured, and when it was over, the physic gave him a sleeping potion that put him out within a few minutes of drinking it. *A brewed flower,* the physic said. Whatever it was, Jareth was snoring in little time.

And with that, his care was over for the moment.

"What do I do now?" Desdra asked softly, pulling a coverlet over Jareth. "Is there anything he needs?"

"Just let him sleep," the old physic, a tall man named Willow, said as he put things away into his medicament bag. "We've done all we can for now. The next few hours should tell if it is going to get worse or better."

Desdra nodded, standing at Jareth's bedside with a worried look on her face. "What shall I feed him when he awakens?"

"Anything he wants."

That seemed to settle it. Orion took one last feel of Jareth's forehead before escorting the physic down to the entry level, where Heracles and Orpheus were on their regular shift at the entry. Zeus was having his usual sleeping period and men were coming in and out of Aphrodite's Feast, conducting business with their lady of choice.

It was just another normal day.

Once the physic departed, Orion headed back up to Jareth's chamber, where he found Desdra sitting beside the bed, simply watching him. He could see by the expression on her face how worried she was. Truthfully, he was concerned as well. Fevers were never a good thing where wounds were concerned, and there had been pus in the wound when they cleaned it out.

Enough to see why Jareth had a fever.

Truthfully, if it got worse, Orion didn't particularly want Desdra to be the one that had to see it first or, worse, deal with it. He would feel better if he were the one on watch and not the woman who was clearly enamored with Jareth. Given the fact that he now had a woman he was rather enamored with himself, he was all for sparing a lady's feelings.

Especially if this situation was going to get worse.

"My lady?" he said, watching Desdra look up at him. "I will sit with him. Surely you have other duties to attend to."

She shrugged. "There are some," she said. "Ledgers must be kept up to date or the task is overwhelming. Since we have been gone, there are some figures I must catch up on."

"Then go and do it," he said, coming into the chamber. "I will sit with him."

"But—"

He cut her off, but not unkindly. "Jareth would not want you to sit and stare at him," he said, a smile pulling at the corners of his mouth. "I'm sure you wouldn't want him to just sit and stare at you were the situation reversed."

She looked a little sheepish. "Nay," she said. "Probably not."

He indicated the door. "Then go," he said. "There is no valid reason for you to just sit here and watch him sleep. He will be out for quite some time. I will send word if anything changes, I promise."

She stood up but didn't move. "But *you're* going to sit and just watch him."

His smile broke through. "Because he has a fever and if it grows worse, I should be here to tend him," he said. "I am not saying that it *will* become worse. Only if it does."

Desdra nodded reluctantly, her gaze moving back to the bed where Jareth was sleeping heavily. "Very well," she finally said. "I will go and finish up my work. But I will return."

"I know," he said. "But do not rush. He's not going any-where."

It was a joke and she smiled, but it was forced. She was genuinely worried for his condition, but Orion was right. There wasn't much she could do except sit at Jareth's bedside and stare at him. Silently, she left the chamber, leaving Orion behind to monitor Jareth's febrile condition.

There was nothing either of them could do now but wait.

CHAPTER EIGHTEEN

T HE GUARDIANS WEREN'T leaving.

That was the conclusion Ciaran had come to. He'd spent several days watching Aphrodite's Feast, those coming and going. He'd even seen his own daughter return in the company of several heavily armed knights who weren't The Guardians. So many comings and goings, and none of them involved The Guardians actually leaving their posts.

Time was ticking away.

At that point, Ciaran was trying not to panic. Although there had been no actual timeline on the missive King Dagda would send to Aphrodite's Feast, he had mentioned seven days. Those seven days had come and gone, so Ciaran was at the point of wondering if he shouldn't simply work the situation out for himself, get the money, and run.

But there were still the little matter of The Guardians.

The truth was that he knew the schedule of the commander of The Guardians, the man who called himself Zeus. Zeus was as vigilant as a watchdog, remaining up all night long and well into the morning before he took a rest. Truth be told, Zeus was the only one that Ciaran really worried about. He'd been the one to throw him out when he and his daughter had gotten into a physical altercation, so Zeus was well aware of his threat to Desdra. But unless he passed that concern on to the men under his command, no one would question Ciaran's visit to his daughter. The more Ciaran thought about that, the more he realized that was the path he was going to have to take. If King Dagda wasn't going to send that missive, it didn't mean the man didn't want his money.

Perhaps he was testing Ciaran.

Perhaps he was looking for a reason to take everything he had, property included.

In any case, Ciaran was starting to feel betrayed. He was also beginning to suspect why King Dagda had been so agreeable to this rather elaborate plan. Perhaps the man was simply being agreeable so he could go back on his word in the end and then blame Ciaran for failing to secure the money.

Well, that *wasn't* going to happen.

Ciaran was going to get inside Aphrodite's Feast and he was going to get the money that he knew his daughter had access to. It infuriated him that she wasn't more forthcoming when it came to giving over her wages to her father, who was not only entitled to them, but was also in serious trouble. Why couldn't she see that? The truth was that Desdra's reasons didn't matter to him. She was going to give him what he wanted.

Any way he could get it.

Several days after his discussion with King Dagda, Ciaran finally left the abandoned cottage he had been sleeping in and made his way to the west side of town, where Aphrodite's Feast sat along the river in all its glory. It was a clear day, with puffy clouds dancing across the sky in rhythm with the breeze that flowed inward from the sea. Birds flew overhead, congregating in the trees, but also wandering around in the gutters looking for something to eat. It was just after the nooning hour as Ciaran made his way up the walkway to the front entrance of Aphrodite's Feast.

Now, it would begin.

"I am Desdra le Daire's father," he said to the young, muscular man at the door. "I have come to visit her."

Another Guardian stepped out from the shadows. The movement startled Ciaran, and he looked up to see a Guardian he recognized. The man called himself Heracles and had been at The Feast for a few years. Long enough to know Ciaran and who he was and probably long enough to know that, in the past, he'd caused some trouble. Ciaran held his breath as Heracles looked him over before finally allowing him admission into the foyer.

"Does Desdra know you're coming?" Heracles asked.

That told Ciaran that Heracles might not be aware of what had happened several days ago. If he were, he might not have admitted him so easily.

"Nay," Ciaran said. "We… we argued the last time we saw one another and I've come to apologize. I am afraid that if you announce me, she might turn me away."

Heracles frowned. "Then I cannot admit you further."

"Please," Ciaran said with the appropriate amount of remorse. "I only want to apologize. You can listen at the door if you wish. I present no threat, I swear it. I only want a private moment with my daughter to apologize for my behavior."

"And if she does not accept your apology? Will you harass her?"

Ciaran looked both puzzled and insulted. "Nay," he said. "But I must see my daughter. Do you have a daughter, Heracles?"

"I do not."

"Then, mayhap, you do not understand my desire, as a father, to speak with my child."

He was begging by now. Heracles wasn't convinced, but Ciaran seemed repentant enough. He did, in fact, know that Ciaran had been run out of Aphrodite's Feast several days ago, but he was walking a fine line. He didn't want to come between a father and his daughter, and it wasn't his job to make a judgment call like that. Only Zeus or Desdra could really do that, and, frankly, he didn't want the responsibility. Family relationships could be so, so touchy and he didn't want to get in the middle of one. Still, he didn't like Ciaran.

None of them did.

Irritated, he simply waved him on.

"Go," he said. "But only for a few moments. Then you must leave."

Ciaran nodded quickly. "Thank you."

"But I *will* be listening."

There was a threat in that. It gave Ciaran a moment of pause, but it was brief. He counted himself extremely fortunate that he'd even made it inside. *Extremely.* Zeus was sleeping, but Heracles was just as vigilant. Ciaran was going to have to plan his next move carefully.

Very carefully.

Nervously, he made his way up the stairs that led to the level where the solar was.

It was quiet on this level, as there were only a few chambers up here, including servants' chambers. Quietly, he made his way to the solar door, peeking his head inside only to immediately spy his daughter seated at the table with her back to the door, writing in a ledger.

The perfect victim.

Silently, he stepped inside and shut the door behind him, very carefully bolting it. It made a noise, something Desdra heard.

"I'll be finished in a moment," she said. "Can you please send word to Sir Orion that I will relieve him at Jareth's bedside?"

Ciaran froze. She must have thought he was a servant, or she was expecting a servant, so he knew he had to act quickly before she turned around and saw him. Rushing over to the table, he grabbed her from behind.

After that, it was chaos.

CHAPTER NINETEEN

ALL DESDRA COULD think about was Jareth.

She knew he was in good hands. She knew he was sleeping. But she was fearful of the fever, knowing how badly those could go under the right, or wrong, circumstances. They never did really get to see Portbury Castle, not the way Jareth had wanted to see it, and they didn't get to see Long Cross Castle, the small garrison across the river, at all. After Jareth had been hit by the arrow, he'd spent the rest of his time in bed, so there had been no inspections for him. He hadn't even met the garrison commander, who had spent most of the time combing the woods again, trying to roust any remaining outlaws who might be a threat to travelers.

With all due haste, they'd returned to The Feast.

She knew that he was probably disappointed about the lack of inspection at Portbury, but they could go back as soon as he was feeling better. She would assure him of that. And she would take him around to all of the other properties that he now owned. Considering she knew everything about them, she was happy to do it. Happy to educate this man who wanted to court her.

That had been the most amazing thing of all.

It was difficult not to daydream when she needed to be completing the tally for the last few days. She had ledgers from the merchant stall in town, among other properties, and entered them all into a master ledger. She hoped that Jareth would allow her to continue her duties after they were married because she very much wanted to. She needed to feel useful, and this was something she was good at. She hoped he didn't expect his wife to sit around and embroider or eat sweets, because she would be bored out of her mind doing that.

Married.

She could still hardly believe it.

Why he should want to marry her was beyond her comprehension. It still seemed like a dream. When he regained his strength, perhaps he would change his mind, though she hoped not. Truth be told, she would be very disappointed if his request to court her had simply been a whim. That strong, broad-shouldered knight had her attention like no one ever had. Just thinking about him made her smile.

She was smiling a lot.

The servants had been in and out of the solar since she'd been there, bringing her food to break her fast or stoking the fire in the hearth. With the mist still hanging in the air, it was both chilly and damp, and the fire kept the solar cozy. It was early afternoon when she began to finish up what she'd been working on as the gulls returned to the windowsill, fighting and trying to sun themselves when little rays of sun would burst through the mist that was still hanging around. She was just finishing up the last ledger when she heard the door click.

"I'll be finished in a moment," she said. "Can you please send word to Sir Orion that I will relieve him at Jareth's bedside?"

There was no immediate answer, which didn't concern her. In fact, she wasn't concerned in the least until someone grabbed her from behind and a dirty hand was slapped over her mouth. Immediately, she went into fight mode as a familiar voice growled in her ear.

"Scream and I will kill you before anyone can help you," Ciaran hissed. "They may kill me in the end, but not before I kill you first. I brought you into this world, girl. I can take you out. It is my right."

Desdra could hardly breathe the way he had his hand over her mouth and on her nose. She realized very quickly that if she didn't calm down, it might grow worse. He might actually smother her if he thought she was fighting. Therefore, she struggled to relax. That made him relax in response.

But he didn't let her go.

"Good," Ciaran muttered. "Do not fight me and we shall get along just fine. I need something from you, something I came to get the last time I was here, but something you denied me. I am back and I want it. I want it now."

Desdra tried to talk, but his hand was pressing down on her mouth. When Ciaran realized this, he loosened his hand a little, but he didn't remove it completely.

"If you scream, it will be your last," he threatened again. "All I want to hear from you is where you keep your money. I want it."

"My money?" she said through his fingers. "You mean the wages I am paid?"

"Aye," Ciaran said. "Bring them forth."

It wasn't as if Desdra had much choice. Her father had her in his grip, the hand covering her mouth now also partially on her neck. If he decided to squeeze, she would find it difficult to fight him off. She had to coerce him to loosen his grip on her somehow. She was trying very hard not to panic, not to start kicking and fighting for all she was worth, because he was stronger than she was. He could overpower her. She had to be smarter than he was.

She had to survive.

"You have to let me move if I am to retrieve the money," she said. "I will not scream, but you have to let me move."

"I will move with you."

"The money is not here," she said. "It is in my chamber and that is on the floor above us. If we leave, someone will see us, so you must let me go alone."

"Never," he snapped, his hand tightening. "You will summon help."

"I could promise not to, but you will not believe me," she said. "The truth is that if you want my money, it is in my chamber."

He paused indecisively for a moment before letting her go. He stepped back, glaring at her as she turned around to face him.

"Then there must be money in here," he said, looking around the lavish room. "Do not tell me that you don't keep money in here, because this is where you keep the ledgers. There must be money in her for you to count."

"There is some."

"Get it."

"It is not my money."

Reaching out, he slapped her across the face. Desdra's head snapped sideways and her hand flew to her cheek as she looked at her father in horror.

"I told you to get it," he snarled. "Get all of it. I want all of it."

Fear was trying very hard to overwhelm her. Ciaran was deadly serious about this because she could read it in his eyes. There was desperation there, and even madness if she looked closely enough. If she could only disable the man, she would be able to make it to the door and cry for help. She was positive that Zeus was on the landing, but the door was closed and voices weren't raised, so he wouldn't be able to hear what was going on.

She had to make it to that door.

"What are you going to do with all of it?" she asked. "Do you owe that much money?"

"Get it. I'll not tell you again."

She could see that. He didn't want to talk. He just wanted money. But that wasn't all that was concerning her. What would he do to her when he finally had what he wanted?

She didn't want to die.

"How do I know you will not try to kill me once I give it to you?" she asked. "For I would know that you stole it. Do you intend to silence me permanently?"

"I will silence you now if you do not do what you are told."

"If you silence me now, you'll never know where the money is," she said. "Furthermore, you will not leave this place alive."

His response was to come toward her, hands out to grab her again, but Desdra bolted.

She began to scream at the top of her lungs.

Ciaran rushed in her direction, but she was faster. She made it over to the hearth and the array of fire implements. She grabbed the first one she came to, which was a spade-like shovel. It was heavy and it was iron. She swung it at her father with all of her might, catching him in the face. The sharp iron edge cut across his cheek and into his mouth.

Blood sprayed.

Momentarily stunned by the pain, Ciaran fell away and Desdra bolted past him, heading for the door, but he managed to catch the ends of her hair as she ran. That long mane of hair, so beautiful and treasured, was her downfall as her father yanked on it, pulling her backward. Screaming, Desdra swung the shovel again, hitting Ciaran on the side of the head. It didn't cut him, but it was a heavy blow. He grabbed it with one hand, still holding on to her hair with the other.

In the fight for her life, Desdra screamed as loud as she could, hoping someone would hear her. In their struggles, they knocked over a chair, a heavy bank of tallow candles, and a stack of ledgers. The noise could be heard everywhere as the fight went on and on.

Little did she know that the cavalry was coming.

⚃

JARETH THOUGHT HE was hearing screams.

They were faint, but he heard them. His eyes popped open and he saw Orion stand up from the chair beside his bed, ears cocked to the sound.

"What is that?" Jareth asked sleepily. "Do you hear it?"

Orion nodded. "I do," he said. "You stay there. I'll go see what it is."

He moved out of the chamber. Jareth sat up in bed, rubbing the sleep from his eyes when he began to hear more screams. There was some banging going on. Given the fact that Desdra wasn't in front of him, but rather out of his sight, there was some concern about her safety. For his own peace of mind, he had to make sure she was well. She was probably fine, and would berate him for being out of bed, but he would welcome the scolding as long as she was healthy and whole.

Very slowly, he managed to climb out of bed.

By the time he hit the corridor outside, there was more screaming. He could hear it. He had to go down one flight of stairs and up a separate flight to get to the solar where Desdra did her work, so he headed in that direction. There was no rush on his part until he managed to descend the stairs and end up in the foyer. There were no Guardians, which concerned him. He could hear more banging, more screaming, and it was definitely coming from overhead. Just as he took a step, Stefan appeared from the reception chamber across the hall. He had a big iron rod in his hand.

"Stefan?" Jareth said, concerned. "What is happening?"

Stefan was in distress. "Come on," he said, rushing over to take Jareth by the arm. "It is Lady Desdra."

Shocked, Jareth made it up the stairs without any assistance. Stefan was right behind him. By the time he hit the landing where the solar was located, Jareth could see a crowd of men standing in front of the solar door. Two of The Guardians were trying to ram the door with their shoulders. The entire Guard of Six was there, not including Hugh, who had gone straight back to Bristol Castle when they returned from Portbury. But Aidric, Britt, Dirk, Orion, and Stefan were present. So were four Guardians, including Zeus. Stefan handed over the iron rod to Heracles, who immediately tried to use it on the doorjamb to loosen the bolt and the latch.

"What is going on?" Jareth demanded, hearing more screaming and banging. "Who is with Desdra?"

"Her father," Zeus said. He looked exhausted and unhappy. "As you are aware, he was here a short time ago and became abusive with Lady Desdra, so I chased him away. He came back this afternoon whilst I was sleeping and begged for admission."

"He said he wanted to apologize," Heracles said as he struggled with the rod and the doorjamb. "He begged for the opportunity to speak to her and I told him he only had a few moments. I was on the landing the entire time. He must have gone into the solar and immediately bolted it, but I did not hear the bolt. I would have acted sooner if I had."

It began to occur to Jareth what, exactly, was going on in that chamber. Horror and panic began to set in. Heart in his throat, he pushed his way to the door, putting his hands on it.

"Desdra?" he shouted. "Desdra, I'm here! Unbolt the door, love! Unbolt it!"

She was screaming something he couldn't make out, which only fed his sense of panic. He swung around to The Guardians standing behind him.

"Is there another way in?" he demanded.

There was a huge sense of urgency and concern, from all of them. He could read it in their faces. But none were more concerned or anxious than Zeus.

"Unfortunately, that is part of the security of this place," he said, teeth gritted. "Every room can be sectioned off, and it is nearly impossible to get in. Unless we want to go through a window, and it is impossible to get to them."

Jareth opened his mouth but something heavy fell against the door and he could hear Desdra cursing and screaming at her father.

"Jesus," he whispered in an urgent plea, putting his hands on the door again. "Jesus, help me."

"I can try to get to the window," Aidric said. "Do you want me to go outside and assess the possibility?"

Jareth thought for a split second before shaking his head.

"Nay," he said. "I want all of us to put our shoulders into this and ram that damn door open. God, I'd give my soul for a battering ram right now."

Zeus shook his head. "We do not have one," he said. "I would not know where to get one. But we can pound away at the door until it gives. That's all we can do if she cannot open it."

There was more screaming, more things falling. Desdra was putting up a hell of a fight and Jareth was struggling not to lose his composure. Just when he'd found some happiness, it was in danger of being snatched away. He could hardly believe it. He wasn't even worried about himself or the fever that plagued him. Truthfully, he wasn't feeling well at all, but he wasn't worried about himself. He was only worried about the woman inside the chamber that he couldn't get into.

It was like a nightmare.

"Stefan," he said, pointing to the door, "kick that door right where the latch and the bolt are. Ramming the whole panel isn't going to work unless we can loosen the bolt and the latch. Kick it as hard as you can, as much as you can. Right in the seam."

Big, powerful Stefan moved forward. Lashing out an enormous booted foot, he kicked once, twice, thrice. Then he rattled the latch to see if it had loosened. He couldn't tell, and Jareth couldn't tell, so he did it again. And again. When he'd done it a few more times, he stepped aside to rest his right foot and Britt took over. Big, mean Britt. He kicked and kicked and managed to shatter some of the wood in the jamb, which was good. That meant they were making progress. Someone ran to grab an ax, hoping that would help.

All of those skilled knights and not one of them could break down that door. Not one of them could help the woman in distress. When Britt stopped kicking, he backed off and Zeus took over. He kicked and kicked, hearing the commotion beyond the panel like they all were, using it to feed his determination.

And then… the screaming stopped.

The quiet was more terrifying than the shouting. Jareth rushed to the door, calling for Desdra, but receiving no answer. He had his hands on the door as if by sheer willpower he could get it open, but someone pulled him back as one of The Guardians, Orpheus, rushed up with the ax and began slashing at the joint where the latch and bolt were positioned on the door. Three strikes of the ax and the doorjamb suddenly collapsed. Orpheus, Jareth, and Aidric were at the forefront, pushing the door wide open and charging into the chamber.

But what they saw stopped them in their tracks.

Ciaran was over by the enormous lancet windows that faced the river. He had Desdra by the hair and had somehow managed to push her onto the windowsill where the gulls liked to gather. She was unconscious, literally hanging out of the window. If Ciaran let go, she'd fall.

Three stories down.

Jareth stepped forward, cautiously.

"Bring her back inside," he commanded quietly. "Bring her inside and we will discuss what your terms are for her safety."

Ciaran eyed the man he didn't know. "I want to talk to Chester de Long," he said. "Bring him to me immediately."

That brought a wave of confusion. "Chester is dead," Jareth said. "I am the new lord of Aphrodite's Feast. You may speak with me."

That brought outrage from Ciaran. "Do not lie to me!" he said. "I will toss her from this window if you do not bring

Chester to me immediately!"

"Throw her from that window and you will not live beyond that very moment," Jareth said, hazard in his tone. "Why are you even doing this? You are her father. You are supposed to protect her."

Ciaran wasn't moved. His gaze lingered on Jareth, appraising and calculating. He'd just spent the past several minutes chasing his daughter around the solar, trying to grab her because he knew her screaming would bring The Guardians. And these other knights—he wasn't sure who they were, but he recognized them because they had been with his daughter when she had come back into town. He had only arrived in Bristol when she had returned from wherever it was she had gone, so the entire situation was confusing to him.

But he knew one thing.

He was in a precarious situation.

You are supposed to protect her.

Protecting Desdra had never entered his mind. He only wanted her money and any other money he could get his hands on. But those plans were now ruined because of her screaming, so once he'd gotten his hands on her, he'd managed to knock her on the head with the butt of the shovel she'd been using against him, hard enough to render her unconscious. At that point, the door to the chamber was about to be destroyed, so he used the only leverage he could—his daughter's life. Men were breaking in to help her, so he had to keep them at bay as long as he could, and he did that by lifting her into the windowsill. It had worked—the men hadn't advanced on him—but he knew that wouldn't last.

If he was going to escape with his life, he had to think fast.

"Bring me Chester or, I swear, I will throw her from this

window," he said again, trying not to sound desperate. "I must speak with him!"

Zeus, who was feeling extraordinarily guilty about this situation, stepped forward. "He speaks the truth, le Daire," he said steadily. "Lord Chester died several weeks ago. Lord Jareth is now the lord of Aphrodite's Feast. You must speak to him."

He was indicating Jareth. Hearing the confirmation of Chester's death from Zeus, a man who had no reason to lie, only further destabilized Ciaran. He was unsure what to do at that point, and Jareth, seeing the confusion on his face, sought to take advantage of it.

"Tell me what you want," he said, taking a step forward, very slowly. "If you have a disagreement, surely we can come to a pleasing solution. Only let your daughter go. We do not need her if we are to discuss things like men."

Ciaran's gaze darted to Jareth. "That is far enough," he told him. "Come no closer."

"What do you want, le Daire?"

Ciaran began to see a way that this situation might work out to his advantage. They didn't want Desdra thrown from the window and Ciaran very much wanted money. *Any* money at this point. He had a pirate to pay and, damnation, the man wasn't going to wait. No one was going to wait. Not even Ciaran.

He pointed to the scattered ledgers on the table.

"Money," he said simply. "I know there is a great deal here and I want it. Bring it to me and put it on the table. Then you will stand back and allow me passage out of here. I will never return. You have that assurance. But if you do not swear a solemn oath to let me leave unharmed, I will let my daughter fall from this window. This I vow."

Jareth shrugged. "As I said, if you let her fall, you'll not live to take another breath," he said. Then his gaze turned hard as he took another step in Ciaran's direction. "I will personally destroy you. I will obliterate you from the face of this earth and even in death, you will be so smashed, so mutilated, that not even God will be able to put you back together again. Do you understand me? Obliteration is something I give my most hated enemies, something not even your soul will recover from. Now… I will give you some money simply to be rid of you, but make one more threat against her and you'll not like my reaction. You are not in command here. *I* am. And I will tell you how this is going to end."

Ciaran's features tightened. "I do not know you," he said. "I do not care. But understand me when I tell you that I will throw her through the window if you take another step. Get out of here and get those men out of here. Bring your money back to me. I will not wait forever."

"You'll wait as long as I tell you to wait," Jareth said. "Remove her from the windowsill and release her. If you do that, I will get your money and you will be allowed to leave, unharmed. Those are the terms."

"You do not dictate terms. I do."

Jareth cocked an eyebrow. "Clearly, you do not know how this works."

"Do as I say or—!"

He never got the chance to finish. Desdra chose that moment to awaken and, though groggy, quickly became aware enough to realize that she was being hung from a window. She didn't know how she got there, or why, but she immediately screamed and started to panic. Kicking her legs, she hit her father in the face, which caused him to lose his grip.

After that, everything seemed to happen in slow motion.

Jareth, seeing that Desdra was coming around, made a break for the window to grab her. She slammed Ciaran in the side of the head with her foot, which forced the man backward. He had been holding her by the back of her garment and his grasp on her slipped. Jareth could see this happen as he ran at her. God help him, he could see that she was now falling, headfirst, out of the window. He could see everything right before his eyes, and as fast as he moved, he wasn't fast enough. He managed to grab part of the hem of her dress as she tumbled out, but it wasn't enough. It slipped through his hands, and she right along with it.

Screaming all the way, Desdra fell three floors to the hard-packed earth below.

Then… silence.

CHAPTER TWENTY

"H E HASN'T LEFT her side for three days," Orion said. "He will not sleep. He will not eat. He just sits there, holding her hand and watching her face. The man is a mess."

He was speaking to Hugh, who had been out on an errand for the garrison for a few days when the incident with Desdra happened. Everyone in the city knew what had occurred. He'd heard about it the moment he returned to Bristol Castle. It was a tragedy on so many levels that it was difficult to know where to start.

"My God," Hugh muttered. "What about her father?"

"Dead," Orion said. "Zeus and the other Guardians took care of that. They felt guilty about even admitting the man so that he could attack Desdra, so they took his behavior personally. The last I saw, they'd put the body on one of the de Long merchant vessels and were going to dump it at sea. Ciaran le Daire can become food for the fish. It is better than he deserved."

Hugh nodded. "That is the truth," he agreed sincerely. "But what about Desdra? What is her condition?"

"Grave," Orion said, shaking his head. He was exhausted,

having not slept over the past few days, just like Jareth. "Fortunately, she did not fall on her head even though she went out the window headfirst. The yew tree in the front, near the entry, broke her fall and flipped her onto her left side, so she fell on that. Her ribs are broken, as is her left arm and her left shoulder, and she is very bruised on the left side. I suspect something may have ruptured inside of her, but there is nothing to be done. We must wait and let God's will be done."

Hugh grunted with great remorse. "God," he said. "What a horror. Is there anything I can do? Fetch another physic, mayhap?"

Orion shrugged. "We've already had the physic who tended Jareth's shoulder come to The Feast," he said. "Willow is his name and he seems competent enough. He has packed her entire left side with cold rags to minimize the swelling and the damage. He's also packed cold rags around her head and neck. He's trying to take her temperature down so the body will have time to recover. As I said, we must wait now. That is all that can be done."

It was pitiful that no one could do more. Hugh seemed particularly pained about it.

"I told Jareth that Aphrodite's Feast would be good for him," he said. "He was so reluctant to accept the inheritance, so I feel as if we had to convince him that it would be worthy. And we could all see how he and Desdra were falling for one another—something quite unexpected, I might add. I've never known Jareth to be a fool for a woman."

"Desdra is no ordinary woman," Orion said softly. "Go and see him. He'll be glad to see you. He's in the chamber across the landing."

Hugh simply nodded and headed up the stairs from the

entry. There was an incredible pall of depression hanging over The Feast, so much so that they'd closed their doors since the incident between Desdra and her father. The muses didn't feel like entertaining anyone and The Guardians felt as if the incident had been their fault, so they simply shut the doors and refused any visitors. That had never happened in the history of The Feast, but it was indicative of a group in mourning.

It was in everything about them.

As Hugh went upstairs, Orion wandered outside, to the window that Desdra had fallen from. He looked up, seeing the broken limbs that had kept Desdra from killing herself in the fall, but it was still a long way down. She had landed in dirt, but it had been hard earth. With a sigh, he turned in the direction of the river. Beyond the tree was the road and then the riverbank, with the silty waters of the River Avon as it made its way to the sea. The gulls were crying overhead and people were down on the riverbank, pulling in the boats from the fishermen. Everything seemed normal, but it wasn't.

Nothing was normal these days.

"My lord?"

Orion turned to see Anosia standing a few feet away. She looked wan and strained, as all of the muses did. Something happening to Desdra had affected them all. But he smiled at her and extended his arm in her direction.

"Come," he said. "Keep me company. I was simply thinking for a moment. Where have you been?"

Anosia came toward him, beneath the shade of that big tree. She was dressed in a simple garment, something that was unlike her. There were no ribbons in her hair, no jewels around her neck. She was dressed simply and demurely, but nothing could detract from her astonishing beauty. If anything, the plainness of her garb enhanced it.

"I have just been in to see Desdra," she said. "Lord Jareth says she has not awakened yet."

Orion nodded slowly. Then he reached out a hand to her, and when she looked at it in confusion, he simply took her hand and brought it to his lips. He smiled; she flushed.

He laughed softly.

"You must become accustomed to that," he said. "I will again ask you if you will return to your cottage and allow me to provide for you. A woman of your beauty and talent should not have to entertain for money. Let me take care of you."

She cocked an eyebrow. "As your kept woman?" she said. "Your concubine? Nay, Orion. I will not be kept."

"But you *are* fond of me."

"You gave me no choice."

She was grinning as she said it, and he grinned in return. "I did not say you would be my kept woman," he said. "I will return and marry you at some point, but not until my position with the king is solid."

Her smile faded. "Why is it not solid?"

He shrugged. "Because I am relatively new," he said. "These men that I am part of, the Guard of Six, do not like me very much. They are a tight unit, and a unit like that must work together with complete trust or it will fail. It is difficult to trust someone you do not like, so the king may decide that I do not belong with them. That is the only reason I do not marry you now—it is because I do not know what the future holds yet."

She caressed his fingers. "They simply do not know you yet," she said. "When they come to know you better, you will become part of them. I know. I watched my husband and his men as they trained and prepared for war. If you work enough with men, and do your part, it is inevitable that they will accept you."

He smiled faintly. "Wise words, lady," he said, but his smile quickly dwindled. "Will you not tell me your real name, love? I cannot call you Anosia when I know it is not your name. But I promise I will use the name when we are in front of people. Please?"

Anosia considered that request, one of many such requests he had made to her. Truth be told, she was weakening. He was sweet and he was sincere, and she couldn't help the attraction she felt toward him. She'd been at The Feast for a long time, and in that time, no one had broken down her walls like Orion had. It was difficult to resist him.

Difficult, indeed.

"Very well," she said softly. "If you are going to cry about it."

He nodded firmly. "I *will* cry," he said. "I'll cry buckets and then you'll be sorry."

She laughed. "No need," she said. "The name given to me by my mother is Olivia."

His smile blossomed. "Olivia," he repeated as if it were the most beautiful name he'd ever heard. "Lady Olivia, it is a pleasure to finally meet you."

She dipped her head demurely. "And you, my lord," she said. "I will tell you more if you wish."

He knew telling him her name had been a supreme act of trust. He appreciated it deeply. But he didn't want to push her.

"I will listen to whatever you wish to tell me," he said. "If your name is all you wish to share, then I am satisfied."

She was still holding his hand. Or perhaps he was still holding hers. Whichever it was, she released his fingers and looped her arm through his elbow companionably. She just stood there, holding his arm, gazing out to the river beyond.

"Desdra has made me realize something," she said.

He was enchanted simply watching her profile. "What is that?"

"Time is short," she said simply. "There is no time to waste in life with rules or hesitation or resistance. I learned that life was short enough when my husband was killed. His name was Brenner le Kerque and he was a knight for the Earls of East Anglia, the House of du Reims. You see, my father is Humphrey de Bohun, the Earl of Essex. He was allied with du Reims, and Lord du Reims used to visit my father all the time, especially when Simon de Montfort was gaining power. Brenner used to come with Lord du Reims, as his most trusted knight, and I fell in love with him. My father was horrified, of course, and disowned me when I announced my intention to marry him. We had a few very happy years, and two beautiful girls, before he was killed at Evesham."

Orion had been listening intently. "No wonder you have such elegance about you," he said. "You are an earl's daughter."

She turned to him. "I am," she said. "I was expected to make an advantageous marriage, but instead, I married for love. Now you know why I cannot go home."

Orion understood that. He understood very well what it was to have a family you could not return to. After a moment, he grunted softly as thoughts rolled through his head, thoughts he'd not entertained in years.

"I will tell you something I've not told anyone," he said. "I, too, have a father I cannot see. My family name, officially, is Payton-Forrester, but the man I call my father was not the man from whose loins I sprang."

Anosia looked at him curiously. "What do you mean?"

He sighed faintly, looking out to the river as he collected his thoughts. "As I said, I've not spoken of this to anyone," he said. "I am not even supposed to know."

"Know what?"

"That I'm the bastard of a great northern knight."

That didn't clear up her confusion. "I do not understand," she said. "Your father is not your father?"

He shook his head. "He is actually my uncle," he said quietly. "My father, to the world, is William Payton-Forrester. I look enough like him that there are no questions, but the truth is that I am his sister's bastard child. She had an affair with a knight by the name of Paris de Norville, who is the captain of the army for the Earl of Teviot. It's a massive army. They are allied with the House of de Wolfe, who has the largest army in the north. Paris de Norville and William de Wolfe are family, as their wives are cousins."

She nodded in understanding. "So your uncle raised you as his son to spare his sister from the shame of bearing a bastard?"

"Aye," Orion said. "She died in childbirth, with me, and my true father, de Norville, does not know about me. He was never told."

"Then how do *you* know?"

He smiled ironically. "Because William Payton-Forrester told me one night when he'd become ragingly drunk," he said. "As it turned out, it was on the anniversary of my mother's death, so he got drunk and was making threats to kill Paris de Norville. When I asked him why, as I thought they were good friends, he told me everything. He does not even remember doing so."

Anosia gazed up at him, giving his arm a little squeeze.

"And how do you feel about that?" she said. "About the life you have led as another man's son?"

He shrugged. "I do not blame de Norville," he said. "He does not even know. And I do not blame my father, Payton-Forrester, because he did the right thing by raising me as his own. He is a good man. I am not entirely sure why he never consciously told me the truth, however, though I suspect it was to protect his sister. I can understand that, I suppose. How do I feel? Fortunate. Fortunate that I had such an upbringing by a good family who loved me."

Anosia smiled at the sweet sentiment. "You are, indeed, fortunate," she said. "I was brought up in a big family by a father who was only concerned with his sons if they could make him proud. He did not give much thought to his daughters until one of them displeased him by marrying the man she loved. I cannot imagine what he would think if he knew I was here, at Aphrodite's Feast."

Orion put his hand over her fingers as they held his elbow. "You did what was necessary to ensure your children had food in their bellies and a roof over their heads," he said. "Even though I do not want you entertaining for money, even I cannot fault you for being determined enough to do what was necessary so your children would not starve."

She laughed. "Thank you," she said. "Sometimes I, too, wish circumstances did not drive me to this, but I will always be grateful to Aphrodite's Feast for an opportunity few have."

"And I will always be grateful that it brought us together."

She laid her head on his big bicep, feeling things she hadn't felt since Brenner was alive. It was a sweet moment between them. Orion kissed the top of her head and was preparing to speak when something down the road caught his eye.

He was watching a tide of people move toward Aphrodite's Feast, toward them. Hundreds of them. Shocked, he and Anosia watched the crowd of people move closer and closer.

"Who *is* that?" Anosia asked with concern. "What are they doing?"

Orion shook his head. "I do not know," he said. "I do not see any weapons or battle implements. It does not seem to be an army."

Anosia could see both men and women in the crowd. "I wonder where they are going?" she said.

Orion wasn't sure. He just shook his head, watching the crowd. When it became apparent they were heading for The Feast, he broke for the entry door, pulling Anosia behind him.

"Get inside," he said. "Let me see what this is about."

She nodded, somewhat fearfully, as he pulled her into the foyer. The Guardians at the door had seen the tide, too, and were most curious. As they began to discuss how to handle the situation, Anosia went into the reception chamber, to the window, and watched the approaching crowd. So many of them coming. It was most puzzling.

But she was about to discover the truth.

CHAPTER TWENTY-ONE

"J ARETH," AIDRIC WHISPERED. "Are you awake?"

Jareth was, sort of. He was sitting in a chair, his head on the bed next to Desdra, when Aidric spoke to him from the chamber doorway. Instantly, his head was up.

"Aye," he said, quickly rubbing his eyes with his good right hand. "I am awake. Why?"

"You'd better come," Aidric said. "Do not ask me any questions because I do not have any answers. But you had better come."

Puzzled, Jareth sat up. "I cannot simply leave her," he said. "Someone must stay with her."

"Orion will," Aidric said. "But you must come. Now."

He sounded alarmed, which had Jareth on his feet. He was weary, and his left arm and shoulder were still wrapped up, but he was no longer suffering from a fever. Thankfully, that episode had been brief. But he was still recovering from the wound and his left arm was still useless. Any movement still greatly pained him. But he forced himself to wake up fully, to focus, because there was evidently something that required his attention.

He headed down to the foyer.

Hugh and Orion were there standing alongside Zeus and Heracles and Orpheus. Once Orion saw Jareth, he turned and headed back up to Desdra's chamber, but Jareth and Aidric joined the crowd at the entry door. He had no idea why until Zeus pointed to the approaching surge of humanity. Bewildered, Jareth stepped into the doorway, watching.

"What am I seeing?" he finally asked. "Who *are* those people?"

"Townsfolk, I think," Zeus said, coming to stand alongside him. "I recognize several."

"But why are they coming here?"

Zeus shook his head. "I do not know."

"Should we secure the building?" Aidric asked. "If they get any closer and charge, we will not be able to hold them all off."

"I'll run back to the castle," Hugh said, turning for the rear of the building. "I'll bring the garrison."

"Nay, Hugh," Jareth said, stopping the man in his tracks. "Hold for now. Let us see what they want. They are not armed, so I do not think they pose a threat."

Hugh wasn't so sure, but he remained, watching the group as they came off the road and headed up the stone path that led to the entry door. They came within about fifteen feet of the door before they came to a halt.

"My God," Jareth muttered. "There has to be hundreds of them."

Zeus didn't even know what to say. He was watching the same thing, as puzzled as Jareth was. He had never seen anything like it. As they stood there, watching the crowd, a man that Zeus recognized as a local fisherman came forward.

"My lords," the man said. He was young, with dark hair,

and a thin but strong body. "We heard about the lady. We've come to see how she fares."

Jareth looked at Zeus in surprise. In fact, they were both surprised. "She is still unconscious," Jareth said loudly. "I do not understand. Why have so many of you come? Do you all know Lady Desdra?"

The man smiled. "If we do not know her, we still know The Feast," he said. "It is something special, my lord. A place of comfort, of caring. Lord Chester was a good man. He took good care of us when we needed it. He never let us suffer if he could help it. Bread to the needy, boats to the fishermen who had lost theirs… The list goes on."

Jareth could see that everyone in the crowd seemed to have the same attitude—there were smiles, mostly. Truthfully, he was touched by the words.

"Chester de Long was my uncle," he said. "My name is Jareth de Leybourne. The Feast is mine now, and I promise to carry on my uncle's legacy. Any in need will always be welcome here."

That seemed to please those who heard him. The young fisherman looked at those around him, nodding, before he took a few steps forward and focused on Jareth again.

"The Feast is unique to Bristol, and there's not one of us who hasn't been touched by it at some time," he said. "We came to tell you we are sorry for the misfortune, but we also came to offer our own comfort the best way we can."

With that, he stood aside as several women came forth bearing trays of bread. So much bread. Little children were running alongside them, carrying loaves under their arms, and they came up to Jareth to hand them to him, but he could only take one tray. Zeus had to take another, and then others came out of The Feast to collect the rest.

But that wasn't the end. More people were coming forward, carrying baskets of eggs or vegetables or fish. No one could take them, however, because their arms were full, so the people simply set the gifts on the ground at Jareth's feet. As he stood there, awed by what was going on, a woman came forward with a basket of kittens.

"This is for Lady Desdra," she said. "She saw me in church one day, asking for alms, and she stopped to speak with me. She wanted to know why I was begging, and I told her because my husband was a farmer who had been injured and could not work. We had nothing. Lady Desdra spoke to Lord Chester and he arranged to have men work our farm and bring in our crop. They also paid for a physic to tend my husband. I have thanked her many times, and we paid our debt to Lord Chester with the money we made from the crop, but when I heard that Lady Desdra had been badly injured, I wanted to bring her something that would make her smile. She told me once that she was sad to have left her cat behind when she came to Bristol. Mayhap these little friends will make her smile again."

Jareth smiled at the cute kittens, three of them, in the small basket. "I will make sure she receives them," he said. "Thank you for your kindness."

The woman shook her head. "I can never fully repay her for what she did for us," she said. "And all of these people—they have similar stories. Without Aphrodite's Feast, many of us might not have survived."

She handed Jareth the basket of kittens and walked away, leaving others to add their tribute to the growing pile around Jareth. He was truly touched by what he was seeing. Someone beside him reached over to take the basket of kitties and he turned to see Melaina, grinning at him when their eyes met. As the woman took the cats and headed back into the interior of The Feast, more people came forward to tell Jareth what Chester de Long had done for them.

It was an astonishing moment.

One man was thankful because he was a smithy who lost his stall to a fire and Chester had rebuilt it for him. Another was a fisherman who had lost his boat in a storm and Chester had given him a job working for him on another vessel. The priest that everyone called the Pope came forward, without his mask or disguise this time, and conveyed his thanks for the beautiful church that Chester had built. Still others came forward to show their thanks for the universitas that Chester had commissioned and what it had done for their lives.

On and on it went.

One of the last people to come forward was a small man with flowing white hair who introduced himself as Marston. Jareth hadn't had the time to get over to the merchant stall yet to meet Marston, so it was a welcome introduction. Marston Crewes was his full name, and he was quietly spoken but seemingly bright and articulate. He and Jareth engaged in a discussion about the merchant stall, officially called The River, but Marston kept having to stand aside while more people brought forth some kind of gift for Desdra and The Feast. They finally had to stop talking because there were so many people who wanted to offer their thanks. So many gifts that Jareth was quickly becoming overwhelmed with it all.

"This has been a remarkable moment," he said, looking at all of the tributes around him. "I feel as if I knew Chester so little. He was my mother's brother, but I hardly knew him. He lived in such a rich world that I'm only just beginning to see."

Marston, standing nearby, smiled in agreement. "Chester and I grew up together," he said. "I knew your mother, the fair Ophelia. You look like her."

It did Jareth's heart good to hear that. "So I have been told."

"Chester never had any children, as you know," Marston said. "He spoke fondly of you and now I see why. You must have reminded him of his sister, whom he adored."

"I think so," Jareth said. He paused before continuing, gathering his thoughts. "It's ironic… when I first heard of this inheritance, I did not want it. I made no secret of that. All I knew was that it was a brothel and I did not want to be associated, but now… now, I am ashamed of my attitude. It's truly much more than a brothel. I did not believe it until I saw for myself."

Marston seemed to understand that. "The legacy of the House of de Long is not a brothel," he said. "Or a merchant fleet. Or the fine manor at Redcliffe. Or anything else, really. The legacy of the House of de Long is the good that it has done for the people of Bristol. That is what everyone has come to show you today. It is gratitude for what Chester and his forefathers have done for them. Lady Desdra has become part of that since she has been here."

Jareth nodded in understanding and in agreement. For a man who had been denied the de Leybourne legacy, he had inherited something far better through his mother. He was to carry on a greater legacy than his brother or father could have ever hoped to achieve. He could see that now, and for the first time since he'd come to Bristol, he was proud.

Proud to be chosen to carry on the legacy of the House of de Long.

"When I am fully healed and Lady Desdra is recovered, I

hope you will come here and sup with me," he said to the old man. "I should like to speak to you more about Uncle Chester. I wish I had known him better. Mayhap you can help me."

That seemed to please Marston immensely. "I should be happy to, young lord," he said. "May I ask how Lady Desdra is? We heard terrible things had happened."

The warmth faded from Jareth's eyes. "What did you hear?"

"That there had been a fight," Marston said, lowering his voice. "Some of the fishermen saw The Guardians bring a dead man to the riverbank and put him upon a vessel. One of them said that the man had harmed Lady Desdra and was paying the price. Some say she is near death. That is all anyone really knows. But that is why we came to pay our respects, to show those at The Feast what it means to us. What *she* means to us."

Jareth felt as if he could trust the man because of his longstanding relationship with Chester. "Her father tried to kill her," he said quietly. "She fell from a window in the process and her injuries are severe. We are hoping for the best."

Marston closed his eyes briefly, sickened by the news. "I am very sorry to hear that," he said. "Is there anything I can do?"

"Pray," Jareth said softly. "I think that is all any of us can do."

Marston understood. As he turned to others standing behind him, people of the community, to relay the request for prayers, Anosia came up behind Jareth.

"My lord," she said quietly, "Orion says you must come. Quickly."

A bolt of fear shot through Jareth, as strongly as an archer releasing his bow. It was quick and jolting. He ran back to The Feast as fast as his legs would carry him, rushing up the stairs to Desdra's chamber. By the time he hit the chamber, he could see that Melaina and Limenia were in there as well as Orion. He could hear Orion speaking as he entered.

"You see?" he was saying. "Jareth is here. He's right here. He's not left you, I promise. Jareth?"

Jareth stumbled over to the bed, astonished to realize that Desdra was awake. She was pale, and had evidently been crying, because there were tears on her face. Jareth dropped to his knees beside the bed, taking Desdra's fingers in his big, strong right hand.

"I am here, love," he said, kissing her hand. "I've been here the entire time. How do you feel?"

Desdra gazed at him. When she blinked, more tears fell. "I thought you had left me," she sobbed softly. "I awoke and you were gone."

He leaned forward, sweetly kissing her forehead. "Nay, sweetheart, I have not left you," he said. "I simply stepped out for a moment. Never were you alone, I swear it."

She sniffled, letting him wipe the tears from your face. "What happened to me?" she said. "Everything hurts. I cannot move."

The warm expression faded from Jareth's face. "You had a fall," he said simply. "Your left arm is broken. That is why it hurts. Can you move your toes and your legs?"

She did, a little, bringing a huge amount of relief all around. "It hurts," she said again.

"I know," Jareth said, kissing her cheek this time. "It will probably hurt for a while, but you are going to heal, I promise. Do you remember how you fell?"

She seemed to be calming now that he was there and she knew what had happened. She blinked at him, still groggy and dazed. "My father came to see me," she said, then suddenly stiffened. "Where is he? He tried to kill me! I fought him and fought him, but he was too strong!"

Jareth tried to ease her. "You will never have to worry about him again," he said. "He will never again be any trouble."

"Is he dead?"

"What makes you ask that?"

"Because I cannot imagine you would let him live after he threatened me."

Jareth smiled faintly. "You would be correct, madam," he said, winking at her. "No man threatens the woman I love and lives to tell the tale."

Desdra stared at him. She was still groggy and her head hurt, but she was far more aware than she had been even moments earlier, so his words had an impact on her. Words she'd never thought she'd hear, ever. It was like a dream.

The woman I love.

She was in awe.

"You… you love me?" she managed to say.

"Of course I love you," he said, gently stroking her head. "You love me, so, of course, I was compelled to love you in return."

A slow smile spread across her lips. "How did you guess?"

He laughed softly. "I did not guess, I knew," he said. "One never guesses when it comes to love. One just knows. And I knew within a few days of knowing you that I loved you. That will never change."

She sighed faintly. "Nor will my love for you," she murmured. "Until the ending of the world and beyond, it will never change. But what happens now? Will I live?"

Jareth struggled to keep a positive attitude. "Of course you will," he said. "You will live and we shall be married. Uncle

Chester will have a great legacy in us and our children."

"Children?" she repeated, closing her eyes because the mere act of speaking jostled her broken ribs. "I never thought I would have children."

"We will have a dozen."

Her eyes flew open. "A dozen children?" she said, mildly aghast. "We must discuss this, Jareth. That is a lot of children for a woman to bear."

He leaned over, his mouth next to her ear. "Given how often I plan to bed you, I would say it is a low number."

As predicted, her pale face flushed. He laughed, she laughed, and soon they were laughing together, only she couldn't laugh too much because her ribs hurt so. He kissed her on the lips once, twice, laying his forehead against hers as he reveled in the reality that she was awake and talking. She sounded like herself. He knew she wasn't on her way to a complete recovery yet, but the signs were positive. He would take what he could get, when he could get it.

For the moment, she was his and he was hers.

All was right in the world.

"You should also know that the entire town turned out to bring you gifts when they heard of your misfortune," he said. "It seems that many, many people have been touched by Aphrodite's Feast, and when they heard about your injury, they came to show you their support for a full recovery."

Her expression washed with surprise. "Me?" she said. "But I have done nothing."

Eyes twinkling, Jareth turned to Melaina, who still had the basket of kittens. "Untrue," she said, coming around the side of the bed. "You have helped many people, Desi. Goodwife Aames brought you this because she knows you missed the cat you left behind at Ridlaw. Look at these beauties."

She set the basket down carefully next to Desdra, lifting a sweet white kitten out of the basket and showing it to Desdra, who was immediately smitten. She then put the kitten down on Desdra's chest so the woman could pet it a little, followed by another white kitten and then an orange-striped one. Desdra was thrilled with the little creatures, and Jareth backed away so Limenia and Anosia could come alongside the bed and admire them. He stood back, watching, as Desdra's friends gingerly hugged her, so very glad that she was alive.

So was Jareth.

"Do you remember when you first came to Bristol and I had to talk you into at least inspecting your acquisition before denying it?"

Jareth looked over his right shoulder to see Hugh standing there, smiling at him. A very knowing smile that was quite annoying, but also triumphant in a sense. Triumphant in that Jareth saw the value of a place he'd originally thought to be simply a brothel.

Jareth couldn't argue with him.

"You were right," he said, watching one of the white kittens walk on Desdra's neck and cheek as she giggled. "You were absolutely right. I'm very glad I listened to you."

Hugh chuckled. "Always listen to your friends, Jareth," he said. "You are almost always the smartest man in the room, but sometimes, we know better than you do."

"You certainly did this time," Jareth agreed. "What I saw today… people bringing tribute to give back to the place that had given them so much… I've never seen anything like it. It was truly remarkable."

Hugh nodded. "That is what I was trying to tell you," he

said. "Aphrodite's Feast isn't a brothel. It's so much more than that. The question now is if you are going to let it continue on with what it does best."

"And what's that?"

"Generating money, of course," Hugh said as if Jareth were an idiot. "The gambling was halted when Lord Chester died. Are you going to resume it?"

Jareth shrugged. "I do not see why not," he said. "It generates more money to be used for good."

"My thoughts exactly," Hugh said, putting a hand on Jareth's good shoulder. "The community depends on the donations, the alms. Do you want my advice?"

"Probably not, but speak."

Hugh snorted. "Talk to the Pope," he said. "That priest who visits here disguised as someone else. He knows this community. I've heard rumors that he wants to start a foundling home, so that might be the next good thing this place does for the community."

Jareth thought on that. "Desdra and I would have to oversee it," he said. "I've heard horror stories about those places and I would not allow that with anything I put my name or money behind."

"Good man," Hugh said, giving his shoulder a pat. "I wouldn't expect anything less from you. Chester was right to leave this to you. He knew it would be in good hands."

Jareth simply smiled. He thought on his uncle, leaving him an empire that was so much more in reality than it was on paper. He watched Desdra with her friends, the women of The Feast, women who had come here to seek a way to survive. But they did more than survive—they thrived. Jareth was going to make sure they continued to do so.

That inheritance he didn't want?

He wanted it now.

As Desdra petted her kittens and relished in the care and love of her friends, Jareth realized that it wasn't simply the money he had inherited, but the wealth of friendship and love that one couldn't put a price on. He had so much in life. For the second son of a man who had hardly given him the time of day, it was the first time he realized that he didn't need his father or any approval, from anyone. He had everything he needed, right here at Aphrodite's Feast.

Finally, Jareth de Leybourne had a home.

And he was damn proud of it.

EPILOGUE

Redcliffe Manor
Six Months Later

I T WAS A wedding feast to end all wedding feasts.

Jareth and Desdra were literally entertaining the entire town at their wedding feast. They had friends at Redcliffe Manor, including the Guard of Six and about three hundred of Jareth's friends from London, and then there was a spread of food and entertainment set up in front of the church that Chester had built. Still more food and drink was at Aphrodite's Feast and at the universitas that bore the name of de Long. It had cost Jareth a huge amount of money but, as he'd said, what good was money if he couldn't spend some of it to celebrate the best day of his life?

And the best day it was.

Jareth and Desdra had been married at the church with a mass said by none other than the Pope himself. Not the actual pope, but the steady visitor to The Feast. He wore his simple priest robes for the mass, one that was attended by most of Bristol. They spilled out into the streets. Although King Henry couldn't attend, as he didn't travel these days, he sent a few advisors, including William de Valence, and a document that gave Jareth the Barony of Bedminster. As Lord and Lady Bedminster were introduced to the crowd to a host of cheers, Jareth also announced that he would be legally taking the name of de Long to honor Chester and the men before him, men who had created this unique and glorious legacy that now belonged to him. It didn't seem right that a de Leybourne should have it, so the de Leybourne name was put aside as Jareth became Jareth de Long, and his children would also bear the name.

The de Long legacy would continue.

For their wedding mass, Desdra wore a dress of pale blue that made her look positively luminous. Her magnificent hair was left long except for a silver ribbon that secured it at the nape of her neck. The rest trailed down her back. She wore a translucent gossamer cape that was anchored at the top of her head with a bejeweled comb that Marston had given her, and on her ring finger, her wedding ring of gold and sapphires gleamed.

Now, they were back at Redcliffe, at a feast that included not one but two whole sides of a cow, roasting over two spits in the main yard. Old Henbury was in charge of the feast, ensuring everything ran smoothly, and Jareth wasn't hard-pressed to admit that the old man did a remarkable job.

Long after the feast started and evening fell, the new Lord and Lady Bedminster took a stroll out in the yard to get a breath of fresh air, accepting congratulations from everyone they came across. On the narrow wall walk overlooking the river, they could see Aidric, Dirk, Britt, Hugh, and Stefan drinking and talking and admiring the clear night overhead. But they were joined by two other men, original members of the Guard of Six, in Torran de Serreaux and Kent de Poyer.

They'd come all the way to Bristol for this momentous occasion.

"You're going to miss your friends, aren't you?" Desdra asked softly.

Jareth looked at her, realizing that she'd been watching him as he observed the men on the wall. "Not really," he said. "I will see them often enough, but much like Torran and Kent, I now have another life now and I intend to live it."

"No more Guard of Six?"

"Once a Guard of Six, always a Guard of Six," he said. "I will be there if they need me. But let us hope they do not need me for a while. I'd like to spend time with my new wife first."

He winked at Desdra as she giggled. She looked positively radiant after her brush with death those months ago. Recovery had been a little slow, and she still hadn't gained full mobility in her left arm because it had been crushed in the fall, but considering the circumstances, it could have been a lot worse. Jareth thanked God daily for his wife and her miraculous recovery.

"They can come and visit frequently," she said, her arms looped around his left elbow. "In fact, we cannot seem to keep Orion away. He and Anosia are quite a pair."

Jareth grunted in agreement. "She finally gave up her position at The Feast for him," he said. "She was well loved there, but I suppose she loves him more. Now, he needs to marry her."

Desdra nodded firmly. "I agree," she said. "I've told him so. He just smiles and says 'soon.' That is all he'll say. It is most annoying."

Jareth laughed softly. "The truth is that he's not entirely certain about his position with the Guard of Six," he said. "Henry moved him in, but he could just as easily move him out, so I believe he wants reassurance from the king that his situation will be stable before he marries a woman and brings her, and her children, to London to live. I am proud of the way he is thinking of others before himself. The Orion I knew before our journey to Bristol would not have done that."

"He has changed?"

Jareth nodded as he thought on the big blond knight who wasn't quite so annoying anymore. "Aye," he said. "Acceptance will do that. Love will do that."

Desdra smiled. "Does that mean you have changed?"

"From what? I was perfect when you met me."

She burst into soft laughter. "You are a confident man," she said. "I love that about you."

"Good," he said. "It is too late for me to change my ways, so you had better."

They had made it to the end of the ward, breathing in the cold, clear air, before turning around. "Speaking of ways, I must tell you again that I am sorry I was unable to go with you when you inspected your properties," Desdra said. "You should not have had to go alone, but my recovery has been slower than I'd hoped. Someday, I will visit them with you, I promise."

He patted her hand. "I was not alone," he said. "Remember? I had Aidric and Britt and Dirk, Stefan and Orion with me. They inspected everything right along with me. Moreover, there was no possibility that I was going to allow you to go, since you were still recovering, so it worked out for the better. And do not forget that Marston was an enormous help. I like him."

"He likes you," Desdra said. "I'm glad he has resumed his visits to The Feast. He used to come daily when Lord Chester was alive, but after his death, I think that, mayhap, it was a little painful for him to come. I am happy he has returned."

Jareth nodded. "It has been interesting learning of Uncle Chester through his eyes," he said. "He saw a different side of him than most, I suppose."

Desdra thought on the small, white-haired man and how kind he'd always been. "I think he knew Lord Chester best," he said. "There was a great deal of devotion and respect between them."

"I sensed that," Jareth said. "And if he and my uncle were lovers, I hope it was something that made them both very happy. I hope Marston was able to give Uncle Chester comfort in his final years."

She smiled up at him, squeezing his arm gently. "I think so," she said. "They were quite inseparable."

He smiled in return, gazing into that lovely face. "We should all be so lucky as to have someone we cannot be parted from."

She chuckled, laying her cheek on his bicep again as he kissed the top of her head. "True," she said. "I've found my someone."

"As have I."

They continued to walk in warm silence, heading back toward the great hall of Redcliffe, hearing the noise and music emitting from the windows and doors, seeing people spill out into the night, drinking and laughing. The truth was that there had been an entire week of feasting and celebrating before the wedding mass, so tonight was the culmination of a very busy week.

And one that they were both looking forward to.

"Now," Jareth said, "I have a question for you, Lady Bed-minster."

Desdra smiled at the use of her new title. "What is that,

Lord Bedminster?"

He pointed to the manse dead ahead. "Do you think we can make our way through those people to get to our bedchamber?" he said. "Or do you think we should take a short ride back to The Feast and spend our wedding night in peace and quiet? Because that lot is not going to give us any peace *or* quiet."

He was jabbing a finger at the bright, noisy hall, and she started laughing. "I will do whatever you wish," she said. "You decide."

He fought off a grin. "It seems to me that we have earned the right to sleep in our own home and not be chased off by a gang of drunken fools," he said. "But we should go in separately. If we go in together, there will be trouble."

She could see the happy guests cavorting through the open door. "They will try to corner us," she said. "We can go in through the kitchens and make it up the servants' staircase. They will not see us."

He thought that was a rather fine idea. "Good thinking," he said. "Let us hurry, then."

"Why? Are you anxious for something?"

He rolled his eyes. "Nothing at all," he said drolly. "I have a wedding night every single night of my life. There is nothing special about this night."

She laughed and he joined her. Then he put his arms around her gently, mindful of her left shoulder and arm, and kissed her lips tenderly.

"I have been waiting for this moment my entire life," he whispered. "Do not think for one moment you are not the most important thing in the world to me, now and forever. You are the stars that shine in the night sky, the sun rising in the east. I never knew what it felt like to love someone so completely, but I do now. This night belongs to us, Desi."

She held him tightly with her right arm and a little less tightly with her left. Jareth had helped her retrain her muscles again ever since she could start to move it, and it had been hard work, but it was paying off. He'd been so good to her during her recovery, and he'd waited very patiently until she was physically up to the task of their marriage. Therefore, he was right.

This *was* their night.

"Come," she said, pulling away from him and taking his hand. "Let us go in through the kitchens."

She practically ran to the kitchens on the west side of the manse, and he happily followed. The kitchens were working at full capacity this night as they passed through the cramped, steamy rooms. Gustave, the cook, noticed them, wondering why the bride and groom were in the kitchens, but neither Desdra nor Jareth stopped to explain.

They just kept going.

The spiral staircase that went to the upper floors was narrow and steep. Jareth, with his broad shoulders, kept getting stuck, so he laughed and struggled all the way up to the top floor where the master's chambers were. In fact, nearly the entire top floor of Redcliffe was the master's chamber, a complex of four chambers connected, including a smaller chamber with a hearth and an enormous iron pot used to heat bathwater. It was Desdra's favorite room.

Without any interference, they made it.

Anosia and Melaina had spent two days making the bedchamber the most luxurious space they could. There were furs on the floor and luxurious linens on the bed, courtesy of Marston. Heavy curtains hung from the canopy as well as a gossamer fabric that one could see through. A fire burned in the hearth, tended by the servants, and there was already wine, cheese, bread, and fruit on the table.

"Look," Desdra said as she picked up a diaphanous garment from the mattress. "My friends must have left this for me. How beautiful it is!"

She held it up for him to see, a transparent garment with the neckline and long sleeves lined with rabbit fur. The fur was heavy for the lightness of the garment, but once worn, it was a beautiful presentation. She held it against her to see how well it would fit, all the while exclaiming how lovely it was.

Jareth simply watched her.

All he could do was watch her. Over the past six months, he'd come close to bedding her, but her injuries had prevented him from truly doing the deed. That was why they'd waited until she was almost fully recovered to be married. He knew that, physically, it would be difficult for them to consummate the marriage, given her injuries, and he wasn't lusting after her so desperately that he wouldn't be considerate of her recovery. That was the most important thing to him. He wanted to touch his wife when she would feel pleasure, not pain because he forced her into his bed before she was properly healed. But here she was, healthy and beautiful, and he simply didn't want to wait. He wanted to touch her, and be touched. He wanted her to feel his love and he wanted to feel hers.

It was time.

As she fussed over the night shift, the linens, and even the curtains that hung from the canopy, Jareth began to undress. She didn't even notice because she was so busy marveling over everything else. Off came his fine silk tunic, the boots, the breeches. Everything came off until he was as naked as the day he was born. As she marveled at the curtains because they were a very new fabric that Marston had brought over from Rome, something called velvet, Jareth silently went around the bed and motioned for her to turn around.

Desdra obeyed, only noticing he was nude from the waist up because she was still focused on the curtains. Jareth unfastened the ties at the back of the dress and helped her slide it off her body. He did most of the work so she wouldn't strain her left arm or her torso, which tended to still be sore. The ribs were healed, but the trauma her body remembered remained. Once the dress was off and she was left in her shift, he pushed aside her splendid hair and began to kiss the back of her neck, very gently.

That was when Desdra forgot all about the velvet. His touch erased everything from her mind except him. Turning in his arms, she slanted her lips over his.

The magic began.

Jareth laid his wife, still dressed in her shift, back down on the mattress, very carefully, the thin layer of linen the only barrier between their bare skin. He could feel her taut nipples brushing through the material, rubbing against his chest, and it nearly drove him mad. He lay mostly on her right side so that he wasn't hurting her, but also because one hand could move freely. When his lips latched on to her soft earlobe, his left hand went to work.

His fingers snaked underneath her shift, lifting it up as he went. Her skin was like silk to his rough fingers, and he felt that divine deliciousness as his hand trailed up her thighs to her buttocks, moving further to her hip. They'd gone this far before at times, but her garments had stayed on.

This time, there was no such restraint.

He moved her shift higher, and when it came up as high as

her groin, he felt her hesitate. They were going further than ever before and her natural modesty was kicking in. His lips left her earlobe and went to her mouth, kissing her until she could hardly breathe. It distracted her enough that he was able to lift the shift to her waist. His mouth still on hers, he put both hands underneath the garment and lifted it over her head in one clean motion.

In the same action, he pulled the curtains closed, sealing her off from the room and giving her a sense of privacy. It was a considerate thing to do, but Jareth had always been intuitively considerate. Pulling back the coverlet, they climbed beneath the linens. Covered up and with the curtains drawn, they continued their intimate exploration.

Jareth's mouth began to explore the skin beneath her chin. Her shoulders, the swell of her breasts, and her arms were the target for his seeking lips. Desdra lay there, half covered by his big body, feeling great anticipation that this moment had finally come to them. Having never been intimate with a man, the excited tremors in her arms and legs were something she'd never experienced, and every time he suckled her skin, it made her gasp in delight. When Jareth's mouth finally latched on to a nipple, she was thrown into a new world of sensations.

His hot, wet mouth nearly brought her off the bed. He put his hands on her arms, holding her down to the mattress as he suckled. First one breast and then the other. Desdra's head was spinning with delight. Jareth's attentions were becoming more insistent as he held her down, ravaging her with his mouth. Soon enough, his hands joined in the exploration and Desdra lay beneath him, too upswept with the new experience to be of much use. But when his hand moved to the fluff of soft curls between her legs, she instinctively flinched.

"Easy, love," he murmured. "I will be gentle, I swear it.

Have I not been gentle before?"

He had. They'd never quite gotten this far, but Desdra nodded unsteadily. She trusted him implicitly. He shifted his body so that he could wedge himself in between her legs, acquainting her with the feel of his body against her. Her scent filled his nostrils and it was like food to a dying man. There was nothing about her that wasn't beautiful and delicious and desirable. He had to remind himself that this was a new experience for her and he didn't want to frighten her, but it was difficult to restrain himself.

He wanted to feel himself inside of her.

Hand on her breast, he fondled her gently as he kissed her, easing his manhood into her and feeling her wet heat against him. He eased in a little, withdrawing, and then doing it again to make the way easier for her. When he finally coiled his buttocks and thrust deep, the only thing it drew from Desdra was a low, pleasurable groan. That was all he needed to hear.

He began to move.

It had been a long time since Jareth had been with a woman. He could not even remember when last he touched female flesh. But as he gazed down at Desdra's face, he realized that no other woman had existed before her. There was no one before; there would be no one after. This was the woman he was meant to have, the one meant to conceive his children. Even as he thrust into her, he thought on the children that would take root in her womb, a son with his strength and her intelligence, or a daughter with her beauty and his resourcefulness.

Children from the woman he loved.

His thrusting became faster.

Desdra was simply taking it all in, one arm on his shoulder while the other was stretched over her head. She was gripping the headboard as he pounded into her, her legs open wide, her body receiving him as it was always meant to. When she finally had her first release, her legs trembled uncontrollably and her gasps filled the warm air of the chamber. She began to rub her pelvis against his, the innate reaction to wanting to make the sensation last. Unable to hold back any longer, Jareth joined her in her climax, spilling deep into her warm and waiting body.

Even when it was over, he held her buttocks to him, still buried in her, loving the feel of his body in hers. From the angle he was lying, her full breasts were by his mouth and he began to kiss them gently, finally shifting enough so that he could suckle a tender nipple. That brought a powerful shudder through Desdra, and she let him suckle as she slowly ground her woman's center against his groin, his manhood still in her, still mostly hard.

It was the most erotic thing Jareth had ever experienced.

He was so overly stimulated that, at some point soon, he grew hard again and resumed thrusting into her. Desdra threw abandonment to the wind, one arm over her head as she held fast to the head of the bed, her legs open wide for her husband as he did as he pleased. All Jareth wanted to do was make love to her, and he did, all night, at least four times that he could count. By the time morning came, neither one of them noticed the noise from the bailey nor the birds as they gathered overhead.

Dead asleep in each other's arms, they slept until the sun was high overhead.

It was the best sleep either of them had ever had.

"My darling?" Jareth muttered. "Are you awake?"

Desdra sighed. "I think so," she murmured into her pillow. "Unless I am dreaming. Are we in heaven?"

"I think so," he said, his hands drifting to her buttocks and pulling her against his morning erection. "How do you feel?"

She rolled her face out of her pillow. "Marvelous," she said, grinning sleepily. "And you?"

She was lying on her right side, facing him, so his answer was to pull her left leg up and over his hip. A little angling of his pelvis and he was able to thrust into her again, listening to her groan with pleasure as the gulls cried outside and people went about their business in the ward. Jareth made love to Desdra as she lay there, finally rolling her onto her back and dominating her body with his.

It went on the rest of the day.

Therefore, it was no surprise that exactly nine months to the day, a fat, healthy boy was born after a day of rather easy labor. Desdra didn't have a terrible time of it, thankfully, though Jareth had suffered probably more than she had as he waited for his son to be born. No amount of comfort from Zeus or The Guardians could ease him. When he was presented with the dark-haired lad who screamed loudly, the man sat in a chair and wept.

It was the most beautiful sound he'd ever heard.

You are the keeper of my legacy, Chester had once told Desdra. Little had she known what, exactly, that had meant. At the time, she only thought to be the guardian of it.

Never the mother of it.

But for Jareth, it was far more. A legacy he had never imagined, a destiny he could have never hoped for. An inheritance he'd almost refused.

He regularly thanked God that he had the sense not to.

And so did Desdra.

Theirs was the legacy, and a love, of a lifetime.

Cʒ THE END ꙮ

Children of Jareth and Desdra

Damien

Chester

Christian

Benedict

Aurelia

William

Matilda

Gwendolyn

AUTHOR'S AFTERWORD

I hope you enjoyed Jareth and Desdra's tale. I can honestly say that Jareth is the wealthiest hero we've ever had. We should all have such luck with a "rich uncle"! Now, you're probably already wondering if Orion and Anosia/Olivia are going to have their own story told, and the answer is YES! I've already got the plot outlined and it's going to be a heart-wrenching one. Orion's sword is named *Devastation*. Considering the storyline I have plotted for him, it will, indeed, be "Devastation."

Now, back to the "rich uncle" comment. Here are answers to a couple of things you might be wondering about that:

The first is the clarification of the two strangely armored statues in Lord Chester's locked room. Desdra said that they had come from the city of Xi'an, in a land called Cathay. That's China. What they were looking at were terra cotta warriors, dug out of the ground. In ancient times, loot from plundered tombs was, indeed, sold. At this period in time, the Silk Road from China was open. It mostly went to Turkey and Italy, and the Middle East, but such things could make their way to England—especially if you had an import business like Chester did. Far fetched? Not really if you understand the trade of the time. Rare things did, in fact, make it to England.

Secondly, I absolutely figured out exactly how rich Jareth was based on the conversion rate from Medieval money to modern dollars. All of the de Long family endeavors together earn over £12,000 a year in Medieval money. That's a phenomenal amount. Was Jareth richer than the king? Probably close to it in sheer cash flow. King Henry, if you remember your history, was a spender. He liked to spend money on buildings. He spent £10,000 on the Painted Chamber at Westminster alone, so he could spend big amounts. Total of all of Chester's coffers is £808,000, not including the value of the buildings he owns.

For a baseline, £15,000 is about $11 million in today's dollars. That makes Jareth's entire inheritance worth $59,253,332.00 = Fifty-nine million, two hundred and fifty-three thousand, three hundred and thirty-two in today's dollars.

And, no—he never gave Henry any of it!

Love,

KATHRYN LE VEQUE NOVELS

Medieval Romance:

De Wolfe Pack Series:
Warwolfe
The Wolfe
Nighthawk
ShadowWolfe
DarkWolfe
A Joyous de Wolfe Christmas
BlackWolfe
Serpent
A Wolfe Among Dragons
Scorpion
StormWolfe
Dark Destroyer
The Lion of the North
Walls of Babylon
The Best Is Yet To Be
BattleWolfe
Castle of Bones

De Wolfe Pack Generations:
WolfeHeart
WolfeStrike
WolfeSword
WolfeBlade
WolfeLord
WolfeShield
Nevermore
WolfeAx
WolfeBorn
WolfeBite
WolfeHound

House of de Norville:
The Best Is Yet To Be
Castle of Bones
Nevermore

The Executioner Knights:
By the Unholy Hand
The Mountain Dark
Starless
A Time of End
Winter of Solace
Lord of the Sky
The Splendid Hour
The Whispering Night
Netherworld
Lord of the Shadows
Of Mortal Fury
'Twas the Executioner Knight
Before Christmas
Crimson Shield
The Black Dragon

The de Russe Legacy:
The Falls of Erith
Lord of War: Black Angel
The Iron Knight
Beast
The Dark One: Dark Knight
The White Lord of Wellesbourne
Dark Moon
Dark Steel
A de Russe Christmas Miracle
Dark Warrior

The de Lohr Dynasty:
While Angels Slept
Rise of the Defender
Steelheart
Shadowmoor
Silversword
Spectre of the Sword
Unending Love
Archangel
A Blessed de Lohr Christmas

Sons of de Lohr:
Lion of Twilight
Lion of War
Lion of Hearts
Lion of Steel
Lion of Thunder

The Brothers de Lohr:
The Earl in Winter

Lords of East Anglia:
While Angels Slept
Godspeed
Age of Gods and Mortals

Great Lords of le Bec:
Great Protector

House of de Royans:
Lord of Winter
To the Lady Born
The Centurion

Lords of Eire:
Echoes of Ancient Dreams
Lord of Black Castle
The Darkland

Ancient Kings of Anglecynn:
The Whispering Night

Netherworld

Battle Lords of de Velt:
The Dark Lord
Devil's Dominion
Bay of Fear
The Dark Lord's First Christmas
The Dark Spawn
The Dark Conqueror
The Dark Angel

Reign of the House of de Winter:
Lespada
Swords and Shields

De Reyne Domination:
Guardian of Darkness
The Black Storm
A Cold Wynter's Knight
With Dreams
Master of the Dawn
One Wylde Knight

House of d'Vant:
Tender is the Knight (House of d'Vant)
The Red Fury (House of d'Vant)

The Dragonblade Series:
Fragments of Grace
Dragonblade
Island of Glass
The Savage Curtain
The Fallen One

Great Marcher Lords of de Lara
Lord of the Shadows
Dragonblade

House of St. Hever
Fragments of Grace

Island of Glass
Queen of Lost Stars

Lords of Pembury:
The Savage Curtain

Lords of Thunder: The de Shera Brotherhood Trilogy
The Thunder Lord
The Thunder Warrior
The Thunder Knight

The Great Knights of de Moray:
Shield of Kronos
The Gorgon

The House of De Nerra:
The Promise
The Falls of Erith
Vestiges of Valor
Realm of Angels

Highland Legion:
Highland Born
Highland Destroyer
Highland Slayer

Highland Warriors of Munro:
The Red Lion
Deep Into Darkness

The House of de Garr:
Lord of Light
Realm of Angels

Saxon Lords of Hage:
The Crusader
Kingdom Come

High Warriors of Rohan:
High Warrior
High King

The House of Ashbourne:
Upon a Midnight Dream

The House of D'Aurilliac:
Valiant Chaos

The House of De Dere:
Of Love and Legend

St. John and de Gare Clans:
The Warrior Poet

The House of de Bretagne:
The Questing

The House of Summerlin:
The Legend

The Kingdom of Hendocia:
Kingdom by the Sea

The BlackChurch Guild: Shadow Knights:
The Leviathan
The Protector
The Swordsman
The Tempest

Guard of Six:
Absolution
Insurrection
Obliteration

Regency Historical Romance:
Sin Like Flynn: A Regency Historical Romance Duet
The Sin Commandments
Georgina and the Red Charger

Gothic Regency Romance:
Emma

Historical Fiction:
The Girl Made Of Stars

Contemporary Romance:

Kathlyn Trent/Marcus Burton Series:
Valley of the Shadow
The Eden Factor
Canyon of the Sphinx

The Eagle Brotherhood (under the pen name Kat Le Veque):
The Sunset Hour
The Killing Hour
The Secret Hour
The Unholy Hour

The Burning Hour
The Ancient Hour
The Devil's Hour

Sons of Poseidon:
The Immortal Sea

Pirates of Britannia Series (with Eliza Knight):
Savage of the Sea by Eliza Knight
Leader of Titans by Kathryn Le Veque
The Sea Devil by Eliza Knight
Sea Wolfe by Kathryn Le Veque

Note: All Kathryn's novels are designed to be read as stand-alones, although many have cross-over characters or cross-over family groups. Novels that are grouped together have related characters or family groups. You will notice that some series have the same books; that is because they are cross-overs. A hero in one book may be the secondary character in another.

There is NO reading order except by chronology, but even in that case, you can still read the books as stand-alones. No novel is connected to another by a cliff hanger, and every book has an HEA.

Series are clearly marked. All series contain the same characters or family groups except the American Heroes Series, which is an anthology with unrelated characters.

For more information, find it in **A Reader's Guide to the Medieval World of Le Veque**.

ABOUT KATHRYN LE VEQUE

Bringing the Medieval to Romance

KATHRYN LE VEQUE is a critically acclaimed, multiple USA TODAY Bestselling author, an Indie Reader bestseller, a charter Amazon All-Star author, and a #1 bestselling, award-winning, multi-published author in Medieval Historical Romance with over 100 published novels.

Kathryn is a multiple award nominee and winner, including the winner of Uncaged Book Reviews Magazine 2017 and 2018 "Raven Award" for Favorite Medieval Romance. Kathryn is also a multiple RONE nominee (InD'Tale Magazine), holding a record for the number of nominations. In 2018, her novel WARWOLFE was the winner in the Romance category of the Book Excellence Award and in 2019, her novel A WOLFE AMONG DRAGONS won the prestigious RONE award for best pre-16th century romance.

Kathryn is considered one of the top Indie authors in the world with over 2M copies in circulation, and her novels have been translated into several languages. Kathryn recently signed with Sourcebooks Casablanca for a Medieval Fight Club series, first published in 2020.

In addition to her own published works, Kathryn is also the President/CEO of Dragonblade Publishing, a boutique publishing house specializing in Historical Romance. Dragonblade's success has seen it rise in the ranks to become Amazon's #1 e-book publisher of Historical Romance (K-Lytics report July 2020).

Kathryn loves to hear from her readers. Please find Kathryn on Facebook at Kathryn Le Veque, Author, or join her on Twitter @kathrynleveque. Sign up for Kathryn's blog at www.kathrynleveque.com for the latest news and sales.

www.ingramcontent.com/pod-product-compliance
Lightning Source LLC
Chambersburg PA
CBHW071246300726

48975CB00002B/564